# HELIOPAUSE

---

## THE QUESTRISON SAGA: BOOK ONE

## J. DIANNE DOTSON

J. DIANNE DOTSON

# CONTENTS

# DEDICATION

For my husband, James, who never stopped believing in me, and for our children, Daniel and Allen. You are the stars in my heaven.

# ACKNOWLEDGMENTS

While I invented my story, others bolstered its continuation and completion. I thank my husband and children for their loving support and patience. Thank you to Laurie Gibson, my wonderful copy editor. Thank you to Lisa Wolff, proofreader. A huge thank you to beta readers and helpers: Pam Magnus, Nathan Camp, Chris Schera, Gregory North, Amanda Kendall, Ed Campodonico, Jessica Springer, Will Turner, Diane Witt, Lauren Warren, Shelly Ellis, Carter Allen, James Phillips, and Joe Delci. Thank you Dash Creative, LLC, for the updated cover design for the 2nd edition. Thank you to cover artist Leon Tukker for the beautiful cover art. And to my teacher Ms. Phillips of Gray, Tennessee, who wrote to a publisher on my behalf, when I finished my first manuscript as a young teen: I can never thank you enough. While I didn't pursue publication then, I knew this day would come eventually. Teachers matter.

# 1

## AURA

I t was all routine by now. Stretch after the alarm. Shudder from the empty chill. Bounce off the bed plank and into the grey-walled tiny room. Grab the boxers and T-shirt and jumper. Zip and go.

Forster never looked out his porthole anymore. He called it a porthole, but it was more a small rectangle. The view beyond never changed much aside from Mandira Station's rotation, he decided, so he usually chose to ignore it.

Sometimes he projected a view of the station's exterior to brighten his room, and to remind himself of his first sight of it. He watched this projection again as if on approach. From afar, Mandira radiated into the inky void, its brightness obscuring fine details. Closer in, it resembled a great conch shell cast upon a black beach, which lent its nickname: The Conch. Coral and cream and peach, Mandira gleamed from the lights among its turrets and spires and branches, and the windows between them. Three decks comprised the conch-shaped government outpost and waypoint. Top Deck was the crown of the station. The research and upper-management section was filled with laboratories and researchers' quarters. Mid Deck bulged out as the bulbous midsection of Mandira. It housed a conservatory, a large docking bay, mess halls, a viewing area, offices, and the homes of many workers. Bottom Deck tapered down to a point, and several small docking bays pocked the station surface there. That section contained a power center and engineering controls.

Forster sighed and turned off the projection. He padded down the Mid Deck hall with its cushioned floor, curved sides, and sickly oval lights overhead and on the walls. He no longer noticed these things either. But he always dreaded the cushioned floor. No hard footfalls —that seemed wrong. Not much sound to reveal his presence. Just his feet sinking a bit, a spongy sensation. Somehow that rubbed him the wrong way. And every morning and every evening when he returned to his room, he thought this.

On the right, three doors down, Dunstan Gibbons played some tinny music. Always just softly enough that you could never make out what it was. Another piece of white noise for Forster to ignore. Cal Burgess still lay asleep, probably, across the hall from Gibbons' quarters. Burgess always trailed into the mess hall some twenty minutes later than anyone else. Same dark circles under his eyes, and bags below the dark circles. Mornings weren't kind to Burgess.

Down a bit on the right, before sleeping Burgess and Gibbons' quarters, Troy Pinedo kept a tidy hole and arose early. He liked to boil a mug of instant coffee to the point of evaporating away anything resembling the coffee taste and smell. Forster hurried past; Troy had ears like a cat, and if he caught Forster, he'd push his reduced "coffee" swill on him. Knowing its value out here, at the edge of the solar system, Forster would sometimes take the offer. But he preferred to evade this circumstance. That "coffee" smelled like the essence of some ancient cigarette stain, full of the ghosts of tar and ash.

Meredith Brant lived next to Troy on the right side of the hall. One of the eldest of the crew, at seventy-five she seemed more alert and spry than the "young-uns," as she liked to call most of them. She had grown up in the southern region of old America. She retained a whisper of her vestigial drawl, unless she chose to whip it out in anger. One rarely found her that riled, so that was always a shock. Meredith maintained some semblance of routine and sanity by crafting. She made patchwork quilts from old, worn clothes and other salvaged fabrics. She embellished some with embroidery. Despite their simplicity, her quilts were always cherished.

Forster enjoyed talking with Meredith, but he knew she didn't like to prattle on. Sometimes he caught her up in the station's observation deck, aka the Dome Car, facing the blackness of space. Her eyes still gleamed green, green as languid summer leaves long ago and so far away. He often wondered what she was thinking when she would stand there. And then he would think of home.

He moved on and slinked past Efron's door. Thankfully he was already out, somewhere. Efron would give him this eagle stare that sent a shiver down his spine sometimes. Like the man could watch his neurons fire, if he wanted to. Forster was warned about Efron before this assignment.

"This guy," Captain Spears once told Forster at Ganymede Base, "dresses like Nikola Tesla. Maybe he thinks he really is Tesla. I don't know. Weird dude." Spears was huge, maybe six foot eight, built like a refrigerator. But Spears seemed the most easy-going fellow Forster had met during his Ganymede years. He was not easily perturbed, and not one for gossip. So that made Forster's ears perk up when he talked about Efron. He had been sorry to see Spears go after the last docking.

Efron was something of an eccentric. He kept his head shaven and wore spectacles that wrapped all the way around. He dressed spectacularly in black platform boots, waistcoat, and high-collared trench coat. Efron also kept a robin's egg–sized amethyst on a chain around his neck. His sharp features, clear blue eyes, and wild eyebrows invoked an aquiline appearance. Forster tried to avoid him.

Almost everyone else tended to avoid Efron as well outside of work. Forster had seen Meredith talking quietly to him on occasion. He might have heard Efron laugh with her once—although that may have been a cough; laughter didn't seem free to Efron anyway.

The mess hall connected to two other branches of the facility. It served as a social area, one of the few designated on Mandira Station. Occasionally Forster's team held their meetings in the hall during breakfast. Mornings were quiet but usually cheerful. Forster most enjoyed Ella and Darren Varis, a couple in their sixties. Pop Doogan, who was pushing seventy and loud as hell, always got him laughing. Pop would bellow you out of your morning haze in a jiffy.

"Here we go!" Pop hollered as Forster came in. "The sun is up! Coffee time!" Pop rose to smack his hand into Forster's.

The two headed over to the beverage bar for their hot drinks. The station granted a daily allotment of artificial coffee, so if you declined, that was it. But the cafeteria overflowed with teas of all kinds, and juice and cider and milk. So the station beverages weren't all bad. And they all tasted better than the swill Troy made.

The Varises came in and sat with Forster and Pop. Each went over their news between mouthfuls of cereal, protein bars, toast, or swigs of drink.

Ella spoke of her sister's illness flaring up again, and how her eldest nephew was finishing college. Darren reported on his stock trades, and Pop lambasted the tide report, as usual. Forster had little to offer as news; some wind readings and a new particle distribution log update. He was getting a mild headache, but he didn't mention that.

"Oh, hey," Darren spoke up, glancing at Forster. "Spears checked in. Next dock is in four days."

"Yeah, I know," Forster replied. "Guess I'd better get to work." They all smiled. Spears was well liked, so they all looked forward to his visit.

Forster liked to leave after everyone had shown up from his branch of the facility. Efron would sweep in briskly and make a tidy breakfast; Meredith would bring some knitting; Troy would arrive all flushed from his "coffee." Gibbons would blink and smile and offer up polite questions and remarks, and Burgess would drag in last, yawning. At that point, after some routine hellos and back slaps, Forster would slip out and walk through Mid Deck to start the workday.

He had about thirty minutes to set up everything before anyone else came to the Mid Deck offices. He liked it this way. Set up while everyone was still eating or whatever. Out here, there wasn't much left one could control beyond one's own surroundings. But you could pick when you wanted to start work, whether you could choose when to end the shift. Forster ran his fingers across the holo remote command codes and tilted the sensor array. He consulted the system bots about diagnostics and listened to their status updates. He gave some cursory instructions to the station systems, and let the morning roll.

This headache, though. He pressed his hands to his temples. The pain began to creep down into his jaw. This was a doozy. He hoped it wasn't a migraine. He'd lost his med dots the other day. Not like he couldn't request more, but he dreaded that. Getting medicine wasn't a problem or anything, but having to record it? He wondered. Who kept track of that stuff, anyway? Burgess would have laughed at him for this. Burgess, who regularly threw back the caffeine dots, to keep those puffy eyelids open, then threw back the sleeper dots at night to keep them closed. Although, Forster thought with a chuckle, no matter what, Burgess wouldn't tolerate Troy's brew.

*Why do I have this headache?* Forster wondered. The intensity seemed close to that of a migraine. But his migraines usually came on after seeing bright glare or flashing lights. His branch and Mid Deck had no piercing lights. He was hydrated. He'd slept well... Wait, he hadn't. He thought back to last night. In fact he'd had a vivid dream.

In his dream, he had walked down the hall and found Gibbons' door wide open. Harpsichord music flooded the hall; dim red light glowed from within. He poked his head in, curious, and found an amazing sight. Gibbons stood there in red velvet coattails and white knee stockings, like some sort of eighteenth-century gentleman. He danced with a marionette. She looked like a shepherdess, all frilly pink, hoop skirted, her curly head in a bonnet. Gibbons set her dancing on her wee patent shoes. He grinned foolishly, twirling her about, enthralled with her. He did not notice Forster watching him, but the shepherdess had turned her head on her own and stared at him with diamond eyes. Forster jerked awake.

Confused, Forster glanced around. That was last night's dream, and here he had fallen asleep at his office desk and dreamt the same thing again. He wiped the drool from his mouth. His head raged. "Oh, God," he groaned.

"Mr. Forster," someone called crisply.

He wheeled around in his chair. Efron stood in the doorway, imposing and lean, with a sharp birdlike stance. *A curious raven,* Forster thought through his pain.

"Are you well, sir?" asked Efron.

By now, Forster shone slick from sweat and his eyes began to water from pain. A scintillating scotoma had formed in his vision, so that Efron seemed encircled by iridescent confetti. "I—I, uh, I fell asleep," Forster responded feebly.

"You look ill. Shall I call Medic?" asked Efron, with unusual warmth. The bright blue eyes under their bushy brows beamed out from Forster's migraine aura. It was almost more visual stimulus than Forster could stand.

He couldn't remember reaching the door, much less getting to his quarters. But the Medic bot arrived shortly and rolled him along in its chair to his room. The pale turquoise Medic bot spoke in a soothing and quiet tone, diagnosed the migraine en route, and administered the dots to Forster. By the time the bot eased him onto his plank with its slender, gentle arms, Forster felt much better, and like a fool. *Should've got more dots myself. Now it's on record. Damn!*

Efron peered in behind Medic and pursed his lips. "I do think, Mr. Forster, you should rest for the remainder of the day. I will inform the team."

"Okay," groaned Forster. *Now leave,* he thought. Efron's mouth twitched into the tiniest smirk, and he actually bowed and left.

Medic rolled out soon after, reminding Forster in gentle tones to call for help if needed.

Forster pushed himself up and sat against the wall. This time, he peered out the porthole.

He drew in a breath. Something was there. Far out beyond the facility. Something very, very faint, but flashing. Tiny pulses. He called Troy.

"Hey Troy," he rasped.

"Jesus, man! What happened? Heard you passed out."

"Nooo," Forster said, with an eye roll. "Got a migraine."

"Weird! Why didn't you get some dots?"

"Listen—I know. Hey, got a minute?"

"Sure," said Troy.

"Come and look at something, would you?"

Troy took his break and wended his way down to their branch. He gave a knock and Forster let him in.

"Check this out," Forster said, pointing toward the window.

Troy turned and squinted. "What?"

"There's a light outside, flashing. Do you see it?"

"Uh...no."

Forster huffed and looked out again himself. Troy was right. He found nothing but black, empty space, and the slowly wheeling bright stars. No light flashing, nothing. He shook his head.

"Okay, whatever, there was a light flashing earlier."

"Dude, you look like shit. Maybe just lay low today and tomorrow. Need some chow? How about a coffee?"

"No thank you," Forster said with emphatic quickness. "Guess it's the migraine. Sorry, man."

"Hey, no problem. Let me know if you need anything."

"Okay. Thanks, Troy," said Forster.

Forster sat back again. His eyes drifted to the window. Nothing. Even after a full rotation, he did not see the lights again. *Maybe Troy's right,* he thought. *But I'm still not touching the coffee.*

## 2

## BEYOND

F orster slept on and off that day, mercifully dreamless. By the time of his evening schedule, he felt perfectly normal. He cursed his stubborn refusal to order more migraine dots after he lost his. He'd kept the old medicine for several months, from four resupply dockings ago. He shook off his foolishness and showered.

He examined himself in the soft light of his small mirror. His brow lines had deepened since the headache, pinched from pain. No surprise there. Streaks of wiry grey poked out from his wavy brown hair. His face wore a haggard weariness; his hazel-brown eyes were dull and dry. He considered his slim frame and the visible tendons in his neck. *Maybe a bit too lean lately. Gotta hit the gym soon,* he reasoned. *Then some extras at the mess hall.*

He enjoyed the indulgence of this day off, but he still checked on the diagnostics and particle distribution reports. Bandon, his sand-hued, round particle system bot, updated him every half hour. Depoe, his cobalt-blue wind sensor bot and twin to Bandon, updated him on the hour. They were his robotic eyes out here in the void. They were his responsibility as well. He felt subservient to robots at times, but that was part of the gig. There were worse fates in the void.

Late into the evening, he stepped away from his particle systems and threw down the last of some pie Meredith had made. She had a knack for foraging the conservatory gardens and for bartering her crafts in exchange for extracts and spices.

"Pie heals all, y'all!" she'd said, clucking with a hint of that accent coming out, all maternal. She wasn't far from the truth. He'd savored the vanilla cream pie bite by bite, resisting the urge to pick the wedge up and shove it in whole. After the last bite of pie, he went back over a blip on his reports.

*Okay, that's weird,* he thought. He found an anomalous reading. He'd never seen one before, but of course they had occurred several years ago, before the facility had been completed. A wind reversal. But that was just one reading. He shrugged. He'd go over it with the team tomorrow. What time had it happened?

*Oh.*

"Gibbons," he called over his link. Gibbons picked up.

"Oh, hello, Forster, good man. How are you? Feeling better?" asked Gibbons.

"Yep. Thanks. Hey, do you have a sec? I want to run something by you. Readings stuff."

"Sure, do you want me to come down?"

Forster paused. He recalled an image of red velvet and a shepherdess. He shook off those thoughts. "Nah, I'll head your way if that's cool."

"Sure thing."

Forster's pulse raced as he stood by Gibbons' door. But the older man opened his door as casually as any other day, and a quick glance reassured Forster of no red velvet coattails and no weird marionettes in sight. He sighed in relief.

Gibbons noticed. He was an affable enough fellow, always game for a long conversation or good deep chuckle. Auburn hair turning grey, grey eyes, a ruddy face with deep laugh lines. He was about five foot ten and sported a beer gut. Not that he had access to beer out here, but there were spirits.

"Strange day," Gibbons remarked. "Sorry you were ill. Can I get you something?"

"No, thanks," Forster replied, sitting at Gibbons' desk. His room was larger than Forster's, and better decorated. If one chose to style an old-fashioned gentleman's den out here, this was what it would look like. Forster kept things lean and vaguely Scandinavian, but Gibbons channeled an old English manor.

"So Gibbons, I've got this reading from the wind report. You ever see this kind of thing?"

Forster brought out his film, and drew his finger along the little plastic slip until he found his data. He handed the slip to Gibbons.

Gibbons pored over the report. "No, but of course you would expect that from a probe out at the edge."

"But not here, though, right?"

"No," Gibbons admitted. "More than likely a glitch. It's the only one, yes?" Forster nodded. "Then I wouldn't worry about it. You can bring it up at the meeting tomorrow."

*I'm not sure I want any more attention,* Forster thought.

Gibbons' room seemed unusually quiet. He did love his music. "No tunes tonight?" Forster asked.

Gibbons' forehead creased. "You know, I've had problems with it all day."

"Oh?" Forster tried to keep his eyes open. Gibbons kept his quarters toasty, with a fake fire in the wall. Forster almost slipped back into that dream again, but forced himself upright.

Gibbons called forth the music, but they heard only static. "It's been like this since this morning," he went on. "I checked on everything, nothing's blatantly wrong, but obviously it's not working. Just static."

Forster inspected the program. It was displayed on a flat, gold-rimmed panel embedded into a faux wooden desk. Yellow buttons blinked and a red sine wave moved across the panel. Its screen showed Gibbons was right; everything superficial looked nominal. He listened and tuned with the flat buttons. Then Forster held up his hand before Gibbons turned it off.

"Hear that?"

Gibbons shrugged. "More static. Let's turn it off; you've had enough of a headache for one day."

"No, listen closely—do you hear that?" Forster insisted. He heard something. Something in the static: the tiniest sounds, little tones. And a distant, patterned buzz.

"What am I hearing?" Gibbons asked, frustrated. "Or what are *you* hearing?"

"Some sort of tone or buzz or something. Can't you hear that?" Forster focused all his attention on it, strained, even bent a bit downward, to Gibbons' height.

Gibbons concentrated, then nodded at last. Forster sighed again, relieved he wasn't imagining things like that light outside his room.

"Good, I'm not cracking up. What do you think that is?" Forster asked. His mind was nagging him. He strained to remember something that seemed familiar.

"There is a pattern to it. I can hear that buzz, just barely," said Gibbons. "But those little sounds. I don't know. Can we focus on those? Amplify them maybe. Clean them up. Veronica?"

Gibbons called on his AI program to focus on the two sets of sounds, the buzz and the tones. He and Forster watched a screen.

"My God," said Gibbons.

"What is that?" asked Forster, his pulse quickening.

"Well, that one: that is Morse code. You know about Morse code, yes?"

Forster nodded. Gibbons went on, "This other sound, the buzz, is coming in with precise regularity, like a repeater. But the Morse code is erratic."

"Where is this coming from?" asked Forster. But he had an unsettled feeling that he knew.

"The sound's not transmitting from here," said Gibbons, which Veronica confirmed. "Veronica, what is the origin of this transmission?"

"There are two transmissions," his AI's lush voice responded. "The tone transmits intermittently from point four-three-zero-seven-five-alpha. The patterned repeater sound has no specific point of origin."

Forster and Gibbons looked at each other. "What the devil?" asked Gibbons.

Forster asked, "Veronica, can you locate this point you mention, for the tonal transmission, in proximity to us?"

Veronica displayed Mandira Station in the room. Then its image shrank as if to fit in one's hand, like a little souvenir shell, and far beyond it stretched the Border Wall. Beyond this lay a winking light. Forster gasped.

"What is that?" he asked, his finger nearly touching the light.

"Unknown," Veronica responded.

Gibbons spoke up. "This is the point of origin for the Morse code?"

"Confirmed," said Veronica.

Again the two men stared at each other. "It's beyond," they both said together. Beyond the Border Wall, far from the sun's influence, and into interstellar space. Beyond the heliopause.

## 3

# THINKING MAN

Forster and Gibbons stayed up late gibbering, intrigued and spooked. Forster had told Gibbons about the flashing light he had—or hadn't—seen. Gibbons now speculated that the light and the Morse code were somehow related. Forster had begun to suspect this as well. Gibbons slid a glass over to Forster. It flickered in the false firelight.

"Is this Scotch?"

"Of course it is," Gibbons beamed. His face already magenta, he poured more into his own glass.

"I remember when I first came here, you said one day you'd have me over for Scotch," Forster mused. "You were one of the first people —actually, one of the only ones, for a while—who made me feel welcome here. Like I didn't stand out so much."

Gibbons nodded, smiling. "Oh, but I could not get you to take the offer on the Scotch!"

"I know, I just..." Forster turned the glass in his hand. "I know how rare this is. Maybe I didn't feel...I don't know, worthy yet?"

Gibbons laughed. "Good man," he chuckled, "you seemed so on edge at first, eyes like a heartbreak."

Forster raised his eyes in surprise to Gibbon's ruddy face.

"I know that look, Forster. I've seen it in my own mirror a few times. I didn't want you to feel that way, not here."

Gibbons took one more sip and licked his lips. He set his glass down.

"Well!" he continued. "Now what? The meeting's tomorrow. We bring it up, we don't bring it up. Either way, I want to know everything about that Morse code. Veronica! Are you finished translating?"

"Verifying. The transmission appears disjointed and incomplete. It repeats only at broken intervals."

"Well, let's take a look at what we've got, anyway."

The men read Veronica's translation quickly at first, and then more carefully, then over again. And then they sat back and stared at the fake fireplace.

"Well, that was...something," muttered Gibbons.

"Yeaaaah." Forster nodded. He appreciated the pleasant confusion from the drink. Still, a sense of unease crept through him.

Gibbons studied Forster through the facets of his Scotch glass.

"I don't know about you, Forster, but I'm thinking there's no reason to bring this up at the meeting."

Forster gave him a sideways look and a smirk. "Bring up what?"

Gibbons nodded.

But both men sat in silence for some time, mesmerized by the fake flames.

"Forster," said Gibbons, very quietly. "The weekend's tomorrow. What say we let this go for a few days? Think things over. Enjoy ourselves. Spears is on his way; I'll have a new bottle or two. We can talk about this again. But Forster. I...I think perhaps...we should keep this between ourselves. Yes?"

Forster poured the last smoky drop of Scotch from his glass onto his tongue. "Yep." He did not mention his dream.

"Friday! Wooooooo!" howled someone down Third Branch. Forster sighed. Fridays used to mean more. Such an arbitrary decision, the celebration of a Friday. An old tradition, one that didn't matter anymore, especially out here. But everyone clings to such things when flung out far from where they began. Forster thought of it as a sort of delicate thread connecting the scattered web of humanity. More delicate all the time, and more separated.

He thought back to Ganymede Base, his last station before coming out here. He remembered the roaring Fridays and Saturdays, weekends still unstoppable machines. Ganymede was known for its parties. It was the last of the larger bases in the outer solar system. Other bases did exist farther out. Small way stations and fueling stops before the long, dark, remote sail to points beyond Pluto, Haumea, and Makemake. There was a sense on Ganymede Base that you lived to the fullest while you could. Because who knew when you ever would again, assuming you made it to where you were going anyway.

Auna had said a final goodbye to him at Ganymede. Auna with her inky eyes, their long straight eyebrows on her broad brow. He used to swipe his hand across her brow; she always seemed annoyed by that. And toward the end everything annoyed her, every gesture became an irritant. He'd known this was coming, since she announced her new station deployment elsewhere. He'd steeled himself. Forster had revealed he had given up his promotion to someone else. It was the latest in a long string of his wanting to help others, rather than stay with a commitment. Auna had reached her limit.

They were a long way from hiking on the Pacific Coast Trail, seeing how far they could go like in the old days. He'd admired Auna's stubborn refusal to do anything the easy way, cop out of the hike, which many had ridiculed. But their end had been easy after all. Her relief had been palpable. And he realized now, he was glad to give her that relief, at least.

They had said goodbye in the bar, each returning to sleep out the final night and any remaining alcohol in their separate quarters. Forster thought back to the cacophony of the bar. At times he struggled to remember, out here on the edge, the need for the noise. Even at its most raucous, and with its continuous droning of machines, the silence beyond remained too giant a force to fight against. Yet one's sanity demanded it.

He wanted a little more noise and exuberance. Something to remind him that he should care about more than the everyday grind and the nauseating cushioned floor he walked day by day. But the younger, rowdier folks of the station's Third Branch gave him *that look* whenever he tried to join the fun. "Whaddup, Grandpa!" someone had actually yowled at him the last time he'd gone to the bar. He'd snorted. Had they ever seen *his* crewmates? Of course, he knew they likely hadn't, except along the fringes of stationwide meetings.

Forster took the risk of personal insults with him and sidled up to the bar. Why not? He could distract himself with the din of increasingly inebriated youth. Maybe that was just the sort of thing he needed to get his head around what he and Gibbons had uncovered.

"What you having, mate?" asked the main bartender, Guru Puaha.

"Surprise me. Something to help me think," answered Forster.

Guru laughed. "Thought you'd come here to avoid that, same as the rest." Forster raised his eyebrows quizzically, and Guru shrugged. He scooped up a clear spirit and tucked a sprig of an herb into the drink, which he slid to Forster. "Here you go, Thinking Man."

"Thanks." Forster took a tiny sip, then sucked on the rosemary sprig. Guru had followed through on the order well enough; just the one taste had cleared Forster's nostrils like wasabi. "What is this?" Guru just winked and moved over to other revelers.

So Forster took in this concoction hesitantly, his sinuses seared from its volatility. Yet it rested easily in his stomach and warmed him gently. And he relaxed enough to think about the message Veronica had attempted to decode.

Whoever had sent the message had been in trouble. Forster knew that was no proper SOS call, though, and this bothered him. The buzzer tone originated beyond the heliopause where no probe should be, currently. The probes had long ago jettisoned into space beyond the sun's realm. And here was a signal, and a light, and a message. A broken one, but still.

"Changed me. Feared me."

This was all Veronica deciphered from the Morse code, among

broken bits. She had found no other underlying message with the buzzer at present. Forster doubted she would.

Forster trembled. Who sent that code? When? Why? He agreed with Gibbons. They shouldn't tell the others. But would someone else pick up the transmission, or see the flashing light?

"You seem deep in thought, Forster."

He jumped and spilled some of his drink.

"Efron! Hello!" Forster feigned politeness, but Efron's towering form disarmed him.

Efron flicked his coat around his shoulders and perched on a stool at the bar. "I'm surprised you're here," he remarked. His protuberant blue eyes stared at Forster, who merely blinked.

"Well, Friday, you know." More staring from Efron. "Can I help you, Efron?"

Efron laughed, and actually smiled, gaining a stare from Forster. "What's the matter, am I that pale? Have I achieved translucency?" He gestured to Guru, who gave him a nod. Forster understood that Efron must be a regular.

"No, no, I just...uh, this doesn't seem like your sort of place," Forster sputtered.

"Ah," Efron answered, still grinning. "Well, of course, there's a lot we don't know about each other."

"I guess I thought you preferred quiet contemplation," replied Forster.

"What, the sort you were just having? I do. But it does gnaw on you, doesn't it? All of this?" Efron waved his hand. "We're all chatting so we don't hear the emptiness." He received his glass and raised it. Forster raised his as well.

"Friday," Forster said laconically.

"Friday," Efron answered.

They sat in silence for a several minutes. Forster noticed Efron only took small sips of his beverage, whereas in his own unease he'd begun taking heavier slugs. Efron's pale hands enclosed his drink like a sorcerer's phial. There was no getting around it; Efron gave Forster the creeps.

"What do you think, Forster?" Efron murmured. "All the worlds out in deep space, so many as yet unexplored. Do you think that's worthwhile? We know there are likely other living civilizations, but we can't quite reach them yet. Do we keep at it? And if we do, why? There is a great gulf between them and us. Yet we cannot cross it en masse. Should we try?"

"Of course," Forster replied. "That's a big part of who we are. We can't stop now."

"But what about the cost to those we leave behind?"

"Listen, I don't know the answers to any of that," replied Forster. "Staying behind wasn't part of my plan. I wanted to work. Out here. It's my job."

"And that's all this is to you? Just a job?" Efron's eyes seemed fluorescent, pool blue. But then again Forster had emptied his drink, and he grew unsteady.

"Gotta work hard to play hard," Forster said with a smirk. He stood up and gave Efron a nod. "Peace," he said, and he left the bar.

# 4

## ANOMALOUS

Forster stirred, still hanging on to a last trailing vine of green images in a dream of another time and place. Suddenly he shot up. He focused on the window...and there it was. The flash again! Only more rapid, urgent even. He swung from his plank and began dressing. *Got to talk to Gibbons. Ask if there's any new translation from Veronica.*

A muffled sound outside his door stopped him. Then a tapping. "Forster!" someone said in a low voice.

He opened the door and found Meredith, her brows high and crinkled, twisting her hands, clenching her teeth.

"Meredith! What is it? Come in," he said awkwardly. He glanced over his shoulder at the window, which stared at him like a dark eye; the flashes had ceased.

"Forster," Meredith began, and she opened and closed her mouth a few times. Forster guided her to a seat. His pulse bounced. Something was wrong.

"What is it? Efron?"

"Efron? No. It's Spears. I think something's happened."

"Spears? What? What's happened?" Forster cried, and now his sweat sprang out all over.

"You've had no contact with him, have you?" Meredith asked, her eyes darting cautiously. This perturbed Forster more than anything. He had never seen Meredith so agitated.

"No! No, I usually don't until he arrives," Forster replied.

"We can't hail him," Meredith said. She twisted her hands again. "His sensors are giving off strange readings. I just wanted to ask you in case...if there's anything...strange?"

Forster stood straight up. "Did Efron speak to you? What's going on?"

"What? Efron? No," said Meredith. She pressed her hands to her temples and her eyes glowed beneath their white brows. "Top Deck is having a meeting in forty-five minutes. We should all attend. You didn't get the message?"

Forster glanced guiltily at his comm desk. Of course it flashed with a new message. "I just woke up," he answered sheepishly.

"Never mind. You need to be present, and I wanted to give you a bit of warning...I knew you'd probably still be asleep. But this is urgent. Top Deck will decide whether to send a probe to rendezvous. But they'll also want to know if anyone has been in communication with Spears. You've not been, so that should suffice...."

Meredith took hold of Forster's arm. He sat beside her, close enough to feel a bit of her warmth.

"Forster, I know something's going on. I don't care what it is. Please don't ask me how I know...not yet. You *can* trust me. But I have some advice for you. Don't mention anything you might have seen. Please."

"Seen?" And at that moment Forster realized that Meredith knew everything. Somehow. He was about to say "Gibbons!" but stopped himself. What the hell was going on? He sighed and answered maybe too quickly, "I've not heard from Spears. Not since the last docking. Give me ten minutes; I'll get dressed and we can go grab tea and walk together to the meeting."

Meredith gave him a glassy stare with her peridot-colored eyes. Then she smiled, but the smile never moved above her mouth. "That sounds good. I'll be waiting."

She left, and Forster swore. *How does she know? Did Gibbons tell her? But he wouldn't. He just wouldn't.* He dressed and swore and thought, and then inspected himself once more in a mirror before leaving. His reflection showed anxiety, so he began to slow his breathing. His eyebrows lowered.

He headed into the hall and ran into Pop Doogan.

Pop jumped. "Forster! Whew...got me there. Didn't see you." Pop's usual jovial cheeks sagged. "Guess you heard about Spears."

"Yeah," sighed Forster. "Headed that way?"

"Let's do it," answered Pop. Pop was a full head shorter than lanky Forster, and gave Forster the impression of a misplaced Santa Claus. Seeing him with no grin and no light in his eyes underlined the palpable unease of the morning.

"What do you think happened?" Forster asked, unsure how to talk about this ominous situation but unwilling to dwell with his fears in silence.

"Don't know, my friend. Nobody's got answers. What do you think the big rods will say?"

"Top Deck? Who knows? I can guess how it'll go, though. Very by the book," Forster ventured.

"Sure," mumbled Pop. Forster noticed Pop seemed more withdrawn and ultimately gave up.

At the elevator to the conference hall, a small throng waited and rustled and whispered. The Varises and Troy and a few folks from the conservatory milled around. But no Gibbons. No Meredith, and no Efron. Forster nodded at the Varises, and Ella moved over and touched his arm, while Darren spoke with Troy and Pop.

"You were friends with Spears, weren't you?" Ella asked quietly.

"I was and I still am. From Ganymede Base. He's not—" and Forster lowered his voice "—he's not dead, right? I mean."

"I'm sure it's just a malfunction," Ella replied, giving his arm a squeeze, but looking perturbed. "I'm sorry. I just...this is just so unusual."

*Is it, though? How many unusual things happen before that's the new normal? What's going to happen next?* And then he remembered an old lab assistant buddy in college shaking his head and saying, "Never ask how much worse things can get." The hair stood up on the back of his neck.

Up the elevator and amid awkward murmurings, the group made its way to the large conference hall. Forster could not remember the last time he'd been in one room with so many people. Certainly that had never happened here during his tenure. He didn't know everyone at the station, by any means, due to its size and his relative newness. He was surprised by the sight of Guru the bartender pressed up against one wall with a group of Mid Deck folks. He'd never thought about it before, but he wondered if Guru ever had any real time off. Forster guessed Guru knew more about everyone on Mandira Station than anyone else. Which made him curious about how much Guru knew, period.

He thought this within a span of mere seconds, while he scanned the large crowd for Gibbons, Meredith, and Efron. After a few minutes, he noticed the Varises moving toward someone, and he discovered it was Meredith. She linked arms with Ella while Darren spoke quietly to her. Meredith looked unwell, and somehow aged even since Forster had seen her earlier. This gave him a pang of guilt for some reason. Why had he been so wrapped up in this weird crap? Why did he and Gibbons need to keep their discovery to themselves?

*Was this my fault somehow? Did I start this?*

He didn't have more time to speculate for the moment. The room was called to order by the "big rods," Mid and Bottom Deck's nickname for the quorum who managed Top Deck in particular and the station in general.

Dr. Vanita Singh rose, while her cohorts remained seated. She stood with her iron poise and announced with voice magnification, "Thank you for coming. As you may know, an incident occurred with regards to the payload operation earlier today.

"We attempted hailing Captain Spears on board the payload, with no response. The craft is scheduled to arrive in seven hours, and there has been no alteration in its course or change in speed. As is customary, the craft has pinged the station at various intervals on its normal schedule. As far as we can tell, Captain Spears performed his routine checks at predictable intervals, until approximately six hours ago.

"At that time, we received anomalous readings of his health monitoring systems. We attempted to hail Captain Spears at that time, following necessary protocols, and received no response."

Ripples of concerned chatter rose and fell among the crowd. Forster sighed heavily. A burrowing dread plunged in his stomach.

Dr. Singh continued, "We attempted more communications to Captain Spears and again we received no responses. I decided to contact Ganymede Base to determine the captain's condition upon leaving. They found no indications of anything unusual before Captain Spears' departure. Logs show the captain performed all his scheduled duties. No overt health concerns were recorded. Apparently en route he suffered a medical event on board the ship, and we are treating it as such.

"Given the ship's trajectory and speed, we will proceed with its docking procedure and assist Captain Spears upon arrival."

Someone in the crowd yelled out, "Can't we meet him halfway? What's the holdup?"

Dr. Singh almost imperceptibly dipped her head. "Per regulation protocol, if we are not alerted by an emergency beacon, we do not send a rendezvous craft. At this point it is clear that Captain Spears experienced a medical crisis, yet he made no distress call. His medical status is classified, but I can tell you, Captain Spears is alive."

Everyone sighed in relief, but the chatter increased to a din.

Dr. Singh continued, "The captain's ship continues its course, unaltered, to the station. Upon his arrival, we will meet him with our medical team and assess his status. I ask that everyone remain calm and respectful of the captain's privacy, and be mindful of his speedy recovery. We will provide an update should anything change. Thank you."

The Top Deck officials stepped down and the crowd noise increased to the point that Forster began feeling irritable. He wanted to speak up in front of everyone right then and there, but held back.

Almost as a retort, Pop let out a loud whistle. "What a crock of bullshit that was!" he bellowed. "What the hell was that? I mean, come on. Like they couldn't get somebody out there? Send a bot? Get the fuck outta here."

And that was pretty much the gist of all the conversation around him. Send a bot, send anything, and just get Spears docked. Forster knew Spears was well liked, but he didn't realize just how popular he was (*and still is,* Forster thought hopefully).

Forster moved over to the Ella, Darren, and Meredith. The Varises shook their heads and left. Meredith stared at Forster.

"Let's go," she murmured.

They walked to the elevator. Forster kept trying to fill that strange void of dead air between them, but every glance at Meredith warned him not to. Once they'd returned to Mid Deck, and once on their hallway, Meredith said, "Let's talk. My place."

"Okay."

Meredith invited him in, and while he had been in Meredith's quarters only a few times, her home calmed him. Her small art quilts hung on every wall. The more practical quilts she spent her spare time making lay strewn on her plank and her two chairs. Meredith's space always smelled of green, living things. Leaves, fertilizer, life. She had only two vine plants, but they thrived. She had named them "Kud" and "Zu," her little invasive plant joke.

She swept her straight, grey bangs from her eyebrows and tucked her shoulder-length hair behind her ears. She locked eyes with Forster and said, "They're quarantining him."

"What!" Forster exclaimed. "Why? I—how would you know that?"

Meredith pierced him again with glowing eyes. "Think about it. Why not send someone after him? They're buying time. They want to set up an official quarantine."

"Why? I mean...I hate to say it but, what if Spears had a stroke or something?"

"They'd know that. Something else is going on."

Forster stood and backed up toward the door. He didn't like the sound of this. Meredith was getting carried away, and Forster felt terrible about Spears. It was too much.

"Forster, remember what I told you this morning?"

"Yes."

"I want you to think about what I said," Meredith told him, and she stood and reached out to him. "Please, Forster."

"Of course, of course," he reassured her. "Just...let's try not to worry so much. There could be something wrong with Spears' system after all."

"Do you *really* believe that?" Meredith asked him.

Forster opened the door and stared back at Meredith. "I don't know."

# 5

## THE CURIOUS RAVEN

Forster stared at his closed porthole. After diving into his solar wind diagnostics for hours, he realized belatedly that he was famished. He pretended there was nothing outside that window. He wanted to believe there never had been anything. He kept a firm control over thoughts of Spears, pushing them out of mind long enough to realize that half the day had escaped him. Again and again he thought of Auna. She would have found the right thing to say, would have instantly reassured him with her steadiness. He fell into his own personal argument over reaching out to her. Several months had passed since Forster had spoken to her.

She seemed almost a talisman to Forster now. Auna with her smoldering dark eyes, which always gave him the feeling of baring his soul. Auna with her smooth brow that belied her steely nature. A tough and brilliant and witty woman, nonchalant about her own skills, generous with her resources. He wasn't even sure where she was. This had been their longest estrangement, and today he felt the loss keenly. But again the disappointment in himself arose, the crushing feeling of having let down the best person he'd ever known. He knew she would sort out exactly what to do about everything happening to him, even if she didn't know the reasons behind it. And he believed he couldn't ask her, because he knew he had disappointed her. He felt he had to figure out all this on his own.

He might have wallowed in the quagmire of his memories and feelings, but his stomach ruled that out, so he munched a protein bar and ran some tests. He had almost finished his snack when his door chimed. His gut lurched—had something happened to Spears? No updates had come in so far. He opened the door.

At first all he saw was a movement of black and silver. Shreds of a black cape dancing in a breeze, long silver hair lifted above it, and eyes like mercury boring into him. Forster stood dumbstruck, blinked, and rubbed his eyes. There stood only Efron after all, in his usual odd attire and platform boots, no cape, and no long hair. *What the hell was that?*

He noticed the tiniest shift in Efron's eyes, almost a flicker of a smile.

"Forster," Efron greeted him, with a small nod. Forster stepped back and let him in.

"Everything all right?" Forster stammered.

"Maybe I should ask *you* that. Are you feeling well?" And Efron gave him his aquiline stare.

"Yes. Sorry. Come in, sit down," and Forster sat again, gesturing to a chair next to his desk. "How can I help you, Efron?"

Efron fixed him again with his unnerving pale eyes. "I think it's time we talked."

"About?" And the hairs rose on the back of Forster's neck. "Is it Spears?" he sputtered. "Is he okay?"

"Clearly he is not well. But let's revisit this in a moment." And Efron made an odd movement, as though trying to gather something about his arms. Finding nothing there, he shrugged.

"It's about Meredith."

Forster's heart raced, and he started to rise from his seat, but Efron waved him down. "She is in her quarters, safe. I merely have questions for you, and maybe some answers." Forster fought his anxiety.

"How long have you known Meredith?" Efron asked.

Forster stared at his guest. "I...well, I've worked with her for several months. Prior to that I'd met her a few years ago at a conference. Why?"

"Do you know her very well—do you know her personal history?"

Forster arched his right eyebrow. "I mean, we've talked some, but she's not really gone into her past much or anything. Why are you asking me this? I thought you were close?" He stood to make tea.

"To an extent, we are friends. I wanted to find out how much you knew."

Efron accepted a mug of hot tea from Forster. He took a long drink and closed his eyes.

"Does she know you're asking me this?" Forster wondered.

"She does not. I think it best that you not tell her we've spoken."

Forster felt a crawling unease. "I'm not sure I can help you," he said quietly. "Maybe you should ask someone else...whatever this is."

Efron's eyes crinkled. "Forster, this is not an inquisition; I merely need to get my facts straight. The matter is important enough that I ask for privacy."

"You don't know her that well, do you?" Forster demanded.

"As I said, we are friends," Efron replied. "Meredith is a rare person; she does not exhaust me immediately like so many others. And I understand her needs, as I can relate to them myself. My goal is to help her with those needs. That's where you come in."

Efron stood, and for a moment Forster thought of the vision in the doorway. The air seemed charged, and the hairs on his arms rose. A strong urge of flight seized Forster, but Efron had moved between him and the doorway. Standing above Forster as he sat, Efron seemed unnaturally tall. He stared down at Forster, which shook him as much as Auna's piercing eyes ever had. Auna he knew; Efron could be anyone, or do anything. Forster felt trapped.

Efron spoke, and his words etched into Forster's mind, jolted him into sitting upright. "Meredith needs you. You are the only person who can help her in her search."

"What?" asked Forster.

Efron smiled with some warmth now, and Forster relaxed. Forster had felt gripped by the neck, like a mother cat, and then released.

"Meredith has been searching for her daughter," Efron continued. "She went missing after enrolling in a program that's now defunct, and there had been no trace of her. That was nearly twenty years ago."

Forster gaped. Meredith always treated him so warmly, with such a motherly affection. She knew that his parents had passed away during his late teens. When he first settled into Mandira Station, Meredith checked in on him occasionally. Not once did he suspect her sad history.

"I had no idea," he said miserably.

"I've assured Meredith I would help her find her child. She realizes it's possible we never will. Ariel was twenty-one when she disappeared, and of course, she may have perished. Or she went on with her life elsewhere. But Meredith and Ariel were close, so that seemed unlikely."

"Why tell me this?" Forster wondered aloud. "This is personal. If Meredith wanted me to know, wouldn't she have told me? I mean, it's terrible. I feel for her, and I wish there were something I could do. But I'm not so sure I can help."

"Forster, you've already helped her. She's valued your friendship. I think eventually she would have told you," said Efron, still looming. "It wasn't clear you *could* help her. Until recent events."

Forster knew what he meant by "recent events." Again he experienced the urge to run, but he sensed on some deep level, there was no way to get past Efron to leave. He had him cornered in his own room.

"Yes." Efron nodded. "The signals. The messages."

Forster almost asked if Efron had talked to Gibbons, but stopped himself.

"How?" he gasped.

"I have ways," Efron answered. Forster grew pale. Efron walked over and placed his hand on Forster's shoulder. "Fear not," he said, and Forster felt warmth flood through his body.

His eyes darted up and again, fleetingly, someone else seemed to stand before him. A figure beyond time, silver and black, swirled in the wind of another world.

And at last Forster felt reassured. Not off his guard entirely, but certainly more confidant. He felt a strange comfort, as though he were in the company of a trusted older relative.

"So you know about the signals. Does that mean you know what they are? Where they're from?" he asked urgently. His pent-up anxiety burst forth into excited relief.

"I suspected for some time. And I might be wrong," Efron told him, "but I think it's Ariel."

Forster's mouth fell open.

"What, she's out there? Out *there*?" and Forster yanked open his porthole cover as if expecting a woman to be staring in at him.

Efron joined him. "Somewhere."

"But...I mean...good God, she could be anywhere. How can we know that's her?"

"We need to find out."

"Meredith knows about this?"

"I told her I have a lead. She knows it involves you. Forster, understand this," Efron warned, and Forster's former confidence extinguished. "Without being absolutely certain, I cannot tell Meredith we've found her child. What I can do, if you are willing, is tell her we have the best lead so far, that you are willing to help, and pursue it from there.

"And this might have been easier, had Spears not appeared at this very moment. I can tell you, I'm aware of his status."

"How?"

"I know. That is all you need."

Efron's voice turned cold and low. "Your captain walks at death's edge. I am not sure he can be saved, and in fact, death may be the best thing for him at this point."

"What the hell?" Forster bellowed. "He's my friend, he's a good man, and he should be saved!"

"Forster, you do not understand what may be at work here. He is not merely unconscious. He is trapped in great suffering. I have no means to release him."

"You're right. I don't get it," Forster conceded, frustrated. "But what does this have to do with Meredith's daughter?"

"I'm still unraveling all this," said Efron. "I think this is clearly related somehow, which is why I'm seeking you out now. If there were any implication Meredith's daughter led to Spears' condition..."

"Yes," Forster admitted. "That's too much."

"Quite. So I'm asking for your help now. We need answers."

"But what can I do? Sit here and wait for signals?"

"I have an idea about this." Efron produced a tiny silver piece in the shape of a diamond. "I'm not sure this will work with you, but it's worth a try if you are willing."

"What is that?"

"This is a conduit through which I can communicate with you privately. And that's going to be necessary if what I suspect is true." Efron held out the object. Forster hesitated.

"That's it?"

Efron smiled. "No. It's also a receiver, of a fashion. You'll be able to record any signals you receive. And I'll receive them in turn."

Forster ran his hand through his hair. "Why me? Why is this happening to me?"

Efron's smile faded. "That's a question I have no answer for. We must go with what we know, and what we suspect. Will you help us?"

Forster closed his eyes. He thought back to Ganymede Base. He could almost see Captain Spears' jovial, round face. He had patted Forster on the back after his breakup. Spears told him, "Don't beat yourself up over it, man. Auna will come around. You've just got to figure your shit out. When you do, she'll be ready, and so will you. Don't give up! I've seen you two. You've got that history. Can't get rid of that."

Then he remembered again the maternal fondness Meredith had shown him. He felt an almost electric sensation ripple through him. All his years wanting to help others crystallized in that moment.

Forster stood. "I'll take it. I'll help you. But only if it can help Spears too."

Efron nodded. "That's unclear, but it's better than doing nothing."

"Then I'm in." He took the silver diamond. And when he did, it leaped to the inside of his forearm and stayed put, and turned to his skin color. He lifted his eyes up in amazement, but Efron had vanished.

# 6

## SILVER AND PURPLE

Within one hour Forster bounced between anxiety and euphoria. The latter took over at last, to the point he kept smashing into things in his Mid Deck office. Not that there were many things to smash into. After the fifth time swinging his arms around like a windmill, his elbow and a lamp collided. He ogled in amazed shock at a developing bruise on his right bicep. But exhilaration coursed through him, endangering anything not anchored down in his office. His shin met his desk corner and he barely noticed. His ears rang and his eyes darted and he caught himself flexing in his porthole reflection. *Still got it!* he glibly thought, before he stepped backward and tripped over his own shoe.

Undaunted, he played music, finished his work, devoured his snack bar, and ran in place once back at his own quarters. Eventually he settled into stretching. He'd ridden a high on a sense of purpose and action such as he hadn't in years, but now he must calm down. By this time it was late in the afternoon. His shift over, Forster decided on a trip to the bar. He threw off the jumper, donned pants, and was pulling a shirt over his head when he noticed the diamond on his forearm. It had turned silver again.

Forster swiveled around, half expecting Efron to appear. *I mean, why wouldn't he? He would totally do that.* Of this, Forster was convinced. A quick search revealed no Efron, but the silver diamond shone. Nonetheless, a deep blush worked its way up his neck, and he watched in his mirror as it erupted in splotches on his face. *Is he watching me?*

He had worked out the possibility when a stabbing pain ran down his head and through his jaw. He approached the porthole window and spotted tiny lights far from the station. *It's happening again.* He watched them, but his migraine had begun. He fumbled for his dots and swabbed one on his tongue. He knew what to expect, and soon enough the shimmering aura crept through his vision. But he still watched the lights closely. He eyed the diamond on his arm.

"Are you seeing this?" he whispered. He felt like he was talking to a tattoo, but his urgency and his pain overcame any embarrassment.

Then his door chimed.

He opened it and said, "Oh good," and then realized he was staring at Gibbons.

Gibbons stood with hands on his hips, his face flushed, and he smiled, but the smile seemed forced.

"Gibbons!" Forster exclaimed, and his friend nodded. "Come in."

"Forster, I've not got much time, have to meet someone at dinner," Gibbons huffed, and he settled himself in a chair.

"Where have you been?" Forster blurted. "I didn't see you at the announcement."

"Oh, I was there," Gibbons assured him, fussing over the tea Forster handed him. "Big crowd, you know. Pity about Spears."

"Um, yes," Forster replied flatly, staring at him. Not sure what to say, he asked, "Any updates?"

"Not that I'm aware of. Sorry, but that's not why I'm here. Are you all right? You look pale."

Forster drew his fingers along his forearm. The silver diamond had vanished. He rubbed his temples.

"Another headache."

"Ah. Just in time. Veronica alerted me to new data." As Gibbons took a long draw of tea, he avoided Forster's gaze.

"Did she?" Forster asked, trying not to wince.

"Yes. Want to take a look after dinner?"

"Sure."

"Good." Gibbons then stood and gave Forster's shoulder a slap. "Feel better, good man. I'll see you around eight?"

"Okay," replied Forster, and Gibbons puffed himself up and left the room.

Forster leaned just out of sight from the door and watched him go. Gibbons had headed off the hall and was leaving the deck. Forster had just gone in to grab a vest when his door chimed again.

"Efron!" he cried, and he saw the silver diamond appear.

Efron stood staring down at the diamond inscrutably. "Ah, good. It works," he said crisply.

"I...guess? Did you...were you able to record anything?"

"I was." Efron gave a funny twitch with his hands, as Forster had seen him do earlier. *Like he's reaching for a coat or something,* Forster thought.

"Can we talk here? I have an update," Efron said in a hushed voice.

Forster gestured and Efron entered the room. Forster watched as he made his way in a long stride to the porthole and gazed out. "The lights are gone. Yes?"

Forster looked. No lights.

"What did Gibbons want?" Efron demanded.

"He knows about the lights," Forster confessed, his eyes avoiding the man.

"I suspected as much. So has he deciphered the signals?"

"I...some of it, I guess. Through his AI."

Efron smirked. "Ah yes. I am aware of her." Forster raised his eyebrows. He watched Efron's smile spread.

Then Efron noticed Forster's pallor.

"Another headache?"

"Yes."

Efron then reached for the amethyst pendant on his chest. "Here," he said, and he pulled the gem up and touched Forster's temple with it.

The oddness of the action threw Forster for a moment, and he had just enough time to say, "The pain's gone!" when Efron withdrew the stone and pulled Forster over to his desk.

"I need to show you something," he said, and he brought up Forster's screen.

An image appeared, and Forster cried out. It was Spears.

Spears, his friend, who had been hale and blustering and jolly and more full of life and vigor than anyone else...this image now in front of him could not be Spears. Forster refused to accept it. Whoever this was, curled into an unnatural shape, his arms clenched in fists in front of his face...this was not Spears. This man, whose face seemed carved in a frozen and incredible pain, screamed in silence. A man warped by and trapped in agony.

"What is this!" cried Forster.

"That's Spears. Yes, it is. Don't back away!" Efron grabbed him and stood him in front of the screen.

"*Look!* Take a good, long look."

Forster's heart hammered in fear and revulsion, yet he did as he was told. "Is he dead?"

"As I said before, he is not."

"How are we seeing this?"

"I have ways," said Efron.

Forster covered his mouth and nose, and peered over his fingers. "Why show me?"

Efron bent to face Forster at eye level, within centimeters, and hissed, "You need to see this! You need to *understand*. This is what has happened to your friend! He is trapped in suffering and he is beyond our reach. If he could choose, he would wish to die. Everyone on this station is at risk. This could happen to all of us."

"How? Not...not Ariel?"

"This is what I'm unsure of, Forster. I don't want this to be true, but we must take precautions. Forster. Gibbons knows this."

"What!" Forster gasped.

"Why would he be so interested in these signals of yours? Why involve his Veronica? Yes, I do know her name as well." Efron nodded. "In fact I feel better learning more about this...Veronica. That may be one weakness. And we should use it."

"Stop. Stop right there. What in the hell are you talking about?"

And then Forster remembered the first code translation and went cold. *"Changed me. Feared me."*

Efron saw Forster's face fall. "What?"

Forster snapped, "Can't you read minds?"

And Efron actually tilted his shiny head back and guffawed. "Ah, Forster! I'm not that skilled, I'm afraid. Wouldn't want to be. I'm just asking."

"The signal. The code Gibbons—er, Veronica—translated. It said, 'Changed me, feared me.'"

Efron inhaled rapidly. And that one gesture shook Forster to his core. *Oh shit, what now?*

"It's Ariel. It has to be," Efron said quickly. He loped to the door. "I need to go."

"Are you telling Meredith?" Forster asked. They stared at each other.

"Not yet. I have something I need to do." And Efron stopped and turned back. "Forster, take a break. You've more than earned it. I'll be in touch."

The door shut. Forster didn't need to be told twice. He combed his hair and left for the bar.

# 7

# THE SHEPHERDESS

Guru caught Forster's eye. "Thinking Man!" he shouted over the din. Forster ambled to the bar and squished between customers.

"Crazy tonight!" Forster said loudly.

"Yes, people are in a mood," Guru called back, serving up some drinks.

"Because of Spears?"

"Must be," Guru replied. "Your usual?"

"Sure."

Forster closed his fingers gratefully around his glass. Its contents smelled sharp and woody, a whiff of Douglas fir. His minded drifted to acrid damp forests and scaling stony ridges.

"Back in a bit," Guru said, and off he went to his clamoring customers.

Forster took a sip. He turned around and found the bar thronged. Nobody he knew well in sight. Voices rose and fell, and he sensed this wasn't a joyful crowd. It wasn't subdued, but he sensed an undertone of nervousness. The chattering and raised voices all tried to mask the unknowns. Forster thought, *if they knew what he did, they'd be asking for thirds at least.*

He lingered over the drink and thought, *longest, craziest day ever.* He wondered why he'd agreed to meet with Gibbons. He wanted to skive off, but he felt an obligation now. He also felt apprehensive. Gibbons was a quirky fellow, but had never once seemed anything other than a jovial coworker who liked a good drink and a fine, cozy home. Except ...Veronica.

"More?" Guru offered, ready to refill Forster's drink.

Forster raised a hand. "Got a meeting in a while. I might be back tomorrow, though."

Guru sighed. "Terrible about Spears. Do you think he had a stroke?"

"Don't know," Forster said evenly. But he thought he knew more than just about anyone else. What were the doctors doing with him? Could they heal him? Forster wondered how Efron knew so much and how he'd accessed the feed that showed the horrifying image of Spears, which Forster willed from his mind. Forster quivered with unease and dreaded meeting Gibbons.

"A real shame," sighed Guru again. "And you know what, we don't even know if we can use the supplies yet!"

"What do you mean?"

Guru lowered his voice and responded, "Word is, they're trying to figure out if there's a pathogen or not. Doing a sweep."

"Oh," said Forster. He'd not thought of that. "Bet we don't have another ship scheduled, either."

"Nope. Not for ages. Running low on things here, for the infusions, and with a testy crowd, that's too bad," Guru mused. "I'll make do, of course." He winked. "Still. Just hoping Spears pulls through. Strange and sad."

And Guru headed off to the other end of the bar. Forster realized it was time to meet Gibbons, and he took the long way around. He wanted to delay the meeting, but also, he wanted to stare at the stars. He went to the Dome Car and found himself alone, staring out at the blackness, sketching the outline of Ophiuchus. Maybe one day he would head to Bernard's Star, he fantasized. Have a look around.

Anything to move on from the disquiet he felt about what had happened to Spears. An urge to escape surged through him.

On he went, through the corridors to Gibbons' quarters. He hesitated outside the door. He rang, and Gibbons opened it. And there she was. The shepherdess from his dream!

But she was no marionette. She was a gorgeous woman, with scarlet lips and sleek black hair. And she turned to smile at Forster. No diamond eyes, but lustrous, dark blue ones shone at him. Forster goggled at her. Gibbons laughed at him, and Forster exhaled.

"Come in! Come in!" Gibbons cried thickly. His face shone with sweat and his cheeks bulged in purple. He chortled at Forster's expression.

"Forster, dear man, it's only Veronica." He roared with laughter. "She's something, isn't she? You should see your face. Maybe you'd like some time alone with her?"

"Now Gibbons," murmured this beauty, "don't abuse our dear Forster."

"Oh Veronica, what can we do, though, so low on our drink and no new supply! We're terrible hosts." Gibbons began playing music.

*Dear God. Harpsichord.* And Forster nearly turned and ran, but Gibbons had him by the arm and sat him down, and pushed a glass into his hand.

"I insist," said Gibbons, who swayed as though he'd had a few drinks himself already. "Never know when we'll get more!"

Forster stammered, "About that. Any word on Spears?"

Gibbons' face fell. "No. Pity. I can't believe it, can you?"

"It's upsetting," Forster said flatly. "I wish we knew more."

"Indeed," said Gibbons vaguely. Then he perked up, rosy and rotund and gesturing. "But the good news is, new signals! Veronica picked them up and was so kind to translate for us. My darling," Gibbons cooed, and he held out his palm to this remarkable woman and kissed her hand with its blood-red nails.

Forster felt sick, embarrassed by this display. He'd assumed Veronica was no more than vocal AI, and realized now that Gibbons had been holding out on him. He wondered what else the man had kept from himself and the crew.

"Forster, dear," Veronica purred seductively, and she reached out and touched him! Forster recoiled in shock.

"Are you an android?" he asked. Veronica grinned, stunning white teeth glinting at him.

"My dear, I'm simply Veronica. I'm so glad you're here. I found more signals, and you picked them up as well, didn't you?"

Forster grew alarmed as Veronica pressed her body against his. Despite all her frilly shepherdess finery, she seemed quite real. Forster stepped back instinctively.

"Y-yes," he sputtered.

"Good, darling. Let's talk about them." He watched, stunned, as Veronica began undressing. First she removed the outer layers, then finally the inner petticoats, and then she stood in a tight, revealing, red corset, her long legs in black stockings held up by a garter belt. She crawled onto Gibbon's bed and began to writhe.

While she did this, she said, "Well, dear, we knew about the previous message, and the new one seems to corroborate it."

Gibbons, smiling like a fool and sweating, was now removing some of his own clothes and moving toward his bed. Forster set his drink down and edged closer to the door.

"And?" gulped Forster, desperate to leave, but wanting to gain any information he could.

Gibbons began unlacing Veronica's corset, and they both laughed as he spilled his drink on her bosom.

"Just two words today, darling," whispered Veronica. Forster almost couldn't hear her over the plinking harpsichord. "*Help me.*"

Forster closed his eyes and ran out the door. Gibbons' laughter grew muffled behind him, and Veronica giggled.

He made it to his quarters, nauseous, horrified. He glimpsed something shining and discovered the diamond on his arm, brilliant and revealed.

"Oh my God," he wheezed, shaking. "I hope you got that."

And the diamond returned to flesh color again. Forster curled up on his bed plank, feeling sick, but managed to fall asleep. He did not dream.

# 8

## AN UPDATE

Forster woke abruptly. His message chimed, and he jumped from his plank and whipped his eyes around wildly. He had slept deeply for the first time in recent memory, and it left him disoriented. Then everything crept back to him, the wild day prior, and its insane ending. He couldn't quite process it.

The message chimed again, this time with a voice. For a full minute he tried to remember who this was, and then Forster called, "Ella! So sorry. What's up?"

"Good morning, Forster, we're waiting on you at the meeting," Ella's clear, warm voice replied.

"Oh!" he exclaimed. "Be there in five."

He hastily cleaned up and then rushed out and down the hall, heels pushing into the soft floor. He slowed when he realized Gibbons would likely be at the meeting. *Oh God. What do I say? I can't look at him,* thought Forster, and he hung back for a minute. He sighed in resignation, set his mouth, and entered the conference room.

Everyone was there. And he was late. He blushed.

"Good morning, sorry I'm late. Overslept, if you can believe it!" he said sheepishly.

"That's usually my line, Forster!" laughed Burgess.

Soft chuckling answered him from everyone at the table. Forster stared for a moment at Gibbons, who seemed incredibly at ease. The only tell were his eyes, which appeared more paunchy than ever, and his cheeks bloomed with splotches. Somehow this made Forster even more uncomfortable. A frown began burrowing into his brow and he fought it. If Gibbons could give good poker face, so must he.

Forster grabbed a muffin and tea and sat down. Ella called the room to order and with her long, slender fingers entwined, looked at each person in turn.

"I've been given an update on Captain Spears," she said, the lines in her face deepening as she seemed to fight back a grimace. The team members glanced at each other. No one smiled anymore.

"He is...still alive," Ella went on carefully. "He is, however, in what appears to be a state of catatonia. Etiology unknown. And a scan of the ship revealed no pathogens, so freight is being unloaded."

Sighs and murmurs circuited the room. Troy shook his head. Pop curled his fists. Meredith sat in stony silence, avoiding everyone's eyes. Efron maintained a downturned mouth but remained otherwise inscrutable. Gibbons flushed to an even deeper magenta.

"This is terrible news. Can you clarify this...catatonia?" Gibbons asked.

Ella shook her head. "I'm afraid I wasn't given any more details. If I learn anything I'll pass it along to everyone."

"Thank you, Ella," Meredith said quietly. Forster met her eyes briefly. He noted her pale and drawn face, and how the gleam had gone from her green eyes.

"Yes, thank you," Forster said also. He sighed. Then he asked, "Are visitors allowed?"

"That's a good question," Ella answered. "I'm not sure. I'll get back to you on that."

Forster nodded. They reluctantly moved on to the normal group meeting agenda and work plans for the week. It felt like a chilling fog had entered the room, muffling everyone, causing them to speak in lower voices, huddling closer. Gibbons, however, seemed completely normal. This bewildered Forster.

*He doesn't remember last night!* he thought suddenly. Indeed Gibbons spoke lucidly about his work, and contributed to the meeting as normally as anyone could when the aura of bad news hung about. Forster sat astounded. He dared not look at Efron, though. Efron presented his usual perched raven visage, and did not look at Forster either.

As they filed out of the room after the meeting, the Varises remained behind with Forster while everyone else left. Ella watched Forster with sympathy.

"Are you all right?" she asked gently. The Varises were the nicest people, revered, respected, and always kind. Forster felt guilty for lying to Ella.

"I'm fine. I mean, I wish Spears was okay," Forster answered evenly.

"Yes. I'm sorry. I wish we had better news."

"Yeah," Forster said sadly. "I can't imagine him like this." And he fought himself, lest he recall everything Efron had warned him of. The intense suffering Spears was experiencing. Forster hoped against hope Efron was wrong about this, but suspected he probably was not. This sickened and saddened him further.

"I will definitely let you know if you can see him," Ella reassured him. She and Darren hugged him and left.

Forster walked along the hall and thought he ought to head on to Mid Deck and start work. As he approached his office, a dark shape obscured the light in the hallway. He approached, confused for a moment, and then he relaxed. It was Efron concealed in the shadows.

"Sleep well?" he asked, with a note of sarcasm.

"Yes, I—wait. Was that your doing?" Forster asked suspiciously.

Efron smirked. "I thought you might appreciate the break."

Forster scowled at him. "Let's talk in the office."

Once they were inside and the door had closed, Efron declared, "By the way, yes: I got everything."

Forster sighed. "Good. I'm pissed you're messing with me, though.

I don't need help sleeping. I thought you said you couldn't read minds."

"I can't," Efron responded with a look of injury. "You need help remaining strong, that's all."

"So...that all really *did* happen?" Forster said, almost to himself. "Gibbons acted like he didn't remember it."

"Oh, it happened. I recorded it," Efron replied. Forster saw with amazement that Efron grinned impishly.

"Um, you'd better not use that," Forster said hotly.

"Oh, calm down. The look on your face, though!" And Efron laughed, which startled Forster. The man's head tilted back and his eyes squeezed together when he laughed, in a deep, rich voice. Forster noticed Efron's stiff regality subside in that moment. "Honestly I'm relieved. Everything worked. Now we know a few things."

"Such as?" Forster asked, flipping through his readings, irritated.

"Well, we can assume Gibbons is held in sway by this...thing of his, his AI," Efron replied.

"Maybe he was just drunk," muttered Forster.

"Certainly he was. But the man is a drinker, yes? Did he not seem out of character last night? You do know him better than I."

"Definitely. Here's the thing," mulled Forster. "I don't know Gibbons *that* well. But I've never seen him like that before. Now I'm not sure if I can talk to him again. This is...awkward."

Efron nodded. "I sympathize. But I would suggest," and his aquiline face and striking pale eyes riveted Forster, "you do maintain contact with him. Play along, only as far as you feel at ease, of course. Try to find out more about this...Veronica. I believe there is more going on than mere recreation."

Forster winced. "Fine. I'll keep it up. Now, what are you doing with the recordings?"

Efron's eyes shone. Forster spied some roguish glee in the man's odd eyes. "Insurance. Now, I'll be in touch later. It's important we talk to Meredith soon." And he swiftly left.

Forster shook his head and set about his workday.

At lunch, Forster sifted back through his records and found the solar wind aberrations from the previous days. He calculated back to Spears' ship docking and realized all the aberrations correlated to the strange events. Yet while the wind reversals were anomalous, they were not an impossible scenario. Only someone as interested as Forster in this remote pocket of the solar system would even find them intriguing. Except for what had happened. What could explain the connection? It made no sense to Forster, even as he reviewed everything several times. And he found himself obsessing over whether or when things would happen again.

He finished his food and went up to the Dome Car. He beheld the blackness and the star shine, and wondered what would happen next. He thought that Top Deck had no reason to suspect anything strange at this point, beyond the medical incident Spears had experienced. The shipment had been clean, but what of the records? Would they have found anything in his log? This bothered Forster. Whoever was out there kept trying to communicate something, and now he knew it was a form of mayday. But how did that injure Spears? Surely if it were Meredith's daughter, Ariel, sending this odd coded mayday, she would not intentionally harm anyone trying to receive it?

And just what the hell had happened in Gibbons' quarters? Veronica had in the past seemed a pure AI assistant, not a fully formed virtual being. Forster guessed that Gibbons had some sort of relationship with this AI, now that he knew what she could do. Or as Efron had said, she controlled him. That thought disturbed him. Especially when the man seemed so unperturbed this morning. Fortunately, Forster relaxed in one way: Efron had recorded the whole incident. So Forster didn't have to question his sanity on that point.

Forster felt overwhelmed. He sighed and his shoulders slumped. He folded his arms and contemplated that void, which he simultaneously loved and loathed. The emptiness now punctured by these strange phenomena. Again he wondered why he should be part of any of it. Why did he experience these flashes of contact?

"Here you are," a quiet voice spoke. He turned to face Meredith. She, too, stared out into the dark. This time she seemed more animated. Even a small hint of a smile dimpled her face, the first real smile he'd seen on her face in days.

Forster glanced around. The Dome Car was empty except for them.

"Should we talk now?" he asked. "Where's Efron?"

"All in good time," answered Meredith, in a soft voice. "I just want to look out there. I...I think she's there."

Forster watched her. "Ariel?" he asked delicately.

Meredith did smile openly then. A smile for her daughter.

"I think so. Forster I...can't thank you enough," Meredith said, and her voice quavered. "All these years. I wondered."

Forster studied his hands. "We still don't know for sure."

"I believe it's her."

She and Forster stood and stared out. "I came here, years ago, not really hoping anymore. I'd given up hoping long ago. But I knew she wouldn't have wanted that. My girl was always a strong one." Meredith's grass-green eyes shone, full of tears that never spilled.

"She was so excited, when she left. Knew she was doing something no one had ever done before, a part of something great and new for all of us," she went on. "I was never worried for her, because she was always so self-confident. Sure that she was doing her very best, and *fearless!* So fearless. But a little fear is a good thing, Forster."

Forster, although crushed by her words, knew that he could not quite understand. This was Meredith's child, vanished perhaps forever. If the presence out in the void was not Ariel, how would Meredith cope then?

"I'm sorry," Forster said. He didn't know what else to say.

"There's no need for that, dear," Meredith assured him. "I never felt she was truly gone; I always knew she would take care of herself and find some way. I can tell what you're thinking," she said, looking at him fondly. "You're thinking if that's not Ariel, I'm gonna drop right here and die, and it's all your fault." She gave a funny little laugh. "Oh, Forster. You really need to work on that face of yours. Anyone can read you so plainly!"

Forster blushed.

"No, don't be sorry, Forster dear," she said to him, giving his hand a squeeze. "I admit I was pretty floored when things started to happen the other day. You go so long with nothing but memories and questions...and something comes up and...well, I was pretty shaken over it.

"But I feel now, for the first time, this...hope. And for that, all I can do is thank you." Meredith gave him a quick hug, averted her full eyes, and left him standing alone.

His eyes stung. He turned back to take in the view of stars. He whispered, "I hope it's you out there, Ariel. I really hope it's you."

# 9

# DREAMING

After an uneventful afternoon, Forster settled down for the night. His mind still jumped from Spears to Gibbons to Meredith to Efron, and back again. He found himself peering out the porthole several times, hoping for a new flash. None came. He wearily eased onto his plank and instantly fell asleep.

He dreamed again, for the first time in a few nights. In his dream, he approached the window to find several large, brilliant dots in all directions. Not the size of the stars, but larger, some spherical, some pulsating. One of the pulsating lights spun and flashed, like a lighthouse beam sweeping continuously. He watched this light, and it began to grow. He realized it neared his porthole. Still dreaming, he made his way to his window and gaped in amazement. This brilliant, oscillating light moved just beyond where he stood. Only the window separated them. The light appeared larger than a person, and so bright it was almost unbearable to look at. But Forster did look, and he found inside the light something suspended. It moved closer to the porthole, and he focused on the object.

A young woman floated before him, her dark hair and pale raiment flowing around her as though she were underwater. Her eyes were closed, but she looked peaceful. The light around her still shone and pulsed, but Forster continued to stare at her. Then the light, and the woman inside it, darted away, back among all the other lights. And then they all extinguished, so that Forster could only see the usual star field.

He fought against waking; he wanted the dream to go on. But his messenger chimed, and so he swung his legs over his plank and threw on pants. It was Efron.

"Yes?" he asked, yawning.

"Time for a chat?" Efron asked.

"Mmph," Forster agreed.

Soon his door rang and Forster bellowed, "Come in!"

He raised his head and once again his mind swam with a black, rustling figure. Yet when Efron entered he presented as his usual lean, birdlike self. Efron smirked at him, his spectacles flickering.

"Well?" he asked. Forster crinkled his brow at him.

"Oh. Take a seat. I mean, I think we're beyond all that, aren't we?" Forster quipped.

"Don't give up on civility just yet," Efron tutted. He made a show of sitting down and accepting a cup of tea from a visibly annoyed and groggy Forster.

"It's five in the morning," croaked Forster.

"Good," Efron replied. "We've plenty of time for a chat then."

Forster sighed. Efron scowled at him and went on, "So. Tell me about this dream of yours."

Forster went owl-eyed. "What? I thought you couldn't read my mind!"

"Oh stop. Of course I can't," snapped Efron. He inspected Forster's arm. "I have all the data I need from *that*."

Forster sighed. "Fine. What's so interesting about my dream then?"

"Well, you tell me. Your brain was in an unusual state. So let's hear it."

Forster obliged, mainly to get rid of Efron, and grew more irritated that he should even be doing this. Talking about his dreams and about his strange visions. So he began talking faster and grew redder, until Efron held up a hand.

"Forster, are you quite all right?" he asked. And he sounded truly concerned.

"No. *No.* I'm not fucking *all right!*" Forster fumed. "What is this shit? Why is this happening? Why do you give a shit, and who even *are* you?"

He got right up in Efron's face, but Efron did not flinch. Forster backed off and turned away and muttered, "Fucking *bullshit,*" as he made his bed. Efron sat and watched, with his long, pale fingers interlocked. Forster practiced some deep breathing for several minutes and calmed himself. Efron stared off at the porthole.

After some time, Efron said in a soothing voice, "There's nothing wrong with feeling uneasy about one's abilities, or lack thereof. You have something unique, and once latent, and now you're waking up. Give it time."

Forster rolled his eyes. "It's not that I don't want to help. I just don't know what—I mean, it's not like I can control this."

Efron raised his brows and held Forster in the sway of his eerie eyes. "You *are* controlling this," he said.

Forster snorted. "Sure."

"The dream, Forster. You dreamed of her, didn't you?"

"Who?"

"Ariel, of course," answered Efron.

"What? I've never seen her, how would I—" And Forster's face went white.

"You knew that was Ariel the minute you saw her," murmured Efron. "You *found* her, Forster!"

"My God," whispered Forster. "But I didn't find her, not yet. She's out there." His eyes drifted to the porthole. "And we have no idea exactly where."

"I think you could find her if you went looking for her," Efron said casually, and he took a long drag of tea.

Forster laughed. "Oh yeah, sure! I'll just head right out there. I'm sure Top Deck won't mind."

"Top Deck won't know." Efron's eyes twinkled.

Forster frowned. "Hoooooold on. No. *No way.* We'd never be able to pull that off."

It was Efron's turn to laugh. "My friend, you want to think inside a little box. It's a very fine box, and has such nice corners. It has a lovely bow on it. Delightful box. But it's useless. Your mind doesn't work that way, despite your ever wishing it did, I suspect for your whole life."

Forster gaped at him.

"Did I lie?" hissed Efron savagely.

The color came and went in Forster's face as he shifted from outrage to anger, to horror, to shame. "Goddammit."

"I thought so," Efron said silkily. "Now. On to business. The time has come for you to go out and find Ariel, before anything else gets in the way and things get more difficult here."

"I don't suppose I could commandeer the drones for this?" Forster muttered hopefully.

"The drones aren't *you,* so no, that won't work," replied Efron. "That's not to say we couldn't use a few of them for something else. Hmm. But my point is, Ariel is a telepath. And she sent out a beacon that only *you* picked up. You should be there. Maybe she would try to make contact again. We could find out if she's responsible for what happened to Captain Spears."

Forster crossed his arms and rolled his eyes.

"Come on, how would I go out there? I'd need a craft, and I'd need to go undetected, if we're doing this in secret."

"Of course we are. No one is going to lend you a vessel to go gallivanting about in, especially right now. And it needs to seat three."

"Oh, so you're coming? Joy," drawled Forster. His irritation foamed up again.

"Well, you never know when you need a bit of extra...ah, help." Efron winked. "Tell you what. I'll have a look at the station's inventory. Meanwhile, keep up your work. Check on your own drone fleet, too, and take precautions with them. I'll leave you to your day."

Forster slouched in relief after Efron left, but then he crawled with dread at being discovered by management. He wasn't used to covering up things, but knew at this point he probably had to. Forster stared at himself in the mirror. By and by, the dread eased and the sense of hope he'd felt the other day came back to him. He would rescue Ariel.

## 10

# THE GOLDEN HOUR

A day went by. Forster became so involved in his work, he didn't realize until well after lunch that he hadn't experienced anything strange or had any visitors. Mid Deck was quiet, as some of the staff were at group meetings that did not involve him. He leaned back at his desk after a distracted meal and thought, *This is how it feels to have a normal day.*

Of course, no day ever seemed normal to him, lately. But he felt some tension slide for a change. He had sent his probes on their routes and repositioned them for various readings. They reported back with nothing noteworthy today. He wished he could send them even farther afield, and see if they might detect anything at a greater distance from the station. He knew, however, that this would attract attention and breach protocol. Also, he wasn't sure anything other than anomalous wind readings could be picked up. He knew, deep down, Efron was right: Forster himself would have to go out into space. Whoever sent those signals needed him as a proxy.

And Efron had his own station duties to perform; he had gone to some of the meetings scheduled. So Forster knew Efron had limitations on time for finding a suitable craft. "I'll bet he doesn't even sleep, though," Forster said to himself. "Bet he's doing this at night."

Depoe chimed to ask for clarification. "No, sorry, Depoe, just talking to myself," Forster answered. "Hashing things out, little buddy."

Forster shivered. Could he trust his drone bots? He had not considered that before. Could someone be recording his conversations with Efron? He discovered the diamond remained hidden. He'd felt uneasy about having this thing on him, but since it caused him no discomfort, he now was reluctant to try and take it off. He wasn't even sure he could do that himself. He longed for the day when he wouldn't need this thing. But he thought better about complaining, and he even thought it might help prevent any surveillance. *Paranoid,* he thought. Yet he felt justified in feeling unsettled.

Finally he left his office and meandered back to his quarters. He kept thinking about how they might leave the station to seek Ariel. He thought a lifeboat might be the best answer, but those vehicles offered minimal controls. After all, he had no idea what might be needed when or if they reached Ariel. What kind of vessel was she in? Could they even extract her from it? What tools would he need? Thinking about this made Forster feel suffocated. Goose bumps spread up his arms and neck. He shook his head when he reached his quarters, backed away, and decided to go for a walk instead.

Forster walked beyond the bar and one of the cafeterias to the other side of Third Branch. There the massive conservatory separated Mid Deck from Bottom Deck. He slid in through the air shower and into the gardens, enveloped immediately with their warmth and humidity and bright ambient light. He took a deep breath, smelled growing things, felt fresh oxygen entering his lungs. He exhaled in relief. He had waited too long to visit the gardens, he realized. They were just what he needed.

He squinted at the bright ceiling above the fruit trees and grappled with that familiar sense of displacement. On the other side of that brilliant light lay infinite darkness, but in here he felt a child of Earth again. The ground undulated away from the crops, to give weary residents a place to amble. Flowers and vines reached up and down on the leisure trails. A few visitors strolled along, and some sat on the ground and picnicked. The light grew warmer in hue, as the facility entered the golden hour of late afternoon. Forster walked along and took everything in. He wrapped his hand around a tree branch and pressed a leaf in his palm. He had forgotten the feel of these simple things.

He strolled over to admire the food gardens, where workers were finishing up the day. Some were human, some robotic, and all frenetically harvested and cleaned. Forster knew some of the workers by sight, having seen them in Guru's bar. Gardeners held coveted positions, and were often touted as the happiest workers at the station. Forster wondered how different life might have been for him had he chosen to farm.

As he watched the workers, he fell into remembering what Auna had said to him, more than once. But the last time he had not realized how long they would be apart.

She tossed her own tears off her fingertips, blinking, as she took his scruffy chin in her hands.

"I love you, I always will, and I love that you have this—this *need* to want to help people. Or rescue them. But one day, I want you to help yourself first. Make yourself happy. I can't be with you until you do that."

But he realized now, for the first time, that he felt he belonged exactly where he was. Had he not been doing his own work, he might not have seen those flashing signals. He might not have been able to help Meredith, and he hoped, Ariel. And he hoped he could somehow help Spears. He knew it was still a long shot, but he loved that rush of being needed, of helping. His mind drifted to the memories of giving up his own chances so that others could have theirs. The promotion he had passed up. And yet, he had not been there for Auna. It had been a long time since Forster had felt proud of anything. Now here he was, watching the light of the day fade into twilight all around him, and someone needed him. He liked this new feeling.

## 11
---
# RECRUIT

In the morning, Ella Varis came by Forster's office. She greeted him with a sorrowful smile. Forster held his breath in fear.

"Spears?" he said.

"He is, remarkably, still alive," Ella replied. She sat across from him and searched his face with her dark eyes. "I asked the medical team if he's allowed visitors."

"And?" asked Forster.

Ella sighed. "They declined. He's still in an unexplained mental and physical state. I saw him myself," she said, and Forster noticed Ella shiver.

"Forster, he's hooked up to a machine to feed him. He's basically quarantined. He seems paralyzed and somehow locked in a...catatonia, but his brain reading shows this as pain signals."

Forster shuddered. Efron had been right. "Will he live?" Forster asked, almost an entreaty to the Universe rather than to Ella.

Ella dipped her head. "They aren't sure. They think he surely can't survive in this state much longer. They've...they've contacted next of kin. And you probably know, he doesn't have much in the way of family."

"Yeah, I know," Forster said, saddened. "His work was his life. His friends were his family." He closed his eyes. Ella pressed her hand on his shoulder as she stood to leave.

"I'm so sorry."

Forster nodded but couldn't speak. Ella left and Forster sank into his chair, his face in his hands.

After a few minutes he shook off his feelings and touched his arm. He muttered, "Can we meet?" and the silver diamond appeared.

His door chimed. Efron marched in and sat where Ella had been just moments before. He regarded Forster with an inscrutable face, but not a cold one.

"I take it Spears has not improved," Efron said.

"You knew that, though," answered Forster dully.

"Yes."

"So, what's next? He dies in agony?" Forster asked. He looked straight into Efron's eyes, and for once, Efron flinched and turned his head.

"Let us hope not," Efron responded.

"You can't wave this away, can you?" Forster pressed him. "You can't put your necklace on him and make him better?"

"No, he's beyond my help right now in that regard, I am sorry to say. I hope you realize that. I would help him if I could. That's where you come in. If we find some way to reach Ariel and break this connection, maybe he could be released."

"But," Forster replied, "we still aren't sure Ariel is doing this, right?"

"No," admitted Efron. "But you know she's out there. And that's all we have to go on until you find her. And I suggest you do that soon. Another ship is coming."

Forster stood up. "You're kidding."

"I wish," Efron said, frowning. He stood as well. "It came from Ganymede, of course. I didn't check the manifest to find out who's on board. No one is leaving the station, notice. So something's up.

"I did look at the station's inventory. Lifeboats, small drone repair modules, that sort of thing. A few upper management shuttles, some diplomatic ones as well. These are secured more than others, of course. There is a med-evac shuttle, so that's a possibility."

"Would it have everything we would need?" asked Forster.

"I'm not sure. I suppose. But I...don't feel comfortable taking that," Efron hesitated. "So I'm thinking let's take the ship least needed."

"And that would be...?"

Efron grinned. "Spears' ship, of course."

"Oh. Sure, okay. That'll be easy." And Forster rolled his eyes.

"It's got to be his ship. It's spacious, and has potentially useful tools."

"Let me guess: you're the pilot," snorted Forster.

Efron feigned offense. "I can fly a ship I do think, and a number of other, far more impressive vehicles, if I may say."

"Good. I'm a shit pilot."

"I knew you would be," laughed Efron.

Forster considered. "It's a helluva heist, so I'd love to know your plan."

"We'll need a bit of distraction," Efron reasoned, "so we're going to have to ask for some help."

Forster nodded. "Okay. I'm in."

The two men left the Mid Deck office and rang Meredith's quarters. She didn't answer, so they tried Troy's. And right on cue, when he opened his door, he greeted them. "Hey! Come in! Want some chow or coffee?"

*"No!"* both responded in unison. Forster coughed to keep from laughing.

Troy shook his white head. "Tough customers," he chuckled. "What's up? Anything new on Spears? Forster, you look like a smacked cat turd."

"Wow, *thank you,*" Forster said. Troy laughed and slapped hard him on the back. Forster winced at the acrid scent of Tony's quarters. *It's like someone hosed down a dive bar with old coffee.*

"We do have news of Spears," Efron said. Troy tilted his head and squinted at the odd, tall fellow. "He's not well, Troy," Efron continued. "We need to help him. And we might have a way to do that."

Troy sat across from the two of them at his table and poured a thick stream of rank-smelling brew into his cup. Forster swallowed back the urge to gag. He tried to focus on the "art" in Troy's room, much of it some depiction of scantily clad women in impossible positions. The man kept his quarters' lights a dim, sallow color, which reminded Forster of a seedy dive bar. Troy certainly enjoyed his surroundings, however. He sucked in a long slurp of the coffee and regarded both of them.

"Well, I'm all ears, boys," Troy said. "What did you have in mind?"

Forster and Efron glanced at each other.

"We think," Forster said slowly, "that Spears is in a state of shock caused by something out there. Something he came across on his way here," and he gestured to Troy's porthole window. Troy wrinkled his eyebrows in confusion, but Forster continued.

"We think he encountered something on the way here. And we think we know what it is, and we want to go and stop it from...doing this again."

"And what is this 'something,' fellas?"

Troy watched them through narrowed eyes.

"A person," Forster said. "A person trapped outside, with some kind of telepathy. Who may have attacked Spears; we don't know for sure."

Efron turned aside and cleaned his spectacles.

Troy stared at Forster and set his coffee down with a *clunk*. "What in Billy hell," he muttered.

Troy turned to Efron and saw his stony, sharp features set in seriousness. "What?" he said again. "Hold up, hold up. Forster. Did this have to do with that light you saw?"

"Yes!" Forster nodded. "That's right. I've seen it a few times."

Troy's expression morphed from astonishment to confusion to suspicion, and then he laughed out loud. He tapped his right temple.

"Space madness, boy!" he roared. "You had me going. Come on now, though, that's not funny. What's the joke?"

"There is no joke," said Efron with eerie calm. He stared down Troy to the point the old fellow began to tremble. "We could go into more detail, but this is urgent. Another ship is coming, and we fear an attack will happen again. Such as happened to Captain Spears. Not only to whoever is on that ship, but to all of us here. We need to stop it, as soon as possible."

"Now, wait a minute, I don't know what this is," Troy cautioned. "You sound, and I mean this sincerely, like you're a few bricks short of a load." He picked up his mug and pointed it at them. "Even if this is true, then why tell me? Why not just tell Top Deck to send out a team?"

Forster and Efron exchanged troubled looks.

Forster said, "Because we think Meredith's daughter is out there, doing this. And if we can get to her before they do, maybe we can help her. If they reach her first..."

"Myyyyy God!" Troy said. His face went pale.

"Do you believe us?" Forster asked, trying not to sound desperate. "You can talk to Meredith about this if you want. But please, please: for her sake, please don't tell anyone else."

"Guys," Troy replied, agitated. "I don't know. I mean...you realize this sounds crazy, right? Like, actually soup sandwich crazy?"

They both nodded.

"But I've known Meredith a while," Troy went on. "And I knew she hadn't seen her daughter in years. How could she be out *there*? How are you so sure about all this?"

Forster shuffled his feet and a muscle in his right cheek twitched. "She's communicated with me. Through signals. Telepathy, I guess. Listen—yes, this sounds nuts. I get it. It *is* nuts. But I think she's in danger, and I think we are. Can you help us or not? Can we trust you?"

Efron stared again at Troy, unnerving the poor man so that he spilled his precious coffee. Forster knew what it felt like to have that laser focus on him, as if Efron might slice him open with a thought. He had to admit, Efron wielded a pretty effective way to make someone pay attention.

Troy took a deep breath. Then he took a slurp of his coffee. "Well, what happens once she gets here? Is she going to do what she did to Spears, to all of us?"

Efron replied, "She's made a connection with Forster. I am certain the connection will be stronger when the two meet, and Forster can try and get through to her."

"*If* she's the one doing this," Forster muttered.

"So you don't know if she's doing this or not, but you know she's out there, and she might be doing this...and you want to get her and bring her back here?" Troy asked, wrinkling his brows.

Forster's skin crawled. The plan was sounding like a terrible idea, now that Troy had laid it bare. He shrugged at Efron and said, "He's got a point."

"Look," Efron snapped, "we're going. I am sure you can connect with Ariel. If it's *not* Ariel causing Spears' condition, we need to find *that* out as well. We have another ship coming, so this can't wait. We must know! And for Meredith, we have to save Ariel."

"Jesus, you're both nuts," Troy said, shaking his head. He heaved a massive sigh and continued wagging his chin back and forth. "But I figure we have to get Meredith's girl. Maybe that means something bad happens to us, but we owe Meredith to try. Top Deck's gonna roast our asses. We might end up in the brig. But one thing at a time."

Then he rolled his eyes, saying, "Fine. I'll do it. What the hell do I have to lose? Can't resist another rodeo—it's not like I get many chances at my age! I'm not gonna go sailing into retirement! Now what do you want me to do?"

"Help us steal a ship," Forster replied with a smile.

Troy made a sound between a loud groan and a caw, and ended up coughing and muttering, "Dios mío!" and "Shit!" a few times. But he was in.

# 12

## PIE AND PLANS

I n the evening, Meredith invited Forster and Troy to her quarters. They found Efron already present, and Meredith gazed at them all with a gleam in her eyes. They sat surrounded by her quilts and embroidery. In the soft, warm light of her room, calmness fell on each of them. A feeling of rightness. Forster recalled his walk in the gardens; here he felt a similar sensation of belonging.

Meredith offered them all chess pie, which they exclaimed over. Then she gazed at each of them in turn, and smiled.

"Thank you," she almost whispered. They bowed their heads.

"You're taking a great risk," she went on. "Efron's told me the plan. If there's anything I can do to help, I will."

Troy spoke up. "Merry, I want to help. I just worry there's more going on here, and we might open up a can of worms."

"I know," replied Meredith. Her voice quavered. "I can't imagine Ariel would harm anyone. But we don't know what her condition is, and how it's affected Spears, or if it could hurt anyone here. Or even if she's caused his illness. I just want her back. I'll take full responsibility for anything. I just want her to get help."

Troy sighed. "Of course, Merry. We'll do whatever it takes."

"Thank you, Troy," she murmured. He nodded.

"Forster," she said, turning to him, "as you are aware, Ariel is... special. Efron's told you she was part of an experimental program. Project NEEDLE."

And Meredith turned on a projection from a button on her desk. An image flickered and showed in great letters: "PROJECT NEEDLE," followed by a smaller footer, "A Subsidiary of Badenhorst Biostructures."

Forster blinked in surprise and burst out, "Wait, Badenhorst? The same guy who designed materials for stations out here? Like Mandira?"

Meredith nodded. "The same man. He had more interests than a jellyfish has tentacles!"

At that moment the image of Clegg Badenhorst shone from the projection. He was wizened from age, with tiny white hairs on a mostly shaven and deeply tanned head. Forster remembered that he had died in a questionable circumstance at age 109.

Dr. Badenhorst spoke: "Greetings and welcome! Today I'm going to talk about an exciting opportunity for young persons with tremendous skills and talents. This—" and his image held his hands out toward the camera, "is Project NEEDLE: Neurological Enhancement Expedition for Detecting Local Extraterrestrials.

"We all know that eventually we will communicate with species beyond our solar system. When we do, how can we remove potential barriers to that communication? I created Project NEEDLE to bridge that gap of knowledge. What better sentinels could humanity have than those so gifted that they can read minds? Think of the potential for our burgeoning telepaths to detect communications that our computers could not. They could then, in turn, be able to help guide us in making peaceful contact with those *out there*."

And Dr. Badenhorst smiled with sparkling teeth. Meredith cut off the projection.

"Ariel signed up for Project NEEDLE because of its benefits and its importance. She volunteered for the job, she was excited about it, and she thought she might make a difference. The crews were to rotate out, so that none of them stayed suspended in space for long.

But after she disappeared, I of course wondered for years what happened.

"I was told there'd been an incident, and she hadn't made it out," Meredith went on, her voice now hardened. Years of heartbreak edged into her tone. "I never once believed that, and I put forth an inquiry. Other families joined in, because she wasn't the only one who didn't make it back from the mission."

Forster crinkled his brow at Efron and shuddered.

"How many others?" Forster asked.

"I never knew how many, but I think several," Meredith replied. "I knew she had made many friends. She had that way. Many of them were introverts, she'd say, but she was different. I think she made them all feel at ease."

Meredith smiled, her pride in her daughter clear on her careworn face.

"Wha—wait," Forster interrupted. "Didn't Badenhorst die right around that time?"

"He did," Meredith said curtly.

Forster raised his eyebrows and shook his head.

"So Merry," Troy asked, "are others out there? With her?"

"I have no idea. We have no way of knowing."

Efron spoke then. "Let's focus on Ariel. If we recover her, she may tell us more."

They all murmured in agreement.

Efron continued, "We are two days from a docking." He considered their troubled faces. "I think we need to act immediately. We want to prevent another situation like Captain Spears."

"And if we don't?" Troy asked.

"Let's just get his ship, go outside, find Ariel, and bring her back," Efron insisted. "Then we'll understand what we're dealing with."

"When?" Forster asked.

"Tonight," Efron declared. They gaped at him.

"Seriously?" Forster replied.

"Yes," answered Efron. "Troy, let's talk distraction. I'll go over the plan with you in your quarters. Meredith, I've already discussed it with you, so be ready with what we discussed. Forster, you'll be with me."

Troy whistled. Forster paced. Meredith twisted her hands.

"Ad astra," Meredith said to them all, and each guest hugged her and left.

# 13

# THE HEIST

Forster battled waves of nausea as he fidgeted in his quarters, waiting for Efron. He left his dinner unfinished. He paced and stretched and obsessively scanned the void outside his porthole. *Like she's going to send me some signal right now. Sure,* he thought with a bit of self-loathing. He tried not to think about what would happen when Top Deck found out he and Efron had stolen a ship. He sweated and fought the urge to retch, and his abdomen clenched in pain from anxiety.

His door chimed and he jumped. He opened it and gasped with relief to find Meredith holding something in her arms.

"Hi," he said, his voice in tremors, "come in."

"No." She smiled at him. "I'll leave you to your evening. Just... please. Take this with you."

Meredith pressed the bundle into his arms and gave him a strong, quick hug, and hurried back down the hall. Forster opened his arms over his plank, and out tumbled a soft fabric mass. His eyes streamed, and he blinked many times as he took in what he saw.

She had brought him a quilt. He realized immediately the quilt was more exquisite than any other she had shown him. She had stitched each piece and embroidered it all throughout. *Did she make it here?* he wondered. He thought perhaps not; none of the fabric resembled any material he had ever seen on the station. He wondered how long Meredith had been working on it.

Forster smoothed the quilt and swallowed as his tears ran. Meredith had embroidered flowers and vines and ruby-throated hummingbirds within her quilt pieces. He traced some of the green-stitched vines and found the name "Ariel" spelled among them.

With great care, he folded the quilt back into a bundle. He then grabbed his rucksack and carefully placed the quilt inside. He took deep breaths, and his anxiety waned. In its place he felt purpose, and determination. He would do whatever he must, to take this quilt to its owner. He was ready.

His door chimed again, and Forster sprang up. His eyes popped wide when he opened the door. It was Gibbons.

"Forster!" Gibbons cried. "You look exhausted, my friend."

"I—well, it's kind of late," Forster replied. "What's up?" he said, feigning nonchalance.

Gibbons opened his arms and asked, "Can I come in?"

"Sure, sure," said Forster, trying not to panic. "But just for a couple minutes, if you don't mind. I'm wiped out."

"I know that feeling too well of late," Gibbons answered.

Forster realized how haggard the older man appeared. He offered Gibbons a seat.

"What's up?" he asked again.

"Well, Forster, I'm a bit troubled," said Gibbons, studying Forster with sunken eyes. Gibbons looked like a man awakened after a long sleep.

"What about?"

Gibbons fidgeted with his sleeves. "Well, about those...signals," he said. Forster's spine tingled. "You've not had any more, have you?"

"N-no," Forster replied. His heart pounded, thinking of the night he saw Gibbons and Veronica. "Have you?"

"What?"

"I mean, have you...has Veronica had any more transmissions?" Forster asked delicately.

Gibbons seemed to Forster to be confused and bewildered.

"No," Gibbons replied, creasing his forehead. "In fact I've had a lot of trouble with Veronica lately."

Forster's right eyebrow twitched. "Oh?"

Gibbons raised his hands in exasperation. "Damnedest thing," he growled. "She was working so well until that last time you stopped by. I can't figure it out."

"Sorry I can't help," Forster said firmly. "Good luck getting it fixed. Maybe Pop can fix it? He's good at those things."

Gibbons chuckled then. "Heavens, no," he said. "She's too delicate for that man's touch."

Forster coughed.

"Well," Gibbons said, "I'll be on then. Tell me if you pick up anything else, will you?"

"Sure," Forster replied, and it was all he could do not to shove Gibbons out the door. Luckily the man left without urging, though he did seem reluctant. Forster caught a glimpse of him shaking his head and muttering. He watched as Gibbons walked farther down the hall, out of sight, and then he dashed back inside.

"Christ!" he gulped.

Forster had calmed himself after the uncomfortable visit, when he heard a message tone. He walked over and saw Troy's face. Troy gave him a simple nod, and the image went dark. Forster hoisted his rucksack and waited.

In the distance, a pulsing sound began to screech through the hallways. Forster laughed out loud. Troy had set off an alarm. The ultimate distraction.

The door rang, and when Forster opened it, Efron grabbed him by the arm. "Ready?"

"Ready," said Forster.

They waited until everyone filed out of their quarters in response to the alarm. Irritated and confused but not frightened, the station's inhabitants ambled to their safety zones. Then Forster and Efron hurried in long strides in the opposite direction.

"The lifts are frozen," Efron told him. "Up ahead, a hatch. Let's head up."

They found a ladder heading to a square hatch in the ceiling and climbed up. Efron turned the hatch open, and they began to climb again. It was a maintenance hatch, connecting spaces between floors and ducts. These spaces thrummed, hissed, and smoldered from piping and cables and controls. Efron found other ladders in one of these between spaces, and they were able to keep climbing without using any hallways.

They climbed and scurried as fast as they could, until Forster dripped sweat. The machinery noises squelched the alarms. At last they emerged, mole-like, stunned by the brighter lights. A few people were leaving the area, so the pair waited until they were out of sight. Efron's shiny head swept right and left, and finally he pointed. They sprinted down the hall as the claxons continued. Then suddenly the alarms stopped.

"*Shit!*" hissed Forster.

"Never mind, we're here," Efron said, and he opened a large door.

"No security?" whispered Forster.

"Well, this is a research station in the middle of nowhere, after all," said Efron.

They entered a spacious docking bay, with three docks. Two docks were empty. One of them was covered with a shiny film. "That's it," said Efron.

"What is that stuff?" Forster asked as they walked toward the bay.

"Some kind of protective covering," Efron observed. They pondered this for a moment, and then Efron whisked out a knife from his coat and stabbed into the material. He tugged at the tear. "Help me get this off."

"You keep a knife on you?" Forster gaped.

"Be glad I do," snapped Efron.

They tore away the film and stood back. Captain Spears' ship rested there, a bulky, stained, grey freighter, boxy and unglamorous. Large, cursive letters spread above the ship's rear door: *Siren of Conaree.* Forster sighed sadly at the sight of the ship's name. A flare of hot rage squeezed his throat. Spears didn't deserve what had happened to him.

Efron worked on the control panel next to the ship's door. A long hiss sounded, and a *thunk*. He motioned to Forster. The door swung open and a ramp extended down with a *scree* and then a *thoomp*.

"Let's go," said Efron, and they walked up the ramp and shut the door behind them.

Forster blinked again in the dim light, with small auxiliary lights winking on around him. Efron touched a control panel, and the main lights came on. They crept through the silent ship, Forster almost tiptoeing. Spears had been here, just doing his job, and then something had happened. Forster hoped the bio-sweep had been accurate and there truly were no pathogens. It was too late to turn back now.

"Hook up," Efron commanded, seated in Spears' chair. "Ready?"

"Yes," said Forster, seated and strapped in.

Efron ignited the ship's engines. Instantly, an alert blared on the screens: *"Unauthorized launch. Please stand down."*

Efron placed his hand on the screen, which then went blank, as did several other lights on the controls.

"What did you do?" Forster cried.

"I like a little peace and quiet when I fly," Efron said.

"Will they stop us?" Forster asked, and he tried to glimpse the station.

"Too late," Efron replied, and they shot forward, rapidly leaving the station behind them. Ahead of them lay open space.

## 14

# BURGEONING

An hour passed, and then another. Efron kept an eye on the ship controls, and Forster occasionally watched the windows. Every once in a while, Efron would ask, "Anything?" and Forster would shake his head.

"How far should we go out here?" Forster asked eventually.

"Well, as far as it takes, yes?" Efron replied with a grin. "Go nap, if you wish."

"There is *no* way I can sleep right now," Forster retorted.

Forster had come down off of his adrenaline rush from stealing the ship. Now he faced everything about what had happened. *How the hell did I get here?* he wondered. *We stole a ship!* He worried about Troy and Meredith back on the station. But mostly he worried about what would happen when he returned.

"They're going to jail us, aren't they?" Forster mumbled.

"Possibly," Efron answered, avoiding eye contact.

"You don't seem too concerned by any of this," Forster noted.

"I'm not," replied Efron.

Forster stared at the back of the man's bald head and seethed. *This man, this* freak, *how did I agree to do anything he said? What's he getting out of this?*

"So, what's your plan when that happens?" Forster asked. "I'm guessing you have a plan?"

Efron turned and stared at him over his spectacles. "I'm not worried, Forster," he replied. "One thing at a time, yes?"

"Well that's pretty slick of you," snorted Forster, frowning. Efron raised his eyebrows, and Forster lost it.

"Listen, *asshole*. I'm probably going to jail for this. Maybe you're not concerned. I'm concerned. So why aren't you?"

"We'll figure something out, Forster," said Efron. "We aren't certain we'll be jailed. We'll have quite the case for ourselves, with this rescue mission, after all. And Meredith will vouch for us."

"That's a big assumption," snapped Forster.

"You agreed to come along," Efron responded coolly.

"Yes. To help Meredith. And Ariel," answered Forster. "But then what? I had a job at Mandira. Am I going to lose my job?"

Efron shrugged.

"Oh," said Forster. "Oh, okay. You don't care. Why are *you* here?"

"What?" Efron asked, switching again to his analyzing manner.

"What were you doing before you worked at the station?"

"Oh, Forster, you'd find it all rather uninteresting I think."

"No, I'm interested." Forster's cheeks flamed. "You owe me explanations. I've gone along with this because Meredith is one of the only friends I have out here. I trusted her enough to listen to you.

"But you're holding a lot back, and I want some answers. I'm out here. I'm playing your little game, or whatever." Forster stood up. "So, you've got me. I've agreed to do this. I can't go anywhere. But neither can you."

Efron raised his eyebrows again and took a deep breath, saying, "Let's not get worked up."

Forster raised his hand and pointed at Efron.

"No, you don't tell me that. I *am* getting worked up. I've questioned my *sanity*, for God's sake. All this crazy shit that happened to me, I wondered what it was. Then you pop up and tell me I need to help someone I've never met. No. Answer me."

"I don't understand why you're upset," Efron said innocently.

Forster roared, "*Why the hell not?* What's wrong with you?" He got up in Efron's face and his spittle flew onto the man's specs. "How could you *not* see why I'm angry? Are you insane?"

Forster backed up and gripped his own hair. "You're gonna give me answers, you *freak*. I've had enough of you and your bullshit! Tell me who you really are! I know you've been hiding who you are. Tell me! Then tell me why you're out here messing with us!"

Efron straightened his back and lifted his chin. "You're not ready for too much too soon, Forster," he answered in a level voice. He wiped off his spectacles. "Calm yourself. I will answer your questions in time. Can we just finish our mission? Can we rescue Ariel? Then I will answer anything you want."

"I don't believe you," panted Forster. "You've followed me around, you put this...this communicator thing on me. It feels like you're stalking me. Then you don't want to answer my questions, you keep deflecting. I'm not doing anything else, you got it? I'll help get Ariel, then we're done."

Efron frowned, unblinking. "Forster. I'm not doing this to harm you. I'm trying to *help* you. You've got a newly discovered talent, and I've been trying to guide you through it. I admit this has been—ah—turbulent. And I'm not the best teacher. But perhaps you can learn from Ariel. Now can we please get on with this?" And he wheeled back around to pore over his controls.

"You son of a—" Forster hissed, ready to grab the man's high collar. Then he gasped and fell to his knees with an "Ugh!"

Efron turned around quickly. Forster moaned, doubled up on the floor.

"What is it?" Efron asked Forster, and almost reached out to touch his shoulder when he himself gasped.

Efron jumped to examine the controls, then peered outside the ship.

"Pain," Forster wheezed, and he lay on his side and hugged his knees. Efron glowered down at him.

"You've not seen any flashes or anything?" he asked Forster urgently.

"No," managed Forster. Sharp pain stabbed his abdomen and began spreading up through his torso.

Efron again found nothing from the control panels. He turned to Forster and grimaced.

"We've got a problem."

Forster groaned. Efron gave a frustrated sigh and bent down and picked Forster up like a child, and hauled him over to a window.

"Can you see anything?" Efron urged. Through his pain Forster heard frustration and maybe even fear. He managed to lift his head and look out.

By and by, in the distance, a winking light shone. "I see it!" he cried. "Oh God, my head..."

Efron then sat Forster down gently, took off his amethyst, and put the entire necklace around Forster's neck. The small, ovoid stone felt cool on his skin. He felt his oncoming migraine vanish, and his abdomen relaxed. He let out a shaky breath. He sat and trembled for several minutes. Efron glanced out again, but found nothing other than starlight.

"You saw flashes?" Efron asked quickly. "Show me. Where?" And he helped Forster stand and walk back to the window. Forster felt drained, but much better than he had moments ago. Forster pointed.

"There," he said. "I don't know. That way," and Efron hurried to his controls and pivoted the ship's engines.

The necklace reached the bottom of Forster's sternum. The egg-shaped purple jewel shimmered there. He picked up the stone and regarded it, and found the craftwork of the pendant and the chain exquisite. The chain's material appeared as simple silver links at first glance, but as he stared at it he found shapes moving in each link. He eyed Efron.

"Thank you," he said. "You want this back now?"

"Why don't you hang onto it for a bit, until we find Ariel," Efron returned, shifting away from his gaze. "You're welcome."

"Can I ask another question?"

Efron sighed. "Might as well. Doesn't mean I'll answer to your liking."

"What is this?"

Efron turned and grinned at him. "It's a necklace, Forster."

"Oh no you don't."

"Fine, you can call it a painkiller," snapped Efron, and this time he twitched, flustered. "It has...special technology."

"Fine. A painkiller stone. Sure. Where did you get it?" pressed Forster.

"It was...a gift," muttered Efron, avoiding eye contact.

Forster raised his eyebrows. *Who would give this guy a gift?* He sat next to Efron and stared out the cockpit window. Wearing the gem gave him almost euphoric relief. He couldn't help but feel greedy about the stone and already wasn't looking forward to taking it off, lest he feel pain again.

Efron noticed. "I'm sorry you can't keep that," he said, "but you'll likely need it for a bit. Do you feel anything?"

"Not yet," said Forster. "Did Ariel do that?"

"No, I don't think so. Look, we're coming up on something."

The ship's lights shone on several small, dim objects floating ahead of them.

Forster stood and gawked. "What are those?"

Efron said, "Some kind of rocks." And he was right. They resembled small, dark rocks, of varying sizes. But one of them was as large as the ship.

Forster felt a surge of warmth as he stared at the biggest rock. "There," he said softly. "That one."

Efron moved the ship closer to that rock. The ship's lights revealed what resembled a large dirt clod, about twice the size of a person. The two men met eyes.

"You're sure?" Efron asked Forster urgently.

"Yes." And Forster again basked in the warmth and certainty from minutes before.

Efron set the ship's controls and moved close to the rock. Then they heard a creaking, clanking noise as the cargo bay doors opened. Efron deployed grappling arms from the cargo bay and gently nudged the controls until the arms captured the rock. Switching to the bay cameras, he maneuvered the object and carefully set it on the floor. The bay doors shut with a reverberating clang. He released one grappling arm and then the other. He and Forster gaped at the onscreen image of the object sitting on the bay floor. The air return signal sounded, and they both jumped.

"Let's go," Forster said. Efron gave a half smile, and they headed for the bay.

# 15

# MESSENGER

T he door to the small bay opened, and the two men entered and stared at what they saw. On the floor lay a large, lumpy rock that seeped and dripped. They approached the rock and walked all around it. The smell of ammonia stung Forster's nose. His eyes watered.

"It's a big, nasty ice ball," Forster said. He felt momentarily crestfallen and embarrassed. He looked at Efron. Efron returned an inscrutable expression. Then the man gestured.

"Touch it, Forster," he suggested.

Forster grimaced, but he reached out and touched the icy surface.

A flood of heat coursed through him, his whole body flushed, and his skin reacted with goose bumps. He drew his hand away, and the sensation left. He stared at his hand, filthy with coal-like residue.

"Do you think it's her?" Efron asked.

"I...I'm not sure. Something's in there. It sent this warm feeling through me. I think it *could* be her."

"Forster, I need the pendant back," Efron said. Forster clutched the purple stone in his hand. His sadness for giving it back overrode his fear of pain. "We need to be sure this is Ariel and not...not what got Spears."

Forster's eyes darted to the large rock again. Efron touched his shoulder. "I'm right here. I'll give it back to you if you need it," he assured Forster. "We need to know."

Forster sighed, and lifted the amulet over his neck and gave it to Efron. Then he took a breath. No pain. He exhaled. He felt normal again.

"I'm fine," he said.

Efron heaved a great sigh and smiled.

"Good," he said. "Now, we need to get this ice off."

Since they had no tools to prevent damaging the inner pod, they worked with their hands. They scraped and chipped away at the dingy ice and made a slushy mess on the floor of the bay. By and by as the ice began to melt, they discerned an oblong, slender shape. The men worked away to uncover more of it.

They stood back to behold a long oval: a black, shiny pod, with small winking lights at one end. Forster and Efron pivoted the pod until it rested solidly on its flatter side. It weighed far less than Forster would have thought. They studied the lights.

"It's a stasis pod," Forster said. "Not like any modern ones."

"I wish we could see inside," Efron noted. He cast his hand across the obsidian-colored object and flung droplets from his fingers.

"We have to open it," said Forster. Efron nodded, and perused the pod's blinking control panel. Then he glanced at Forster. Forster nodded, and Efron pressed some of the screen.

A long, bubbling hiss sounded, which sent shivers down Forster's spine. The pod had cracked open along its equator. "Ready?" asked Efron, and he and Forster grasped the lip of the opening and pulled. The lid snapped off and they set it aside, and peered down inside the pod.

Inside there lay a pale figure, coated in a thick layer of slime. Popping and hissing sounds came from all around this figure, as the stasis pod set about its work. Gradually the slime layer thinned and dripped off, and they realized that this was, indeed, a woman, soaked in fluid and still as stone.

"Is she alive?" whispered Forster.

Efron stared down at her, inspected the controls, and wiped his hands on his pants. He reached inside and almost touched her, but then stopped himself.

"You do it," he said to Forster. "She's not connected to me at all. It should be you."

Forster did his best to clean his hands, then reached down to touch the young woman's arm. A surge of heat flowed through him again, much as before, but far more intense. A visceral and naked connection.

"I'm here, Ariel," whispered Forster, in awe of this feeling. "I'm here."

And this young woman, looking nearly drowned and deathly pale, began to turn pink. Forster instinctively leaned over her and rubbed her arms, and watched her skin turn a pale, rosy hue. She opened her eyes and stared at him.

He felt a jolt of confusion. Not his feeling, but hers. She stared up at him. Forster began to cry. Her eyes! Her eyes were the clearest shade of green, like summer leaves. Meredith's eyes.

"Ariel!" he cried. And she drew a long, sharp breath and began coughing. Forster helped her sit up and she coughed out long ropes of liquid. He wiped away all the fluid from her face and cradled her back.

"She's very weak," Efron said, reaching to hold her head upright. "We've got to get her out."

"*Cold,*" Forster felt or heard her say.

"She's cold," Forster said. Then he remembered his rucksack. "Can you hold her?"

Efron bent, and slid both arms around her back and head. She continued staring at Forster while he yanked open his pack. He pulled out an amorphous shape. Ariel and Efron both gawked. Forster fumbled as he struggled to unroll the thing cautiously, lest it fall in the filthy slush at his feet. He brought it over to her.

"Efron, help me—let's get her wrapped up in this," he said, unwinding his bundle.

He draped the quilt over Ariel. Efron helped him swaddle her, all the while holding her head to prevent her falling back in her frailty. They left her arms out. Her hands fell onto the quilt and she blinked.

Forster shook and his eyes stung. He spread the lettering of her name out for her to see, but she did not take her eyes from his. An astounding, protective instinct overcame him. For the first time in his life, he considered what it must feel like to become a parent.

"Ariel," he said again. "My name is Forster. This is Efron," and he gestured. "You're safe now. We've got you, and we're taking you to your mother."

"Mother?" asked the young woman. Forster and Efron exhaled and smiled. Forster meanwhile sensed a familiar flood of warmth from the girl, and he tucked the quilt about her snugly.

"You can speak," Efron said, with a huge smile. Forster had never seen the expression on the man before: he shone with intense relief and even joy. "Ariel, we are going to move you out of this pod, carry you to the cockpit, and then you can sit and recover. Here we go."

And the two men lifted limp, damp-haired Ariel in her swaddled quilt and carried her between them. Inside the cockpit, they lowered her gently in the copilot's chair and reclined it so that she did not loll. Her color grew rosier.

Efron brought her water. "Please sip a little bit at a time, Ariel," he told her. "You're recovering from stasis, and your muscles are atrophied. You've had no solid food, so you will be weak for a time. We are returning to a station, where you will be given medical care and food. And your mother is waiting there."

"*Mother,*" the word reverberated in Forster's mind.

"Efron," he said, "she's communicating with me."

Efron smiled down at the pale slip of a girl, with her long, matted dark hair and her huge green eyes. "Of course," he answered. "Ariel, Forster is the person who could hear you out here. He is...new at this."

Ariel took her sips of water from a cup Efron held. He set it aside, and he then sat down in the pilot's chair. On the other side of her, Forster hovered restlessly. He kept constant watch on her every move, lest she fall or sag or anything.

"We will leave soon and return to the station, Ariel," Efron went on. "If you are able to, we would like to ask you some questions before we return."

Forster exclaimed, "She's not ready for that! She's barely upright!"

And Ariel jerked her head at him and set her mouth.

"Forster," she said aloud, "I can answer." And she said to him telepathically, *"Quiet."*

Forster swallowed and nodded. Efron smiled again, visibly pleased.

"Very good!" He clapped his hands together. "First, I want to ask you, do you remember what happened to you, how you came to be out here?"

Forster felt her shock at this question.

"No," she answered. "I'm not sure where I am."

Efron pressed on. "Do you remember anything at all?"

"No," she said again. "Just...bits and pieces." She twitched her arms, and her fingers stretched over her quilt. She looked down, as though seeing the quilt for the first time. She blinked and rubbed her eyes. She had found her name, embroidered onto the fabric. "My mother made this?" she asked.

"Yes," Forster replied, kneeling at her side. "She asked me to bring it to you."

Ariel leaned back and closed her eyes. "So she's all right."

"Yes! She's fine. She's waiting for you."

Ariel said nothing. Efron gave her a little more water, and waited several minutes before asking her anything else.

Finally he asked, "Ariel, were you...alone out here?"

She opened her eyes. *"Feared me."* The thought shot into Forster's mind. It was the same signal that Gibbons' AI had translated.

The moment he thought of Veronica, Ariel flailed and tried to sit straight up. Her chest pumped as she gasped.

"What is it?" Efron cried, alarmed. He and Forster held her on either side.

"Veronica!" she said. She was trembling.

Forster and Efron stared at each other.

"Do you...do you know what Veronica is?" Forster asked.

"I know *who* she is," replied Ariel, licking her lips. She reached for more water. Efron gave it to her, and after she finished, she said, "She's out here too."

"What?" Forster exclaimed.

A forbidding expression fell across Efron's face, and his jaw muscles tensed.

"Veronica's a computer," Forster told Ariel. "She's not out here."

"She's a person," Ariel replied with some strength, "and she was with us. She *is* out here, as you say."

"Us?" Forster said.

Efron held up his hand to Forster and asked the young woman, "What do you remember of this...Veronica?"

Ariel tensed. "Nothing much," she stated. "I only knew her a little while. Maybe she's dead now, like the others."

This revelation staggered Forster. What could she possibly mean?

"I don't understand," he said. "Are there others like you out here? And...you think they're dead?"

"Of course they're dead," Ariel responded. She set her mouth in a line. "I mean, I don't know for sure. But nobody's been talking out here. So they must be dead."

"How...how many..." Forster began, but Efron shot him a warning look.

"That will do, Forster," he said, his voice icy. "Ariel, did you sense another...living presence out here? Or do you think you are the only one?"

Ariel turned her head to behold the blackness of space. "There's something. I don't know if it's what you'd call *living*."

Efron clasped his hands, set his chin upon them, and held her gaze. "Do you know what happened to the pilot of this ship?"

She turned back to him and scowled. "No. Maybe she did it."

"Who?" Efron asked. Forster's skin crawled. He wanted to cover his ears, but knew he could not escape from anything this young woman said, aloud or in his mind.

"Veronica."

# 16

# THE RENEGADE

E fron and Forster left Ariel for a few minutes to speak privately out of her sight and earshot.

"Won't she just pick up on our thoughts?" asked Forster.

"She can't read my mind," Efron growled. He held his hand up again before Forster asked why. "Call it years of practice."

"What do you think she meant about Veronica?" Forster asked. "The name can't be a coincidence."

"I agree," Efron replied. "I'm not exactly sure. We can find out more after we get back to the station, and things settle down. We should try not to mention Gibbons' AI again. Try to push that thought out of your mind if you can."

"How?" Forster asked. His frustration percolated again, and Efron's brow creased in thought.

"Think of anything else," Efron responded. "Something that centers you."

Forster thought immediately of Auna. "How about someone?" he asked.

"Yes. A person. Go with that." Efron nodded. "Now. Listen to me. The pain you felt earlier. I noted where we were, when that started."

"Yeah," said Forster, "and?"

"I'm guessing that is the route Spears took. If we pass through that area again, you'll feel pain again. And she will too," Efron said. "You will have to share the stone. By wearing the stone, you will be spared the pain." He took hold of the necklace and fidgeted, and pulled gently on the chain so that it extended by a few feet. "Now it can fit you both."

Forster thought for a minute, and then said, "Wait. How do we know we've made it through?"

"Just keep it on until we reach the station," replied Efron. "We need to warn them, and send the coordinates to that ship arriving tomorrow."

"Tomorrow!" cried Forster.

"Forster, we've been out here for a while. I'm going to pilot us back. Go ahead and sit next to Ariel and tell her about the necklace."

"Will it work?" Forster asked.

"Hmph," Efron said, and he turned and raced back to the cockpit.

Forster followed and walked to Ariel. He said, "Here, put this on," but she pushed back in her chair away from him.

"I'm not putting that on," she retorted. She shifted in her chair and tried to rise, but ended up sliding off onto the floor. Both Forster and Efron helped her stand on wobbly legs.

"Ariel," said Efron quietly, "we passed through something coming out here. A presence, which caused Forster great suffering. This necklace ended that suffering, and can prevent it for both of you. We can try to avoid that area on our return to the station, but just in case it's fluid, we had better err on the side of caution."

Ariel sighed. "That's going to block my thoughts, isn't it?"

"No," Efron answered. "But it will protect you from..."

"From Veronica," said Ariel.

Forster asked, "How do you know Veronica? You say she's a real person, and she maybe caused this thing that hurt our captain? And was hurting me until Efron stepped in?"

Ariel puckered her mouth as if tasting something acrid. She told them, "Veronica was part of our group once. We were a special team. She sometimes did not want to follow mission orders. One day, she broke away. But she was a strong member, so officially they kept her on, and placated her needs so she would stay.

"She left again, and we never knew what happened to her. I was with a smaller group sent out—" and Ariel stopped herself. "She was not part of this group. We had been...changed. I think she envied us. I don't know. I just knew that I could...feel her anger, and her fear, on a basic level. Maybe the way you felt me," she said to Forster. "So I think she is out here, like I was."

"Why would she attack anyone?" Forster asked.

"I don't know. I never understood her," replied Ariel. "She operated away from anything that made sense to me. Wanted to go rogue. And she was powerful, and could have helped people, but she was unstable."

"If she's as weak as you are—no offense—how could she do this to Spears? And then try it again on me?" Forster asked. He sensed the young woman's outrage building in her as she remembered.

"Put the necklace on!" Efron barked at them. "It can only stave off this sort of attack. If you're fully taken, there's nothing I can do for you. Please! You're too important."

This time Ariel obliged, and she and Forster squeezed next to each other in her seat. Forster felt bad for thinking she reeked of chemicals and old sweat. But he could not help wanting to turn away from her. He grew uncomfortable, and slightly afraid, as Efron piloted them.

*You don't smell great either,* Ariel fumed in his mind. Forster blinked several times in surprise. *What do you think I could do to you right now, anyway? Come on.*

*Fair enough,* Forster thought back, with an apologetic face. *I'm sorry.*

"We're through that general area," Efron announced. "I flew below and around it. Let's hope that works for anyone else. We're not far from the station now."

Then he turned to face Ariel and Forster. To Ariel he said, "I am afraid, my dear, that Forster and I will be arrested upon our return. Your mother is innocent of our actions to come and rescue you."

"You mean nobody knows you've rescued me?" Ariel asked, her eyes wide.

"Well, your mother does," Efron conceded, "as does another member of our team, Troy. He provided the...distraction."

"Wait!" Ariel cried. "You stole this thing?"

Efron gave her a nod.

"What's going to happen to me then?"

"You'll go to the medical bay. Your mother can join you there," replied Efron. "You'll be safe."

"I wonder about that. And what happens to the two of you?" Ariel asked.

"Apart from you and your mother making a case for us?" Efron said with a smile. "I do hope the station management will be interested to learn we've got a problem out here, and we might be able to help stop it.

"We're close enough to the station now. I'll need that necklace back. And if you and Forster could not mention how it works to anyone, I would appreciate that. It's—ah—classified tech, after a fashion."

Forster handed the necklace back to him, and he sensed anxiety from Ariel, on top of his own. A speck of light appeared out the cockpit window as the station came into view. Forster watched Ariel, who stared at that light. For the first time, he felt great relief that the only thing he could see out of any window was his station home.

# 17

# HEROES

E fron took a deep breath and switched on all the controls he had turned off when they had left the station. Immediately, alarms sounded. Forster and Ariel jumped. Outside the cockpit, Forster saw a number of drones form an array between their ship and the station.

A voice cracked through their communication screen. "We repeat: stand down. Disengage your engines. You will be towed in."

Efron disengaged the engines. And within seconds, the drones surrounded the clunky ship and attached to it. Their small thrusters set to work and tugged Spears' ship toward the station. Efron turned to Forster and Ariel. Forster looked at Ariel, and back at Efron.

"Efron," he said, hoarsely. His insides quaked. He understood, now, the reality of what was about to happen to them. He thought about his past, about Auna, about everything leading to this moment.

"Yes?" Efron answered.

"I just want to say, you're a pain in the ass," Forster said. He grinned, and Efron laughed.

Ariel reached out and held Forster's hand, while her lucid eyes moved back and forth between both men.

"I don't think I had much left in me," she told them. Her thin face glowed in the reflection of the bright station through the windows. "But you found me. Thank you."

Forster swallowed and turned away. He felt her warmth again, and heard her thinking, *"You did a brave thing."*

"You're welcome," Forster said aloud.

Efron nodded. He turned back to the controls. "Time to dock," he announced. "Hold steady."

The ship docked, and Efron powered it down. He stood, and he and Forster lifted Ariel up between them. Forster began shaking. *We did the right thing,* he thought. *"Yes, you did,"* Ariel answered back. The bay doors opened.

A security team stood waiting for them, in addition to a doctor and a Medic bot. Among them stood Meredith, her hands clenched together in front of her. Her eyes shone like green lamps at the slim young woman seated between the arms of Forster and Efron. Ariel sat upright, and lunged forward. Forster experienced the tremendous pull of love and joy from Ariel toward her mother. Tears filled his eyes as they moved forward with her.

She slid from their arms and leaned into Meredith's waiting embrace. Meredith wept openly, clasping her daughter tight against her. The doctor stepped in to help Meredith buoy Ariel on her atrophied legs. The Medic bot trundled along behind them. They began to leave the bay, but Meredith stopped and turned back.

She stared defiantly at the security team and said loudly, "I'm gonna fight this." Her Southern accent echoed. "You might take them away, and restrain them, but be aware of this. We're in for a fight. They brought me my daughter. To me, they are heroes!"

And Meredith gave Forster and Efron a long, grateful look. "Boys," she told them. "You did good."

Forster felt strong hands on his shoulders, and turned to watch Efron being led away. Efron walked tall and aloof, his bald head shining, his spectacles glinting, and did not look back. A moment of vertigo struck Forster. He beheld another figure in Efron's place: the taller, prouder person in the black cape with the long, silver hair. Then the vision vanished as Efron's guards led him out of the bay.

Forster trudged along, sullen, and the two guards leading him took him down a long hallway and into a room. Efron and Meredith and Ariel were out of sight. The guards, crisp in their deep maroon uniforms with black belts and boots, opened the door.

"Wait here," said one of them, a tall and stout man. "You will be questioned shortly."

The door shut, and Forster found himself in a spare, small meeting room, with a table and chairs. The lights changed from dim to bright white. He sat at the table and blinked, his vision adjusting. He considered his hands, caked with dirt from the ice ball on the ship. He realized he probably looked disheveled and filthy. Then exhaustion took hold of him. All his adrenaline had drained, and he felt shattered. He couldn't remember when he had last slept, when he had eaten, when he'd had any water. His thoughts blurred.

Yet despite his increasing feeling of doom, he basked in a lucid and lingering feeling of joy. He replayed Meredith and Ariel's reunion in his mind over and over, and how Ariel felt, and Meredith's defiance. Forster realized he regretted nothing. Pride overcame his misgivings. No matter what happened next, he would hold onto that feeling.

## 18

# INTERROGATIONS

Forster felt sudden warmth, and he woke with a snort. There, in front of him, next to the table where he sat, stood Ariel, as she had appeared to him before they had found her. She floated, her hair drifting kelp-like to and fro as though suspended in a sea, and her green eyes stared at him.

"*Forster,*" she said. He blinked and almost spoke. She put a finger to her lips. "*Don't act like you see me. They'll be here in a few minutes.*"

He shut his mouth and responded in thoughts, "*Are you all right? Where are you?*"

"*I'm fine. I am tired, of course. I ate a bit, then vomited. But I ate more later. First solid food in a long time. Mama is with me in the med bay.*"

"Good," Forster said.

"*Forster,*" she went on, "*I need you to keep secret how I contacted you. They're going to ask you. Tell them it was the wind readings you found.*"

Forster realized Ariel must have gleaned some of this from Meredith. But the rest she could only have surmised by picking up his thoughts. He followed Efron's instructions in a flash and filled his thoughts with Auna, so Ariel could not pry further.

"*Don't block me too much,*" Ariel told him, her image smiling. "*Will you keep the secret?*" Forster nodded. "*I can't contact Efron,*" she went on.

*"Mama says he will be vague in his answers, and tell them she had asked years ago for his help to find me."*

*"That sounds good,"* Forster replied. He felt bewildered. His head began to hurt.

*"Thank you,"* Ariel said, and she faded away.

Someone gave a tap on the door, which then opened to admit two people. A security guard stood outside. Forster did not know either of the pair who'd entered, but he thought he recognized the man. He looked younger than Forster, clean-shaven, with sculpted dark brown hair and slate-colored eyes, and he wore a crisp, well-fitted suit. The woman appeared roughly Forster's age. She had a sort of bland prettiness, with sandy hair, dull, opaque blue eyes, and a wide, round face. She wore a stiff, navy-blue uniform, similar to what Top Deck administrators wore except for its color.

The man said, "Room, please begin recording."

Forster breathed deeply in and out to calm himself.

"Mr. Forster," said the woman, extending her hand, "my name is Lieutenant Marshall. This is Officer Derry. We will be handling the preliminary investigation into your activities." Forster shook each hand in turn, and wondered at their politeness.

Officer Derry sat ramrod straight and clasped his perfectly manicured hands on the table. "Mr. Forster," he said, "we would like to begin by stating that you have violated multiple station codes relating to the craft of Captain Spears." And the man turned to one of the walls to show a list form of station rules and regulations. Forster stifled a sigh and reluctantly read the list, with font too large to ignore. He nodded.

Lieutenant Marshall announced, "We would also like to discuss the nature of what happened, beginning with any information you had about Ariel Brant. In particular, how you came to receive information about Miss Brant and her whereabouts."

"I—I," Forster stammered, "I noticed something strange while doing my work. I mentioned it to Mr. Efron and Meredith Brant, Ariel's mother."

"And what did you notice, Mr. Forster?" asked Officer Derry in a clinical yet unctuous voice. Forster disliked this man, from his impeccable appearance to his cold eyes. He sensed the officer had never worked hard, but rather influenced his way through life.

Forster replied, choosing his words with care, "My drone bots picked up on a change in wind patterns."

"And this is unusual?" Lieutenant Marshall asked. She also chilled Forster. The blankness of her eyes disturbed him.

"Yes, Lieutenant," Forster responded.

"What happened then?" Lieutenant Marshall inquired. She and Officer Derry stared at him, and his cheeks grew hot as his color rose.

"I...alerted Meredith," Forster replied, doing his best not to think of Gibbons. At every struggle to avoid those thoughts, he brought up the image of Auna in his mind.

"And how did Mr. Efron find out about the readings?" Lieutenant Marshall pressed on.

Forster said, "She told Efron, as he is her friend and we are teammates."

"And yet," said Officer Derry, lightly tapping his fingers on the table, "you did not tell other members of your team?"

"I did not think about it at that time. I was ill," answered Forster. He fought down the urge to slap the man's drumming fingers.

"I see," said Officer Derry. "Did you detect any more wind changes, as you say?"

"Yes," answered Forster. "The drone bots did detect two other instances."

Lieutenant Marshall asked, "Who or what led you to believe these wind changes had anything to do with the disappearance of Ariel Brant?"

Forster took a deep breath and replied, "None of us knew anything for certain. Efron had told Meredith and myself that he suspected it could be Ariel."

"Where did Mr. Efron learn this information?" asked Officer Derry.

Forster felt a creeping sensation. *What does this have to do with stealing the ship? Shouldn't they be asking about that?* he thought.

"Listen, I don't know all the history, okay?" answered Forster, irritated. "I was told she had disappeared, and Meredith had been looking for her for years, and Efron was helping her. He said this was the best lead they had had."

The smug Officer Derry said, "Mr. Forster, don't you think it odd that you would be asked to steal a ship with Mr. Efron, based on wind readings?"

Forster bit back the urge to shout, *Of course, dumbass, but I'm not telling you* shit!

He replied benignly, "Both Meredith and Efron are far more experienced than I am, in terms of what's out here at the edge. I trusted their knowledge. I offered to help in any way I could. That is all I know."

The two interrogators glanced impassively at each other.

"Very well, Mr. Forster," said Lieutenant Marshall briskly. The pair stood. "We may ask to speak with you again, as part of our investigation. Are you sure you have nothing more to add?"

"I'm happy to help," Forster told her. "I have nothing more to add."

Officer Derry told him, "Mr. Forster, a member of your management team will arrive shortly to assess your sentencing. Do tell us if you remember anything else that could be helpful in proving your innocence. Room, end recording." And he nodded and left with the lieutenant.

Forster sighed in relief and ran his hand through his hair. He looked at the wall, where the script of regulations still glowed. On a whim he pulled at his sleeve. The silver diamond shone, but it faded as he hurried to cover up his arm. He dared not make a sound, in case he was still being monitored in some way. A thrill of triumph shot through him. The investigators had not only been dissuaded, they had also been recorded themselves. Forster hoped against hope that Efron somehow followed the entire conversation. That might buy the man some time to think of how to corroborate, Forster mused.

He closed his eyes and thought, *"Ariel."*

He opened his eyes. She floated again in front of him. She

smirked. Forster thought she looked like a child with a secret. He then realized he viewed her as a child, just out of her teens. Though her actual age must be close to his, he thought, after years in stasis. Forster quickly relayed to Ariel everything that had happened.

"*Thank you, Forster,*" she said. "*I'll tell Mama. Good work. She says you'll have company soon from management.*"

"Yes, that's what I was told. Ariel?"

"*Yes?*"

"Did you know who they were? They were very interested in you."

Forster noticed Ariel lower her eyes and scowl.

"*I'm not sure,*" she answered. "*I'll see what I can find out.*"

Forster quaked with anxiety for her. "*Be careful.*"

She smirked again. "*Bet on it.*" And she vanished.

Forster laid his aching head on the table. Communicating with Ariel taxed him, and he was already exhausted. He drifted off, and dreamed he was back on Spears' ship. He stared out the cockpit windows at the blackness and tiny star points, when a stabbing pain shot down through the top of his skull and into his jaw. It coursed down his spine and he found himself curling into a fetal position. Then he woke, sweating, and wiped drool from the corners of his mouth. He shivered. Whatever was out there had wanted him. It wanted him to suffer.

The door chimed and opened. He collected himself. He stood in surprise at the sight of Ella Varis and Burgess.

"Ella! Burgess!" he exclaimed. "Why are you here?"

Ella met him with disappointment in her eyes, which stung him. Burgess set his mouth in a line and shook Forster's hand.

"Well, Forster," said Ella with a sigh, "as your manager just below Meredith, it's my job to ask you my own questions and decide on a consequence. Burgess volunteered as witness. I'll present my findings to Top Deck and ultimately they will sign off one way or the other."

Forster sighed. "Of course. I'm sorry."

"Not as sorry as I," Ella replied with a devastated expression.

Burgess continued looking grim, but managed a small smile.

"We're trying to help you out, Forster," he said. He and Ella sat at the table.

"Thanks, man," Forster said, sitting reluctantly.

"First, I see you received the regulations for review," Ella noted, her eyes scanning the wall. "I want to remind you that for *our* unit, we have our own set of protocols and...expectations. That you should alert all of *us,* the management, whenever something unusual happens."

Forster nodded. "Meredith was told," he said.

"I know this, now," Ella said, giving him a sharp look. "Honestly, I'm so disappointed with how all this has come about. It seems you and Meredith and Efron took it upon yourselves to keep this under wraps."

"Well...it was personal," Forster answered in a muted voice. "I didn't want to talk about the fact we might not have found Ariel, alive or dead. I knew nobody would go for it."

"You're exactly right about that," snapped Ella, a fire in her dark eyes. Her fists clenched on the table. Somehow this was far worse to Forster than the strangeness of his previous inquisitors. "Why didn't you tell the rest of us? We could have sent a probe of some kind out there. Even if it was a long shot. Then you wouldn't be in this situation."

Forster wanted to groan. He felt backed into a corner, but knew he could not say anything about his and Ariel's mental connection. Nor could he mention his confiding in Gibbons. He thought Gibbons would likely not have wanted that either, lest management find out what he was up to with Veronica. And then there was that presence out in the darkness. The malevolence that struck Spears and himself. Ariel insisted on calling *that* Veronica. What did it mean?

Forster managed to say, with deliberate care, "I thought maybe I could do some good, after what happened to Spears. And...I confess, I don't regret it. We *did* do something good. Don't you think that?" he pleaded. "We found Ariel, and now she's with Meredith again. And, I hope, she's getting better."

Burgess began nodding, but Ella shot him a warning look. He froze, opened his eyes wide, and kept his mouth shut.

Ella said, exasperated, "Forster. You've been at Mandira long enough for me to know that you're not giving me everything I need here. Are you sure there isn't more to this? I'm trying to understand. It's serious business to steal a ship. I am well aware of the benefit of what you've done. But consider what could have happened. Will you? What if this hadn't gone so well?

"Think about this. You could have injured yourselves, damaged or destroyed the ship, and even damaged the station. Not only that, but what if you hadn't even found Ariel? Then you simply would have stolen the ship. Not 'borrowed' it for a rescue mission. I am not, by the way, excusing Meredith in this. Her judgment is clouded by this, naturally."

"It wasn't her idea," insisted Forster. He grew miserable over all the considerations Ella had laid out, but on this he stood firm. "It wasn't her idea, and it's not her fault. Efron and I chose to do this. For her. Like I said: no regret. Fine, punish me. I'm sorry we stole a ship. But I believe what we did was important."

Ella frowned at him. She gave a long sigh and shook her head. "Here's what I'm going to do. I'm going to recommend you remain confined to quarters pending further investigation. I am going to authorize release of any data you collected with those wind readings. But ultimately that's not my decision. Top Deck will decide. And I think they might want a little more information themselves, Forster. I'm warning you. If you keep anything else from us, there will be a stronger consequence. You could lose your position and be sent back to Ganymede for further punishment."

Forster swallowed. His throat felt like sawdust. "I understand," he told her.

"Good. I will send up my recommendation, and if approved, you will be escorted to your quarters. There's a meal outside for you, meantime," said Ella.

"Thank you, Ella," Forster said, relieved. She and Burgess, who bowed his head to give him a regretful nod, were leaving. "Wait. How's Spears?"

Ella turned back and faced him with sorrow in her eyes. "He's not improved. They just aren't sure what to do for him, and expect he will die. I'm sorry, Forster." They left him.

Forster lowered his head. *We need to find a way to break Spears out of this. Can Ariel do that? And what about that ship coming? Would they avoid that area? Or would the same thing happen to them?* He hoped Efron had a plan.

# 19

# A WELCOME

Exhausted from the interrogations, Forster laid his head down on the cold table and fell asleep. He dreamed vividly of Auna.

She sat squeezed into a small space, wearing a flight suit and helmet. Her large, dark eyes stared intently at a screen in front of her, its reflection shining on her faceplate. Her broad forehead was fringed in dark bangs, which even in his dream made Forster wonder when she had cut her hair. He could not hear Auna's voice, but he recognized ferocity in her features. He watched her mouth move to swear. He knew that look, though it had been a rare one for her. That always made it more effective. He wanted her to hear him but knew she could not. He wanted to reach out to her, but his arms froze.

Forster woke, sweating, to the sound of someone opening the door of the interrogation room. He swiftly wiped the drool from his dry lips and ran his hand through his unruly hair. Ella reappeared.

She told him, "Top Deck approved. You are free to return to your quarters. I'll walk with you."

Ella frowned at the security guard. The man followed until she turned and said, "That won't be necessary." He halted but did not leave.

Ella pulled Forster along beside her and said in a low voice, "You can expect a word from Top Deck at some point. Right now, lay low. Efron was interviewed and gave a recommendation that your punishment be commuted. I didn't hear all the details, but it was enough for Top Deck to oblige my request."

Forster thought, *What did Efron say?* And wished, for the first time, that he could speak with the strange man. After all, they had pulled off a heist. If they weren't quite friends, they had an understanding at least.

Forster and Ella reached his quarters. "Can I speak to Efron?" he asked.

Ella shrugged. "As long as you remain in your quarters until you hear otherwise. I don't see a problem."

Forster saw a twitch in Ella's left cheek. "Has something happened?" he asked.

Ella blinked. "Forster, we'll be in touch. Get some rest and order something good to eat. You've earned it."

Forster gawked, amazed. He entered his room, and saw Ella turn to deal with the trailing security guard. He felt glad he did not have to face Ella anymore, with the expression she held for the man down the hall. He half wondered if her eyes could set a person on fire.

He turned around in his room and heaved a huge sigh. His first thought was a bath. After taking care of that necessity he gulped down water and ordered a meal. He shoveled the food down, ravenous, and then brewed a tankard of tea. This revived Forster briefly, but then he could not hold back any longer and collapsed on his plank.

Hours later, he woke and realized it was night already. He noticed messages glowing, waiting for him. The first was from Meredith.

"Forster, Ariel and I would love to drop by when you're ready for visitors," she said warmly. Forster grinned, proud to hear those words.

The next message was from Efron. "Forster. Page me when you get this. It's urgent." This unnerved Forster, but he pressed on. A third and final message was from Gibbons.

"Forster! Dear man, my God, tell me when you're settled. I'll pop by."

Forster couldn't help himself and said aloud, "Not likely." After Bandon and Depoe chirped at his voice, he said, "Not now, you two." He rolled his eyes and decided he should contact Efron first.

Efron answered in short order. "Forster. Good." On the message screen, he appeared relieved. "I know we can't meet in person, so I'll do my best with this, and maybe through Ariel."

"Sure. What did they ask you?"

"Well, of course they wanted to know why we stole the ship rather than ask for permission for an expedition. I told them time was of the essence, and they asked why."

"And?" Forster sat straight up. "Did they believe you? Did you tell them everything?"

Efron's face looked sharp and stern. "I told them you had received a sort of coded mayday signal sent by Ariel," Efron replied. "I told them I thought you should go along, since you received the mayday, in case you were contacted again. I also told them they needed to try and halt the incoming ship or at least tell the crew to alter its course."

Forster widened his eyes. "I'll bet that went over well," he mused.

"Oh yes. They asked how much I knew about the ship and its passengers, and of course I knew at least one person was classified. Things got a bit ugly," Efron said, and this time he smirked. "I managed to smooth everything over by suggesting we might have a way to cure Spears."

"Are you ever going to tell me what that is?" Forster asked, feeling his temper rise.

"We need to try and eliminate that presence, basically," Efron answered. He sat back in his seat and glowered at Forster.

"Terrific! Get back to me on how you do that," snapped Forster. "I don't think there's a 'we' anymore. We got Ariel, and we were arrested. I don't think there's anything else I can do."

"You're wrong about that. You and Ariel can work to stop this."

"How? They're just going to let us go right back out there?"

"They may not have a choice," said Efron. Forster could hardly see him, but his eyes glinted in shadow. "That ship is now close enough; we should learn very soon if anything is amiss. And if something does happen, they'll be forced to let us help."

Pangs of dread knotted in his stomach. "You sound like that's unavoidable."

"I've never hoped more that I'm wrong," Efron responded, and he sighed. "Get some rest. We'll know soon enough. I'll be in touch."

The screen went dark and Forster slumped where he sat. Then he remembered Meredith's message and called her.

"Hi," he said to her smiling face, "is it too late? Do you want to drop by?"

Moments later, the door chimed and he found Meredith and Ariel smiling at him. He forgot, for a moment, any dread or worry. Meredith looked smaller and somehow older, yet she beamed in happiness. She stood alongside taller, pale Ariel with her long, now clean hair. Both women's leaf-green eyes gleamed at him.

"Come in, come in!" Forster laughed, hugging them.

Meredith held out a plate covered with a tea towel and said, "Let's have some pie, Forster." And the three of them fell upon the dessert along with big mugs of tea. Ariel winked at Forster and sent him some little rapid, sparking thoughts.

*"You talked to Efron."*

*"Yes. Did you?"*

*"No, but Mama did. I wanted to talk to you first. I can be your go-between if needed."*

*"Be ready. He seems to think we'll be needed very soon."*

*"Mama won't like that."*

*"No, she won't."*

*"I'll do it,"* and aloud Ariel said, "You look a bit more rested."

"And you seem much better," Forster replied. "So good to see you both."

Meredith sat back, folded her hands across her lap, and smiled. Forster had never seen her so happy before. He hated the idea of risking Ariel, especially so soon after finding her. But he saw in the daughter's face a determination he recognized, a stubbornness that no one, not even her mother, could ever dissuade. He sensed at least she would stay the course, no matter what happened. That was a good sort of ally.

The door rang again, and Forster went to open it. Gibbons stood in the hall and craned to peek inside. He slapped his hand into Forster's and shook it. Forster recognized Gibbons was glad to see him, but wondered why he was visiting so late.

"Come in, Gibbons," Forster said, making a show of politeness for his company. He didn't want to, but he did not want to create any more tension.

Forster wrestled between his past friendship with Gibbons and the fact that the man had changed. He knew he owed him some gratitude for having helped translate Ariel's messages. But he felt he could not trust Gibbons again.

"Hello, Gibbons," Meredith called to him. "This is my daughter, Ariel. I am sure you've heard what's happened. Come and have some pie."

Now it was Gibbons' turn to make a show, and he kissed Ariel's hand, and looked back and forth between the two women. He gave a laugh, but his eyes glistened. Forster thought the man might begin to cry. Forster also noted Ariel's reaction to being kissed by this older man. Feeling an inner squirm, he avoided eye contact with her.

"How grand, how grand!" Gibbons kept saying. "It's wonderful, and we can thank our man Forster here for getting the job done!"

"Efron, too," Meredith reminded him.

"Oh, yes, of course, but Forster now." Gibbons winked at Ariel, whose mouth froze in a false grin. "Forster here is the genuine article. My good man!" He clapped Forster on the back. "Oh, and I forgot to bring by the Scotch. Next time. Good to see you, dear man!"

Forster walked with Gibbons to the door, and Gibbons said in a low voice, "It's a good thing that you did, Forster. Don't let anyone tell you otherwise. I only wish...I mean, I couldn't ask you, but... Ah. Never mind. Rest up. I'll try to speak with Top Deck about all this. Hope they let you off soon." Forster again saw Gibbons' eyes water, but the man sped away before he could ask what was wrong.

Instinctively, Forster thought of Auna before turning to Ariel. She had watched the interchange between the two men with intense curiosity. Forster perceived Ariel trying to bend her thoughts into his mind. He focused on Auna. He felt triumphant; he had blocked Ariel from reading him and his thoughts about Gibbons.

"You're an interesting man," Ariel said out loud. "Mama has told me a little about you, but not nearly enough." She and Meredith stood to leave, and both hugged Forster again. "Thank you," said Ariel, and this time she met his eyes. He knew she meant it.

Meredith held Forster's face in her hands before leaving. "You're a dear," she said, and gave him a peck on the cheek. As she and Ariel turned leave, Ariel gave him a sly wink.

Forster realized then that Ariel had gleaned something from his exchange with Gibbons. *She's much more powerful than she's letting on,* he thought. Still, he practiced thinking of Auna and silently chanting a mantra he had learned from Mandira's meditation classes. He repeated, *I put my thoughts aside* before he closed his eyes for the night.

# 20

# OMENS

I n his dreams that night, Forster saw three strangers on a small, rounded white ship with no obvious markings. One of them was dressed in a splendidly decorated uniform, like someone of high military rank. Another was a pilot, and the third a passenger. He watched them talking but could not hear what they said. He heard instead a strange, familiar static. Forster realized this was the same static he had heard in Gibbons' quarters. When Gibbons' AI had relayed Ariel's Morse code, they had also heard interference. And then he watched something that made him desperately wish he could wake up.

The three people on the ship simultaneously grabbed their temples and doubled over.

"No, no, no!" Forster heard himself yell. "Fight it! No!"

The sound of the static faded and the strangers' voices broke through in screams. The pilot slumped over and fell writhing onto the floor. The passenger curled into a fetal position where he sat. The officer groaned, growled, and shrieked; yet he managed to slam something on a control panel. A blaring alert sounded.

Forster woke sweating, his heart bouncing, a wild panic taking him over.

"Jesus! No, no," he cried as he ran to his messenger.

The image of Efron's somber face shone at him.

"It's happening, yes?" Efron whispered.

Forster nodded.

"I'll alert command. But no doubt, they already know."

Efron's image vanished just as the door chimed.

Forster leapt to answer it. Meredith and Ariel stood before him. Eyes feral, Ariel clutched her mother and trembled.

"Tell me, Forster," said Meredith urgently. "Is it the other ship?"

"I think so. Yes," Forster replied. Ariel reached out and clasped Forster's hands. Her touch jolted him like a current.

*"They're trapped,"* Ariel's thoughts pinged in his mind.

*"God. I hoped it was a dream,"* Forster responded, his eyes sad.

*"I dreamt it too. I heard a noise—some static, and then people screaming."*

*"Same here."*

*"What do we do?"*

*"We have to go out there. Are you up to this?"* And Forster searched Ariel's face, then her mother's.

Meredith appeared very aged, every line around her eyes deepened. "Forster," she said hoarsely, "you're going to take her back out there, aren't you?"

Forster reached over and held her hand, which hung cold and stiff. Between the three of them, their hands linked. "I'm not taking Ariel anywhere she doesn't want to go," Forster assured her. "Only Ariel can decide what she wants to do. I'll do what I can to help her, if she chooses to go. I promise."

"I believe you," Meredith said in a broken voice. Forster looked at the floor. It seemed so cruel to do this to Meredith. And yet he knew he could not face the presence without Ariel's help.

"Well," Ariel interjected, "I'm definitely going. I don't want anyone else to get hurt. I've got to try and stop what's happening, and I've got to work with Forster. Efron can get us there."

"I'll go to Top Deck," Meredith said. "Ariel, come along with me.

Let's ring up Ella—she'll be needed as well, since she's interim supervisor. Forster, I'll tell you and Efron what I find out."

"Thank you," Forster told her. They left. He felt a great urgency to begin, no matter what that entailed. He swiftly bathed and dressed. He threw down a snack and went through his wind readings. What he saw made him jump.

At some point in the night, a burst of wind had registered. Depoe and Bandon had duly recorded all the data. This was no slight wind shift, as he had recorded when Ariel had sent her signals. This was a wave that would have buffeted anything in its path. A cold dread overtook Forster. The ship never had a chance to avoid such a force. Whatever that presence was, its capabilities had been underestimated. Was it powerful enough to reach the station? What would happen then? The thought of the entire station being tortured sent his blood pressure up, and his head pounded.

"We have to stop it," Forster whispered.

He programmed his bots to track his movements. "I need you to record me," he told them. "I'm going to take a ship out to the edge. Follow my trajectory so we can mark exactly where I go. Then we can record where this thing is."

Depoe replied, "I do not understand. We cannot travel beyond station boundaries."

"That won't be necessary. Just record *me*."

The bots obliged, and Forster synced his communicator with them.

A few minutes passed, long enough for Forster's anxiety to well up inside him as if he were a bird trapped in a net. He fought his nerves with some success, but knew that ultimately he would need some of that frenetic, primal energy later. He hoped it wouldn't overwhelm him. He didn't know what to expect out there, and even if he could fight when he needed to. But he knew he likely didn't have much time to find out.

His door chimed again. Forster raised his eyebrows. Had they got clearance from Top Deck already?

"Good, you're back, you troublemaker!" Troy grabbed his hand

and yanked on it. He smiled broadly. "Boy, don't you just look like you stepped in a steaming pile!"

"Get in here!" Forster laughed. "Am I ever glad to see you. Thank you so much for helping out."

Troy put his finger to his lips and grinned.

"Ah," said Forster, and he grinned back and nodded.

"I'd love to chit-chat, but something's up."

"Yeah, it is."

Troy stared at him. "Oh shit! More of *that*?" and he pointed at the porthole. Forster nodded.

Troy shook his white head. "Whew! What is going on around here? Honestly, everything's all gone to hell." He seemed to mutter that last sentiment to himself. "Well, listen, man. Seriously, something's not right with Gibbons."

"Tell me about it," Forster replied dryly. Troy chuckled and shook his head again.

"No, listen. I just saw him yesterday and he seemed in a funk. Then I saw him this morning, and..." Troy squinted up at Forster. "He's not right, man. He was talking to himself. I passed him in the hall. Straight up ignored me. It was like I wasn't even there."

"Well," said Forster, "he's in a mood for sure. He seemed glad about Ariel, but sad, too. I don't know what's going on with him."

Troy fidgeted.

"I admit I turned and followed him a bit, from a distance, you know. Just wanted to make sure he was okay. And he went back to his quarters."

Forster nodded, and Troy went on, "He got to his door, and it opened, and...now I didn't look inside, okay, because I was hanging back. He didn't see me at all. But I saw him. And I could hear music. Some kind of old, weird music. He just stood in the doorway and stared in. And he started crying! Like bawling his eyes out. And then he went in." Troy's white mustache wagged as he worked his mouth. "I don't know, Forster. Pretty messed up."

Forster frowned. "No kidding." His thoughts raced back to the time he heard the harpsichord music and saw the vision of the shep-

herdess. And then to the disturbing visit and the very realistic Veronica. He shivered.

Forster said, "When I'm out of here, I'll check on him."

"Keep me in the loop. Anyway, good to have you back."

"Never know, might need you again." Forster smirked.

Troy chortled. "Oh, *hell* no! I've had enough rodeos for now."

"Well, I hope so. Things could get dicey," Forster warned him. He
watched Troy's eyebrows work into contortions.

"Jeeeezus Gawd," Troy said. "In that case I'd better go brew a
cuppa. You want one?"

"Oh, *hell* no!" cried Forster, and he waved away the guffawing
man. "Get outta here."

"Stay cool, Forster," Troy called to him as he left.

Forster felt the tug of guilt that Troy should be in any danger. But
he knew Troy was a stubborn goat of a man and he would not take
kindly to such sentimentality. Forster leaned back and stared out his
porthole at the black field with its bright stellar pinpoints, and
waited.

# 21

# HIGH AIM

Two hours passed, then three, and Forster heard a rare intercom tone. He listened for any related announcement, but none came. Eventually the tone shut off. It was not a station alarm, just an alert. Still, it set him on edge. He was convinced something was happening.

He checked the wind readings: movement had ceased. What was going on? And then out of the corner of his eye he saw something fly past his porthole. He jumped up and craned to see it. A tiny speck of light blew by, but he knew what that was: a drone bot. He watched three more shoot past, all in the same direction. This was unprecedented. The only times drone bots operated were for research, maintenance, or investigation of issues on the exterior of the station. They never moved as rapidly as these, and certainly not into empty space.

His door chimed and he jumped. He twitched it open and his eyes widened. He was face to face with Ella, Meredith, and Dr. Vinita Singh herself. Ariel stood behind the three women, with Efron beside her.

"Dr. Singh," Forster said numbly. "Please come in."

"Not necessary," Dr. Singh replied. "Forster, if you would come with us, we would like to discuss the current situation."

"Am I...am I relieved from confinement?" Forster blurted without thinking.

"Yes," came Dr. Singh's curt reply. "For now."

Forster followed the group, moving next to Efron and Ariel.

Efron looked down at him. "It is happening."

"I know," said Forster. "What can we do?"

"Wait until the meeting," Efron said, his gaze unreadable.

They entered the conference room where Ella's team held their group meetings.

"Please seal the door," Dr. Singh requested, and Ella and Meredith did so with their command controls. Forster lifted his eyebrows.

Everyone sat. Dr. Singh folded her fingers together in front of her on the table, and gazed sternly at each of them in turn.

"What we are about to discuss is a high security clearance conversation. I ask that none of you sitting here relay this information to anyone else. Understood?"

Nods and affirmations rose among them.

Dr. Singh continued, "I am aware of the current incident. At this point, we understand that three crew members on the government ship SS *Alta Mira* were traveling to the station."

Above the table, she brought up a simulation of the station and its surrounding field of space. A tiny ship approached the station and halted. "At this point, in this location," Dr. Singh went on, "we received a distress signal from the commanding officer on board. The ship was brought to a full stop at that time. No further communications were received here at station, and no hailing attempts received a response."

A visible shiver swept the room.

"What we also know, according to data sent prior to the mayday, is that each person on board experienced an extreme reaction to an unknown agitator. I discussed with the medical team here, and we concurred that this same process had also been recorded with Captain Spears on board his own ship. We can infer that the crew has therefore suffered the same fate as Captain Spears. At this point, we have no choice but to prevent any further contact on the station with anyone on board the *Alta Mira*. We must treat this as a quarantine situation."

Forster wanted to speak up, but Dr. Singh's eyes darted to him.

"I understand we have no evidence that this is a known contagion," she told them. "But we must consider this to be a threat to the station. The commander had the foresight to issue a full stop on the *Alta Mira,* so we can be reassured it will not dock at the station.

"I ordered a team of drone bots to investigate anything in the station perimeter that seems amiss."

*So that answered that question,* thought Forster. He caught Ariel's eyes. *"Wait for it,"* she advised him.

Ella spoke up. "Dr. Singh, what will become of the ship's crew now? Won't they require medical care like Captain Spears?"

"I understand your concern," Dr. Singh said evenly. "Naturally my first instinct is that they should receive care, yes. However under the circumstance, and with our limited medical staff, I am reluctant to send any medical envoy to meet with the *Alta Mira*. We simply cannot risk potentially exposing our team and this station to whatever is causing this."

Dr. Singh puffed out a long, frustrated sigh. "I must tell you, the ship was also carrying a medical expert whom we hoped could help Captain Spears. Now that option is lost."

Forster groaned, and Ella and Meredith sighed. Efron's brows furrowed.

"What are you proposing we do, other than monitor the perimeter with bots?" Ella asked.

Dr. Singh spoke to Efron. "My understanding is that you and Mr. Forster, although committing theft, revealed important information that could aid us. And if I may say, welcome to our station, Ms. Brant. I am only sorry it should be under these circumstances."

And Dr. Singh smiled at Ariel, who smiled and lowered her head. Then she raised her hand. Dr. Singh nodded at her.

"I just want to say," Ariel told them, her eyes sweeping back and forth between Forster and Efron, "thank you so much. I want to do everything I can to help you, and I hope you won't be punished anymore for rescuing me."

Forster fought back a laugh at Meredith's scandalized face. However, she chimed in, "Yes. A huge thanks from me, for reuniting us."

"Thank you," Dr. Singh told the women. She did not thank Forster and Efron.

"Mr. Efron, if you would, I would like to hear what we've already discussed and what you think can be done. Again I want to remind each of you, I want no one outside of this room to hear what we are discussing." And Dr. Singh ceded the table to Efron.

Efron sat tall and proudly. He regarded each of them, and Forster knew the pride extended to him. It embarrassed him but also encouraged him. Efron seemed pleased, as if he had collected a set of something he had sought for years.

"Thank you, Dr. Singh," he said. And Forster took note of how commanding Efron's voice became.

"What has happened here, I have been concerned would come to pass. I made my concerns known to Top Deck, and Dr. Singh has been kind enough to hear me out when others would not. I value the lives on board this station, and I want to stop any harm from coming to them.

"The signals sent by Ariel, as a form of mayday over many years, were heard and received by Mr. Forster here," Efron said, giving Forster a nod. "What appeared to be static underlying her message I now think was from something at the edge of the heliopause, not from Ariel herself. A kind of interference. Ariel's signal was translated by an AI construct of Mr. Gibbons, revealing the mayday. The static was never translated, and so was considered just background noise.

"However, when Captain Spears approached the station, he entered a pathway that set him along the source of the interference. He unknowingly fell victim to its source. When Forster and I retrieved Ariel, we also entered the general area where this occurred.

But I was able to protect Forster from the kind of attack Captain Spears, and now the crew of the *Alta Mira,* suffered.

"We took care not to reenter that space on our way back to the station. I alerted Top Deck of the coordinates, and those were relayed to the *Alta Mira.* Unfortunately, despite their alternate path, they still befell the fate of Captain Spears. We must conclude that whatever is out there can move, and may not be avoided. We must assume, therefore, this is an enemy combatant intent on harm. And from that we must presume the entire station is at risk from this entity."

Dr. Singh spoke up. "You were able to shield both Mr. Forster and Ms. Brant from being attacked. Is this something you can provide the entire station?"

Amazingly, Efron stood and held up his purple stone in front of everyone.

"This shielded Forster and Ariel from harm," he announced. His audience stared at him, even Forster, who already knew about the stone's capability. "I was able to drape it over the two of them. But as you can see, this is very small, and will not protect the population of the station."

Forster could see the questions on the brows of the group. Dr. Singh asked exactly what Forster wanted to learn.

"Where can we get more of these stones?"

Efron bowed his head. "This is the only one I have. And so, it can protect only two people at a time, maybe three."

Dr. Singh asked, "Does it protect you?"

"I don't need it, as I am resistant to the attacks," Efron said. Forster's mouth fell open.

"Mr. Efron, would you care to explain first of all, what the device is, and secondly, why you don't need it?" Dr. Singh asked.

Efron appeared irritated, as much as he could in the situation, which for him was remarkable given his usual restraint. He answered coolly, "As I discussed with you recently, Dr. Singh, I seem to be immune to the effects of the presence. And the technology of this device was not developed by me, but seems incidentally to ward off these attacks on its wearer. A friend gave it to me many years ago. I regret there are not more of them available, or I certainly would make sure everyone had one."

"Tell us, if you would, what your...research has taught you about this presence," Dr. Singh commanded him.

Efron adjusted his spectacles. Forster barely contained his excitement. *Finally!*

"I have, prior to my assignment here, conducted research on the far reaches of known space. And I have come across this entity before," Efron announced, as casually as he might describe a walk in the woods. "That research is classified," he added. "What I can tell you is that this presence is amorphous, and as we've seen, it can move. The entity induces a heightened state of intense suffering without killing its victim. In fact I think its ultimate goal is the unending suffering of a host."

"What hope do we have, Mr. Efron, of stopping such a thing?" Dr. Singh asked. Her eyebrows rose.

"We must try to remove it," Efron told them all.

"How?" Forster asked abruptly.

"I'm going to need you and Ariel working together," Efron said. Meredith put her hands to her mouth. Ariel took a deep breath and nodded.

Dr. Singh's brow creased with concern. "What do you need from Top Deck?"

"Another ship," Efron replied. "Or, perhaps the same one, as that ship worked well before. I want to use it to draw the presence away from the station. From there we will need Ariel and Forster to use their...skills to try to fight it off and hopefully drive it away."

"What if that doesn't work?" asked Dr. Singh.

Efron's lips stretched into a thin line. "We must try first and see. And hope that it does. Other measures would be more extreme, so I hope this will work."

Dr. Singh nodded. "I will grant the use of Captain Spears' ship. Mr. Forster and Ms. Brant, do you accept this mission?"

"Yes," Forster said swiftly.

"Of course," Ariel replied.

Dr. Singh looked at all of them again. "I approve this mission. I must caution each of you to keep this confidential until you hear otherwise. Given the potential for this...presence to move, I must proceed with an evacuation plan for every team on this station."

Efron opened his mouth, but Dr. Singh raised her hand.

She said, "I do realize that even leaving this station puts us at risk for attack, but we must come up with alternatives. Meanwhile no other ships, beyond Spears' and the drone net we've dispatched, are allowed in or out of this area until further notice. Thank you."

Dr. Singh hastily left the room. Ella, Meredith, Ariel, Efron, and Forster remained. The solemn mood of each person disturbed Forster. Every one of them stole looks at Efron, with his violet pendant. Efron returned to his seat, and sat still and straight. He looked down at the gem, which he held in his left hand.

Ella said, "Efron, how long have you known about this thing?"

"None of us knew until Ariel's signals were picked up by Forster," said Efron. Forster avoided his eyes just then, for fear he would betray his own doubts about the man.

"And this was...telepathic?" Ella asked delicately.

Ariel spoke up, saying, "Yes. I sent them. I was very weak and could not send anything other than an SOS, basically. My father had taught me about Morse code years ago. That was the only thing left I could do. I'm just glad it worked!"

Ella frowned. "Abilities like this...I'd heard of them, but they're uncommon, and I thought that sort of thing was experimental."

"It was," Ariel replied.

"Does anyone else here know about this?" Ella asked.

Forster shifted uncomfortably. "Gibbons knows, to an extent. He knew about the signals because his AI picked up on them too."

Ella nodded, her face serene. "Forster, can I have a word with you back at your quarters?"

"Sure," he answered.

They filed out of the room. Ella hung back and walked with Forster down the soft-floored corridor to his room. When they arrived, they sat and sipped tea. Forster could smell the spices of Ella's chai more than his own pekoe.

"You're taking a big risk, Forster," she told him. "I thank you for this. I have many questions, but it seems we may not have much time. I understand why you and Efron took the risks you did without asking for permission. That does *not* mean I am okay with you circumventing my supervision. But still. That was brave, and what you're about to do is also brave. I fear for you and Ariel out there. Obviously, Efron seems unaffected, but I wonder."

Ella's eyes glazed as she remembered.

"He and I have worked together for a long time, but he's always shut off, personally," Ella mused. "I knew he had spent years in the field conducting research at the edge of the system. A lonely job, and he seems to have no living relatives. He always evaded talking about family, I remember. At one point he even said his friends were family. Not unlike Spears. But I can't picture Efron having friends, other than Meredith. Would you consider him a friend?"

Forster thought for a minute. "Not at first. I...found him odd." Ella nodded and smiled in agreement. "But...I don't know. He got on my nerves, but the thing with Ariel.... I guess we're friends now, yes."

"He's not...quite normal, is he?" Ella asked in a soft voice, as if speaking her thoughts aloud to herself.

"No," Forster agreed. Both of their brows furrowed.

"Forster, I wish you luck. You've been a great member of the team. I want you to report back to me, okay?"

Forster smiled, appreciating Ella's kindness. "I will. I'll do my best."

She gave him a quick hug. "Darren and I are rooting for you."

# 22

# A NEW MISSION

Forster woke in a haze. Not long after he had bathed and donned his jumpsuit, his door chimed. He opened it to find Ariel, Meredith, Pop, Burgess, and Troy, all with upbeat expressions.

Troy bellowed, "Get on out here, buddy! We're taking you and Miss Ariel here to brunch. Efron's off getting things ready."

They made their boisterous way through the hall, and Forster noted Gibbons' closed door. He said nothing about it and they passed on, headed to the bar. They met Guru, who was waiting for them.

"Here he is, mates! The man of the hour!" he shouted, and about two dozen customers stood and applauded. Forster's eyes grew round and he balked, stunned, at Guru.

The bartender's eyes crinkled cheerfully. "Sit where you like. Everything is on the house for you today."

"How did—" Forster began, but Guru shook his head.

"Mate, everyone heard what you did," he said. "Word got out about the ship, too. And now you're headed back out there? We had to send you off proper." Guru saw Ariel and took a moment to admire her cool, delicate beauty.

"And here's our lady of the hour!" he called out to the bar. "Miss Ariel Brant! Two heroes here among us!"

More cheers, and Ariel's pale face stained into a rosy glow as she smiled sheepishly at Forster and her mother. Meredith grinned, putting on a good face. Only Forster noticed her smile fall away when she turned her head.

The staff served good food and drink, by station standards. Guru brought out his special infusions with much pomp. Laughter and handshakes and backslaps met Forster. Meanwhile some customers peered curiously and—was he imagining it?—suspiciously at Ariel. None came by to greet her.

Ariel made eye contact with Forster. *"Can you blame them? Of course they're afraid of me. Word got around."* She rolled her green eyes and tossed back her cloud of black hair. *"Good thing we're leaving soon."*

Forster frowned. *"We'll be back."*

*"Oh. Okay. Sure, Forster."* And Ariel turned away from him to talk openly with Burgess.

Forster's wrist pinged. It was Efron. He stood.

"Time to get ready." He nodded to Ariel. Everyone else stood as well.

"Go kick some ass, you two!" Troy roared, and the little group clapped and led the two raucously back to their quarters.

Forster stopped at his door. "I'll just be a minute," he said to Ariel.

He left her with Meredith and entered his room. He sat down and engaged his bots. "I'm leaving now. Please sync up." The bots synced with his communicator, and he said, "Keep recording for me," and left them to do their work.

He met Ariel, now in a jumpsuit, and again the gaggle of friends walked along the spongy hallway to a lift. The situation could not have felt more distinct from his and Efron's heist. The march disturbed him. They arrived at the docking bay almost too soon, he thought. He shook everyone's hands, and received another hefty backslap from Troy and a long squeeze from Meredith. Forster found he could not look anyone in the eye.

Behind him and Ariel, a figure swept from shadow, and the size of the shape sent a shiver down Forster's spine. The light revealed Efron as everyone else saw him. He looked so unusual in a jumpsuit, Forster fought the temptation to laugh. His suit gave him a long and spindly affect, contrasted with his broad shoulders. Forster did not see the gem, but he knew Efron must have it. Efron seemed uncomfortable and occasionally tugged at his sleeves. But he presented an appreciative smile at the group.

"Well," said Efron, "this is a bit different from our last adventure." Forster snorted at the understatement.

At that moment, Ella and Darren Varis entered the bay. "Thank you all for being here," Efron told them. "We plan on coming back as soon as we can," he said and turned to Meredith particularly. She nodded to him.

"Good luck," she said, and gave her daughter a long hug and many kisses on her black hair.

Ariel moved forward, her jaw clenched and her hands balled into fists. She stood next to Efron, and Forster joined them.

"Get on with it," Troy said to them gruffly, working his trembling mouth into a smile.

The three nodded and turned to enter the ship. The door closed behind them with an echo, and Forster shuddered. He found the craft already lit and its controls activated, thanks to Efron.

Forster looked all around the corridor of the *Siren of Conaree* and could not help but think of its unfortunate captain, so warped from his former cheer and vigor. Now Forster could only sense the anxiety and strain in the atmosphere. He wished it were Spears at the helm, booming with laughter and doling out encouragement. He sighed.

Efron, meanwhile, walked behind them as they made their way to the cockpit. He stood back, and glanced left and right, and turned around. Forster saw a tiny scowl form on the man's face.

"Everything all right?" he called to Efron.

Efron glimpsed back again, then shrugged. "Everything checks out. Let's head up and strap in."

Forster strapped himself in and watched Ariel as she sat, staring, in her own seat.

"What is it?" he asked her aloud, while Efron disengaged the ship from the dock.

A series of clangs and whines echoed through the craft, and Ariel sat motionless. The *Siren of Conaree* drifted off from the station, and Efron engaged its engines.

"Something's not right," Ariel warned. Forster and Efron stared at her.

"Do we need to turn around?" Forster asked.

"We're not turning around," Efron replied firmly. "We're short on time as it is, I fear."

Ariel shook her head. "No, no, we have to go out there. Just... something feels weird."

Efron squinted at her, then turned back to the controls. Forster began to sweat, and he felt chilled to the core. Between Efron's odd behavior and Ariel's remarks, a simmering fear began to bubble through him. He fought the feeling as best he could, but he realized that now there was no going back. He was strapped in for whatever lay ahead. He looked down at his communicator, where one tiny dot flashed. His bots were recording. This calmed him a bit, so he sat back and waited.

## 23

# ENCASED

A mostly silent ride away from the station gave the ship's crew little comfort as it cruised away toward the blackness. Forster had settled into an uncomfortable, but tolerable, position in his seat, when Efron spoke up.

"We are now out of station boundaries," he told them. "Maybe in another hour, we'll pick up on something."

Efron then unbuckled and stood. He unfastened the neck of his jumpsuit and pulled out a long, silver thread and the familiar purple, egg-shaped gem.

"It's time you two put this on," he said. He had thought ahead, and had Ariel and Forster stand while he combined their seats into a row. "I realize this is a bit awkward, and I'm sorry for that. It might grow more uncomfortable as well. When things get interesting, you need to figure out a way to keep this between you and yet stay mobile."

So Forster and Ariel sat next to each other and worked with the necklace. They decided on entwining Forster's right arm and Ariel's left with the chain. The gem dangled beneath their wrists. It took several minutes for them to figure out motions, but Forster soon realized that having a telepath work with him made things easier. It seemed to click with both of them. He marveled at this.

"*We're linked in our minds,*" Ariel explained. "*So it's easier to deal with our bodies.*"

While Forster didn't quite understand, he realized she was right, and his confidence grew. In a way the chain seemed more symbolic than physical, except for that one small gemstone, flashing its violet depths at them in the cabin's light.

Efron spoke. "I've detected the *Alta Mira*." Forster and Ariel sat up straight.

"Nothing from that ship. No new distress call. No beacon, nothing," Efron continued. "I can see the ship still generates power. Maybe its crew is still alive. But it's anchored."

Forster sighed. "Nothing else?"

"Not yet. You two tell me if you pick up anything."

For a little while, Forster calmed himself, seated next to Ariel. He was able to speak with her telepathically on occasion. But neither had the energy for conversation, and Efron remained fixated on his controls. Occasionally the man glanced over his shoulder, away from them.

Forster began feeling a dull headache. Then his heart began to beat faster. A sense of unease grew in him. Ariel stared straight ahead, her large eyes fixated on nothing he could see. He noticed, however, the pulse in her neck. It began to grow faster.

"Efron," said Ariel, and both he and Forster jumped.

"What's happening?" Efron demanded, standing.

"I'm feeling something, and I think Forster is too," she said.

Forster replied, "I feel like...like I'm slipping, and trying to catch hold onto something."

Efron's mouth went into a straight line. "We're very near, then."

He scanned the surroundings. "As I thought, it's moved again. It's not near the *Alta Mira*, but farther out." He and Forster and Ariel now stared at his control screen. "I'm definitely picking up signal interference in this area.

"There's a fair amount of debris out here," Efron noted softly.

"One of the objects isn't like the others, but which one?" He muttered, "I'm going to approach a cluster of them and find out what happens. Ready?"

"Yes," Forster and Ariel said in unison.

Efron brought up his screen. At first only the field of black space and a smear of starlight met their eyes. Gradually, though, Forster found small patches where no stars shone. Efron was correct; several shapes drifted among the void. The feeling of great dread increased in Forster, and his mouth went dry and his pulse raced. He sensed one of those objects was staring back at them, back at *him*.

"Are they...are they rocks?" he found himself asking, licking his parched lips.

"Yes. Some of them, anyway," Efron answered. "We're close enough now, I can shine light on them."

Forster wished he wouldn't. He did not want to see anything out there. He wanted to jump up, wrestle Efron, and turn the ship around for the station. He felt sweat form on his upper lip.

"Forster!" exclaimed Ariel, and Forster realized he had stood and jerked Ariel's arm, entwined with his, as he did so.

"Sorry," he stammered. Efron turned to them.

"Lights on," he said. "Which one is it?"

And they discovered dark shapes on the screen, suspended beyond the ship into the black.

"There must be dozens," Forster whispered.

"Ariel?" Efron asked pointedly. She stood with Forster to scan the void. He felt a raw surge of fear jolt through her. He followed her gaze and gasped.

One large rock, very like the one they had found Ariel in, stood out from the rest. Not because of its visible features. All these dark, lumpy objects looked more or less the same: like black potatoes. One of them, however, *felt* different.

"It sees us," said Forster hoarsely. Efron's jawline twitched. He pointed where Forster focused. "Yes, that's the one," Forster answered.

Efron checked all his controls.

"I'm not picking anything up from these rocks. No life form, nothing. Only static," he said. "Are you *sure*?"

Ariel nodded. Her eyes began to water. "That's it."

Efron stood in front of them, breaking their line of sight. "Listen to me," he told them. "If I bring this thing on board, I do not know what will happen. I assume that it's dangerous. I assume that if you did not have this necklace on, you would both be writhing on the floor, and then become catatonic. So you must keep that on.

"But I'll need you to help me get the ice off, and we can see what's inside. Only then do we learn what we're dealing with."

"What then?" Forster croaked.

"One thing at a time," Efron responded, and he whirled back around.

Forster and Ariel, already linked by the necklace, found each other's hands and clasped them.

*"Zero hour. We've got this,"* came Ariel's thoughts.

*"Okay,"* Forster responded. A small spark of reassurance trickled through him, despite his inflating sense of panic.

Efron activated the grappler. It reached forth and captured the one rock: the rock that stared into Forster's mind. The ship brought the object gently into the bay. With every creak and grind and clang that came along with the movements, Forster jumped and fidgeted. Ariel swallowed again and again, and shook off an occasional tear. He didn't need a mental connection to her to know her visceral state: terror.

*Oh God oh God,* Forster thought to himself. *Oh shit.*

The object sat on the floor of the bay. Now they had to investigate it.

"Can we just...can we just *watch* as it thaws?" Forster asked, quivering. "I don't really want to go in there."

"Truth be told, neither do I," Efron replied, and he lifted an eyebrow. "But this is what we're—what *you're*—here for. Remember, we have an entire station waiting for us."

Forster took a deep breath. His hand clenched Ariel's.

"Let's go," Ariel said, and her firm statement relaxed Forster.

They walked down to the bay, and Efron only briefly hesitated. He turned around, eyes searching, before he opened the door.

Inside the bay, they found the large, bulky rock on its side. Pops and sizzles echoed through the bay as the filthy ice on the object fell and thawed. Forster found the rock similar to Ariel's, but something radiated from this one. Efron grimaced, and Forster wondered how much of this ominous feeling the man perceived. Forster knew he and Ariel would crumple up if they dared take that necklace off their wrists.

"Let's get it out, then," Efron said.

The three scraped away at the dark ice with their hands, taking care not to damage what lay beneath it. This became cumbersome for Forster and Ariel, who worked as one unit with their free arms, and with limited movement from their joined ones.

One large ice chunk fell from the side and landed with a boom. Ariel and Forster both jumped and Ariel let forth a squeak. Efron looked at where the ice had fallen, and then up and around the room.

"Let's work from that side," he suggested, and they clawed at the ice until they found something beneath it. Larger ice pieces began fracturing and melting off in the heat of bay. An oblong shape grew visible. They stood back, uncertain, and eyed what lay before them.

It was another capsule, very like Ariel's in size. But whereas hers had been smooth and sleek, this one appeared battered. They even found cracks in the glaze, and in fact parts of it were broken off. Efron examined one end and announced, "I found the controls."

Forster and Ariel followed him. Forster discovered another difference from when he had helped uncover Ariel's pod. These controls flickered in faint orange lights. Forster's dread increased. Something had definitely gone wrong with this pod. While it still functioned, it clearly was failing.

"It's broken," Ariel murmured.

"Yes," Efron agreed. "Yet still active. Barely."

"What do we do?" asked Forster.

"We need to try and open it," Efron answered, his mouth scrunched and grim. "Are you ready?"

"Yes," Forster replied, and they tried prying open the capsule.

This soon proved very challenging. Between the damage to the pod, with its dents and cracks, and Forster and Ariel's limited mobility, they struggled. But Ariel managed to wedge her small fingers in far enough so her fingernails tripped the latch. It cracked open, the sound ricocheting off the bay walls. Forster shuddered, Ariel trembled, and Efron began blinking.

A horrible stench erupted from that crack, a wretched, sweet smell of rot combined with an acrid, heady smell of organic solvents. Forster's brunch launched out of him. Ariel just dodged his vomit and covered her mouth and nose with her free hand. They had backed several feet away. Efron moved with them.

"Sorry," he told them. "I can't do anything about the smell. But we've got to open this thing. So let's do that."

Forster, the taste of bile fouling his mouth, nodded reluctantly and the trio approached the pod again.

"Three, two, one, *push*," Efron commanded them, and they all pushed on the pod lid to raise it up.

Forster could not understand what he was seeing. He only partly registered Ariel's shrill scream, even as she took gulps of air and shrieked more. She strained hard from him, tried to run away, but he stood still and stared at the pod's contents.

Dark, cable-like mats and webs extended from inside the lid to inside the pod. They shivered and pulsed as though filled with blood. Inside the pod they coalesced around a long shape. Forster made out a bipedal figure, stretched out flat, covered in this reverberating, slimy web. Ariel pulled desperately on his arm. The necklace tore at his skin as she tried to move him away. But he could not help himself; he moved closer and stared down at the end where a head should be.

He found a small blob, the size of a human head, but enrobed fully in these membranous cords. The jaw was pulled agape. Where a mouth should be, a long cable completely stuffed and engulfed it. Ropes of slime writhed all about. Forster could no longer hear Ariel's shrieks nor feel her pulls as he leaned in closer and closer to look for eyes.

The eyes found him: brilliant, blinding flashes of light with innumerable facets. Beautiful and full of rainbows, two large, egg-sized diamonds stared into his eyes. His mind danced away, surrounded by the sparkle and the light. He heard a luscious, feminine laughter.

Arms yanked him about the waist, and he and Ariel went sprawling onto the floor, sliding in the black slush. Forster lifted his eyes and found Efron staring down at him, with a wild face, and then watched the man look at Ariel.

Ariel lay sobbing, and attempted to crawl away.

"Who is this?" Efron demanded of her. "You know who this is, yes? Who?"

Ariel choked and coughed. She reached for Forster and they held each other. *"Don't look at it again, Forster, please don't look at it again."*

Forster shook his head, and the distant laughter and sparkle left him for the moment.

Ariel propped herself up and stared at the pod. The dirty ice continued hissing as it melted, and a tiny beeping from the pod's controls pinged through the bay.

She took a breath and stammered, "It's Veronica."

# 24

## LOST

A yell and a crash sent Forster and Ariel sprawling again. Forster saw a figure struggling with Efron, and for a wild second he thought maybe the figure in the pod had risen to fight them. Efron had the person clamped around the middle with his long arms.

"Enough!" yelled Efron. "Enough! There's nothing you can do!"

A gurgling yell answered him. Forster saw the bulging, ruddy countenance of a shorter man fighting against Efron's grasp.

Gibbons!

"No! Ronnie, Ronnie!" Gibbons yelled. He managed to slip out of Efron's grasp, or perhaps Efron let the man go. Gibbons skidded and fell in the puddles of melted ice and slush as he tried to reach the pod. He stood again and threw himself onto the side of the container and looked in.

A long, broken wail lifted up and bounced inside the bay walls, a sound of such anguish that Ariel yanked her chained arm up to help cover her ears. Efron stood off, away from Gibbons, his face stern, his teeth clenched. The sounds of Gibbons' sobs echoed in the hollow bay.

"Ronnie-Ronnie-Ronnie-Ronnie," Gibbons whimpered. He

leaned over the dark, entangled being in the capsule and his tears and his snot dripped down onto it. Forster could not see the diamond eyes, nor did he want to.

"Gibbons," Efron said, in a soothing voice that still betrayed an edge. "You cannot help her now. She is lost."

Forster held up his free hand. "Let him have this," he said. He felt a deep pang for Gibbons, who, after all, had been a kind of friend to him not very long ago. Their meeting and camaraderie had brought everything together, to his rescue of Ariel, and now this. But Forster's thoughts reeled over this scene.

How did Gibbons manage to get on board the ship? And why was he not in a tortured state, like Spears and the crew of the *Alta Mira*?

*"Be careful,"* Ariel told him. *"Try to block anything that comes at you, even me if you have to. If she's still alive, she's powerful. Oh, and unstable."*

Forster nodded. He helped Ariel stand and they made their way to Efron.

"You knew he was here?" Forster asked.

"No, but I suspected," Efron answered. "I never would have let him come with us. Now we see why he did, but we don't know everything about our...passenger." He considered the capsule with half-lidded eyes. Forster spied a deep glint in them, a silver spark.

Gibbons lifted his head and stared at Efron, then sputtered, "Can't you do something? Can't you save her?" And he stood and walked toward them. Efron moved in front of Forster and Ariel.

"I cannot," Efron answered firmly. "As I told you, she is lost. This presence seems to have ensnared her, and drained her of most of her humanity. What little is left seems to be keeping you from falling to its sway."

Forster spoke up, "So Veronica is fighting against this...presence?"

"That I'm not sure of," Efron admitted. "I suspect this is more of an...arrangement."

"That doesn't sound good," said Forster.

Ariel stared beyond Efron. "She's deliberately keeping him around," she said suddenly. "As long as he's alive, she's alive."

"But why?" Efron wondered.

Gibbons turned to face Ariel. "Miss Brant, my dear, dear girl," he said, in a soft, pleading voice, "can't you talk to Ronnie? Can't you help me speak to her?"

"I—I don't think that's a good idea," stammered Ariel.

Forster moved between them. He sensed the protective instinct he had felt after helping revive Ariel on this very ship, in this same bay. "She is not going to do your bidding, Gibbons."

Ariel's cheeks turned scarlet. "That's not for you to decide, Forster. I'm just...not sure there's any way I can get through to her, at...at this point."

Gibbons' eyes rolled wildly. "You can! I'm sure you can! Why don't you, my dear, why don't you try? Please, dear. Your mother, Meredith, we've known each other so long. I know how she missed you. You must understand I've missed my Ronnie, the love of my life. I would do anything to help her! Won't you help me?"

The wretched man approached her hesitantly, pleading. But his eyes told Forster his mind had unspooled the moment he had looked into the capsule. He ached for the man on one level, but could sense a growing feeling of alarm that Gibbons might never be well again.

"Gibbons," said Efron briskly, "we have three people adrift out here, frozen in a tortured state. We have another on board the station. The entity controlling your lover could attack anyone at any time. It chooses not to attack you, because of your relationship to her. Can you see that we need to break this contact? Veronica was telepathic, and the reach of her mind is vast. As long as she is under the control of this thing, she can direct her mind and attack anyone. Please. I am asking you to let her go."

"What do you mean?" Gibbons asked, his mouth sagging to pout at Efron. "What do you mean, let her go? I've only just found her. I'm not letting her go. You're going to *help* her, dammit! You're going to *fix her!*" His whole body shook, and he looked as though he might spring at Efron at any moment.

"The only way we can help her, Gibbons, is if we set her free from this entity."

"You mean to kill her!" Gibbons shouted.

Efron hesitated, and Gibbons pounced. "You're not touching her, you're not killing her, you keep your freak hands *off* her!" he screamed.

An alarm sounded, and Efron's head jerked up. Forster, startled, took Ariel's hand.

"What's happening?" she asked.

"Something's changed; we'd better take a look." Efron answered. He watched as Gibbons returned to the capsule and draped himself over the side. "Come on," he commanded Forster and Ariel.

"But Gibbons," Forster began.

"It's not like he's leaving her; he's not going anywhere," Efron snapped.

They fled to the cabin. Once they reached the cockpit, Efron brought up the alert and gasped. Forster and Ariel watched him, alarmed.

"The *Alta Mira*," Efron said. "It's moving."

"What?" said Forster. "How, where?"

They watched the signature of a craft streak in a flash across the screen. "Not toward us, I hope?" Forster asked nervously.

"No, worse," Efron replied. "The ship's headed for the station, a direct line. It's probably being hailed by the station and not answering." Efron covered his mouth. The screen light shone off his spectacles.

"Traveling at high speed and accelerating," he muttered.

"What!" Forster cried.

Ariel said in a low voice, "She's doing this. She's sending it herself."

"Oh shit," said Forster.

"Yeah," said Ariel.

Efron opened a channel to alert the station, but was met with static. "The channel is blocked. We have no way of warning them. But they must know by now, what with the drone net. Unless something happened to that too."

"What's it going to do?" Forster asked, unable to grasp what was happening.

"I think the *Alta Mira* is going to ram into the station," Efron answered.

Forster pressed his own communicator. He commanded, "Depoe, Depoe, if you can read me, alert Ella Varis to an approaching ship. Warn the station of imminent danger!"

"Oh God," cried Ariel, "will they hear us? Mama!" And she folded herself into her seat and closed her eyes.

*"Can you reach Meredith like this?"* Forster asked.

*"She can't read my thoughts,"* Ariel responded with a wave of sadness. *"But I can still try to warn her. I hope this works."*

"What can we do, can we kill Veronica now and break this connection?" Forster asked. At this point he felt desperate enough to try anything.

"I think," Efron said soberly, looking quite aged to Forster for the first time, "maybe we cannot. The presence is keeping Veronica alive, though just barely. By default Veronica is keeping Gibbons safe and alive. It feels threatened. So it's lashing out."

He then got up and stood in front of Ariel and Forster. "Can you focus on her?" he asked them, but he directed his fierce gaze to Ariel in particular. "Try to focus on her, and then try to break through to her. See if you can get her to stop that ship."

"We will need to be close to her," Ariel answered, and she shook.

"What happens to us if this doesn't work?" Forster asked.

Efron groaned. "I have no idea, but I imagine it won't be good."

"Great," Forster retorted. "Well, why the hell not?"

He and Ariel went back down to the bay and padded in silently. Gibbons stood at the foot of the open capsule, wherein the wreck of Veronica wheezed, fluttered, and pulsated. His face shone from tears but his mouth smiled. Forster shook his head. The Gibbons he thought he knew was long gone.

Ariel ventured toward the foul-smelling pod, pulling Forster gently with her. He swallowed to keep from gagging, and the two peered down at the figure. They found themselves drawn to its crystalline eyes. A current of power surged through him and through

Ariel. And though he tried to resist, he could not resist looking into those eyes.

When he did, he felt flung into the air, high above and beyond the confines of the ship, but not into space itself. It was like being in a large room, like a cave with dim light. He sensed Ariel remained connected to him by a thin thread, a silver thread, nearly invisible. Ariel, though, seemed to be far away from him, so far that he could just barely see her. But closer by, he found Veronica.

The young woman, so striking and alluring, smiled at him with open arms. She looked exactly like the AI projection he had seen in Gibbons' room. And all he wanted to do, despite his rational thoughts, was to run to those arms and feel them around him. But he felt the tug on his silver string, and he remembered why he was here.

"Veronica," he said, unsure how to proceed. "Ronnie, yes? Why don't you let that ship go? Those people aren't going to hurt you. You don't want to hurt them, or the station. Why don't you just stop it and be done?"

And Veronica laughed and laughed at him. Such a merry laugh, he wanted to join in with her and laugh too. *Tug, tug.*

"Oh Forster," said this gorgeous young lady, "I've watched you sleeping. My poor, lonely Forster. I wanted to join you, you know. Keep you warm at night. I wanted to crawl in beside you and whisper to you while you dreamed."

And a heat formed inside Forster when he heard this. Yes, oh yes, he would have liked this; he would have definitely liked her in his bed. *Tug, tug.*

"No," he said then. "Please stop this." And he tried to search for Ariel's distant form.

"I don't think so, Forster," Veronica chided him, still smiling. "Let me have my fun. I've been locked away for so long, you see. I'm not going to stop now. Oh no."

And Forster realized with unease that he would not be a match for Veronica. He also realized Ariel must be having her own conversation with this person, so he tugged on his silver thread.

And he was snapped back together with Ariel. The vision of

Veronica vanished, the woman gone and yet the diamond eyes remaining suspended before them.

"She hates me," said Ariel, "and she won't listen to me. We can't stop her from doing this."

They broke away from the trance and stared down again at this pulsating creature in the capsule. "It didn't work," Forster called. The alarm still sounded, but Efron quieted it.

Ariel cried softly. "We can only hope it doesn't do too much damage, and that somehow we warned them."

Forster ran his free hand through his hair. "What do we do now?"

# 25

# ENTANGLEMENT

Forster and Ariel left Gibbons and what remained of Veronica, and hurried back to the cabin. Efron sat hunched over the controls, his head in his hands, but his eyes stared up at the screen.

"As best I can tell, by now the *Alta Mira* has struck the station," he announced.

*Oh, please, no.* Forster groaned. His dry eyes could not tear.

"I'm sorry," he said, his voice cracking. "We tried. She wouldn't listen to us. Said she wanted to have her 'fun.'"

Ariel reddened. "She wouldn't even listen to me."

Efron turned to look up at her. "Oh?"

Ariel grew redder. "I tried, okay? The two of us were never close."

Efron sighed. Forster realized he dreaded hearing a sigh from Efron.

"So now what?" Forster asked. "She's proven she can fling a ship across a pretty good distance and smash it into things. What can she do to the station?"

Ariel winced. She thought to Forster, *"I didn't want to think about things getting worse."*

*"Well, we have to,"* Forster replied.

Efron turned, straightened up, and observed them over his spectacles.

"Our situation leaves few options," he said grimly. "If we stay out here, with Gibbons and Veronica, at least the ship remains intact. But we can assume she won't want us aboard much longer. The entity inhabiting her, whether parasitic or symbiotic for her, clearly wants to use what is left of her to carry out its wishes. But she is in a weakened state. The force is keeping her alive in her own form of suffering, as it wants to do to everything in its path. In this case, Veronica is such a strong telepath, the entity is using her while sustaining her enough to continue. At any point, this could change. But Veronica seems to cling to some small semblance of her former self, just enough to keep Gibbons from utter collapse. I don't see that remaining true for long, however.

"Sooner or later the temptation to overtake Gibbons will be too strong, I think," Efron continued. "This presence was drawn here long ago. I suspected this was the case. Telepaths provide links to other minds, and this entity found a chain of them. From Project NEEDLE. That was enough to draw the presence to this system. It was too delicious a possibility, I think, a link to so many beings it could torture, or use as a conduit to inflect suffering. And while most of the telepaths appear to have died, enough remained with strength to fight off interference. Ariel and Veronica, the two most powerful."

Ariel shook her head. "I wasn't; I'm not all that powerful," she insisted. Efron smiled at her.

"I disagree," said Efron.

Forster looked from Efron to Ariel. "What you're telling us...is that this presence, this entity, came here from somewhere else. Where?"

"I only wish I knew," Efron replied with regret. "That's one mystery I may never solve."

"But it's not from *here*," Forster clarified.

"Correct."

"And you aren't either, are you?" Forster pointed out. He felt a mixture of unease and excitement.

Efron smirked. "Why ask what you already know, Forster?"

"Can we trust you, though?" Ariel asked him. "If you're not...one of us, how can we be sure you're really on *our* side?"

Efron glanced from Forster to Ariel and back again. "You're both braver and stronger than you realize. I'm definitely on your side, and always will be. I'm asking you to trust me, and I understand that's a big ask. But if we don't work together, you'll be overcome. And if you're defeated, all those at the station, and all the other stations and worlds in your system, will suffer. I want to help you."

Forster examined at the small, purple stone between him and Ariel. The chain had loosened just enough so that it did not press hard against their arms. "This stone," he said, "is the only thing protecting us. And you don't have any more of them. It won't stretch over everyone in the station. So what can be done to stop that presence?"

"You're telepaths," Efron said. "You're up against another telepath. You've got to focus like you never have before—ever. You'll have to work together to fight Veronica, to keep her away from the station. With that focus, and this stone, you can fight the presence long enough to distract it, and then I can assist."

Forster and Ariel locked eyes. "I'm new to this mind-power stuff," Forster pointed out. "And I didn't do so well against Veronica today."

"I'll help you," Ariel declared. "Just remember to stay focused, and think of something or someone if you feel yourself slipping."

"But the station. How can we tell them what's going on, with Veronica controlling things?" Forster asked. "Are we stuck out here?"

At that moment, an alarm squawked, startling the three of them.

"What the hell is that?" Forster yelled. Efron brought up his screen.

Forster and Ariel leaned over him. "Not good," said Efron.

"What is it, what's happening?" asked Ariel, and her fear throbbed through to Forster and nearly compounded his. The next moment, though, she calmed herself, and Forster did the same.

"Gibbons took the lifeboat," Efron told them.

"You're kidding," said Forster. "Did he take Veronica?"

"Let's go see, shall we?" Efron replied.

They hurried down to the bay door. Efron opened the entrance, and the three peered inside. Gibbons and the pod were gone, with only the dirty slush remaining on the floor, some of it trailing off in one direction toward the empty lifeboat dock.

"Jesus," said Forster. "He dragged the pod himself to that thing?"

Efron said, "I think we can verify now, Veronica and her passenger have complete control over Gibbons."

Forster gawked at the mess on the bay floor. Ariel pulled on his and Efron's arms.

"We'd better get going then," she said, "and head back to the station to warn them and help out. Can we beat them there?"

"I hope so," Efron replied. They returned to the cabin to strap in, and Efron fired up the engine, turned the ship, and set its course at top speed.

"So where are they?" Forster asked, staring over Efron's shoulder at the screen.

Efron shook his head. "Unknown. They should be close, but this ship isn't detecting them."

"I don't like the sound of that," said Forster. In fact, he didn't like anything about this. Gibbons ferreting the pod away by himself unnerved him. One man could not have done this alone. And so Forster found himself crawling with the idea that Veronica, or the presence, or both, were controlling Gibbons. They forced him to operate beyond his normal strength.

And Forster then remembered the warmth of Gibbons' cozy room, the soporific flickering from the faux fireplace. He visualized Gibbons raising his beloved Scotch glass, its facets winking off his content face. Forster remembered breathing in the liquor's volatile smokiness before he let it sear his throat. *We finally had that Scotch, after all that time.*

Forster then grew enraged. "She...it, whatever the hell," he said hotly, "made him do this. He was a good man." His eyes stung. "He didn't deserve this. He just wanted her back."

"The entity manipulates. It twists. It coddles, it does whatever it needs to do to control," Efron told them. "This is no doubt how it got to Veronica to begin with," and he raised his eyebrows at Ariel. "True?"

Ariel tossed her hair. "No, Veronica was always horrible. *She* was manipulative. She never wanted to follow the rules, and wanted to do her own thing. I think she brought this on all of us."

"I think you are likely correct," Efron said. "And now we know Veronica cannot break free. It's too powerful for her, and yet she wields more power with it than she ever could without. She won't let either of you go for long, regardless of the station."

"Still, I'm not giving up on saving them," said Forster firmly.

"Neither am I, obviously," Ariel agreed.

"We'll be there soon," Efron assured them. "And we need to help ready the entire station for anything."

"How are you going to help the rest of them, whenever she comes back?" Forster asked.

"I mean, it's as simple as this: do they want to live or die? And if they want to live, I have to help them be ready for the consequences," Efron said.

"Wow," said Forster dryly. "Sounds like such a great choice!"

"That's the only choice," Efron hissed.

Forster and Ariel raised their eyebrows at each other.

*"He's crazy as shit,"* Forster thought.

*"I don't think so. I think he knows too much. And I think he's our best hope,"* Ariel thought back.

*"Fingers crossed,"* Forster responded. And they both crossed each other's fingers.

## 26

## IMPACTS

Mandira came into view at last, floating like a giant conch shell in the endless night of space. Forster had never before felt such a relief at the sight of the station's coral and cream branches, its gleaming decks. He stared and stared, searching for any sign of damage. Of course, the *Alta Mira* was a small ship, and this was a large station. Soon the station filled the entire screen, and Forster and Ariel sat staring out the window as they approached. Forster grew uneasy.

"Still nothing about that lifeboat?" he asked Efron.

"Nothing."

"Do we know if it's here or not?" Ariel asked, without reading Forster's mind, but still mirroring his thoughts.

"We do not," said Efron.

"I don't like this," muttered Forster. "There's no way that presence is just letting us all go. And who knows when Gibbons and Veronica will show up?"

"Once we're aboard, I will debrief with Top Deck," Efron assured them.

"Thank you," said Forster.

"Oh!" Ariel gasped, and Forster and Efron jerked to see what she was looking at.

They found the *Alta Mira,* or what remained of it, alongside the station. Small bots were moving the pieces of the ship together into a cluster. Forster shook his head, appalled. His gut roiled.

"Guess they didn't make it," he sighed.

"No, it would appear not," Efron agreed.

Forster looked up again. His eyes bulged. "Dear God! Efron!" he cried.

Efron joined his gaze. The three of them discovered the impact crater where the *Alta Mira* had slammed into the station. Bots were working on stitching the hole back together, which appeared blocked from the inside.

"Oh my God!" cried Forster. "That's our hallway on Mid Deck!"

Efron stood quickly. Forster and Ariel again experienced a symbiotic fear pinging between them.

"Mama," Ariel whispered, and she trembled.

"We don't know anything yet," assured Efron, and he lightly touched her shoulder. Forster squeezed her hand.

"We'll hope for the best," said Forster, but he shook with a sick dread.

They docked soon after, and stood ready for the doors to open. The bright dock lights greeted them, as did a group of several people. The three blinked in the light, and after the doors closed behind them, they moved slowly forward into the crowd. Forster had just enough time to untwist the chain from his and Ariel's hands before she dashed ahead of him with a muffled sob.

Meredith met her in a desperate grasp. Forster threw his head back and exhaled in his own relief. He took in the various backslaps and shoulder punches from Troy and Pop and Burgess, while the Varises smiled and pulled him forward. He glanced back. Efron stood aside, speaking to Dr. Singh. No one else had greeted him. Forster caught his eye and waved. Efron nodded back, and a wry grin worked his mouth.

"Oh, man," said Forster to his teammates. "Am I ever glad to see you turd-brains!"

"Aw, he's a chip off the old block!" cackled Troy.

"We had no idea what happened after that crash," said Pop. "Thought you guys were goners!"

"Glad you're all right," agreed Burgess. "What say we head to the bar?"

"That'll work for me," enthused Forster.

He started walking instinctively in one direction, but Burgess stopped him. "Can't go that way," he said. "It's blocked off from the crash. I can't get to my room either, so I'm staying with Pop until it's fixed."

"Wait," said Forster. "Can I get to my room?"

"Maybe," Troy replied. "I didn't wait to find out when the alarms went off. Pretty sure Gibbons' room is blocked, though."

"And Gibbons wasn't there," said Forster.

The others gawked at him. "How did you know that? We couldn't find him," said Troy. "I went and tried to get inside his quarters before the impact but ran out of time, so I took off. Meredith said he hadn't been there, but she didn't say where he was."

"Let's talk about that later," said Forster. He stopped for a moment and shook his head. He was sounding too much like Efron now. "I saw the repair bots outside," said Forster, as they took a different route to Guru's bar. "Awful, about the ship."

"Yeah, completely smashed," said Troy, wagging his head. "We freaked out, thought it might be you guys. Awful glad it wasn't, but still—this is terrible. Everyone's on edge."

"How bad was the impact?" Forster asked.

"We got a good shake," Pop answered. "Of course, we're made to withstand a fair amount of collision with space junk, but still. Good thing it wasn't anything bigger than the *Alta Mira*."

"What did Top Deck say about it?" Forster asked.

The three other men flicked their eyes at each other. "Why don't we wait until we're in the bar," suggested Burgess. Troy and Pop nodded.

They entered the bar to a great, raucous din. Forster sympathized with the crowd. The crash unnerved everyone to some extent. He let relief surge over him for a moment, that he was here, alive, among friends. Guru lit up at the sight of him.

"Thinking Man!" the bartender called out. He showed the four men to a table.

"So glad you made it back all right," Guru told Forster. He served up the table with four shots and hustled on to the burgeoning customers.

Forster, Troy, Pop, and Burgess held up their shot glasses and tossed them back with gusto.

Forster said, "Okay, out with it, what's the 'official' message?"

Troy squinted at the others. "The big rods said the ship controls had been overridden by some sort of electrical damage. And that 'sent the vessel unobstructed toward the station' or some such bullshit."

"I wish," said Forster. The other men glared warily at him.

"Were we attacked?" Pop asked. Forster grimaced. Pop nodded. "Thought so."

"So where's Gibbons?" Troy asked in a quiet voice. The others leaned in.

"Out there," answered Forster, also quiet. "He stowed away on our ship."

"Get out!" Troy shouted, and then he covered his mouth in embarrassment. "Well, what for? And where is he now?"

"It's...a long story," Forster said. "And honestly, I can't even get my head around it yet. He went looking for his old girlfriend...and—" Forster noticed someone staring at him from the bar. The dim light obscured the person's face, but Forster shivered.

"Listen. He found what he was looking for, and he took off in the lifeboat. We have no idea where he is now." Forster laced his fingers behind his head and stole glances toward the person at the bar.

"Hoooooly shit!" exclaimed Troy. "Well, yeah, maybe let's not go into details here." He turned his gaze to where Forster looked toward the bar.

"He could be anywhere," Burgess mused, scowling.

"And we can't get to his quarters," muttered Pop.

Forster frowned. Something about this bothered him, but in his tired and slightly inebriated state, he could not quite figure out his own thoughts. He stood.

"Fellas," he said to them, "thanks for this. Good to be back. Time to call it a night."

His friends stood as well, and they wandered back the long way around to their quarters. Forster peeked down their hallway to find it completely blocked off by large emergency doors painted with bright yellow chevrons. He shuddered.

When he reached his own quarters at last, he entered and collapsed on his plank of a bed. He stared at the ceiling. He wondered who he had seen at the bar, and thought he had almost figured it out. But then he surrendered to his exhaustion.

Just then a chirp sounded, and he rose enough to listen to his bots' message.

"Welcome home," said Depoe. "We received and relayed your message, as you asked."

"And did you record everything?" Forster asked urgently, sitting fully upright.

"Yes," the bot replied.

"Good," he said. "Thank you. Now please seal the recording."

"Affirmative."

## 27
---

# WISHES

Forster met with his team for breakfast the next morning. Ariel joined them, but everyone glanced from time to time at Gibbons' empty seat. Efron fidgeted in his chair and made that familiar gesture of trying to gather a cape around him, but finding nothing to grasp. Ariel's green eyes had dulled, dark circles shadowed beneath them. Everyone looked fatigued.

"Right," said Ella, after everyone pretended to eat as normal. "We are glad to have Efron, Forster, and Ariel back with us." She smiled at each of them. "But we must acknowledge what has happened."

She spoke mainly to the three who had returned, saying, "The *Alta Mira* struck yesterday in the very early morning hours. We fortunately received word through Meredith ahead of time that something was wrong, so we evacuated our quarters."

Forster turned to Ariel. Her cheeks dimpled in a tiny grin. *Good work!*

Meredith spoke up, saying, "I had felt something was wrong. Then I was alerted by Forster's bots, which sent me a warning. Forster, thank you for that. Smart thinking!"

Murmurs of agreement passed around the table.

Ella then picked up the thread, continuing, "Not everyone knew it was the *Alta Mira,* but we were so glad it wasn't your ship." She lifted her eyes and sighed. "Later on, we realized Burgess' and Gibbons' quarters were damaged by the impact. The hallway was partially blown out, then blocked off by the station controls. So we couldn't reach Gibbons' quarters. But we did find out he wasn't in there, from station logs. So that was a relief."

Efron told the group, "I've informed Ella and Top Deck of Gibbons' stowing away. We lost contact with him after he took the lifeboat, and we haven't heard from him since."

An awkward moment of uncomfortable shifting in chairs and blinking went around the table. No one knew quite what to say.

Ella spoke anyway. "Should anyone receive any contact from Gibbons, you must notify me immediately. I ask that you not engage with him more than you have to. We fear he has been compromised."

Troy shook his head, and Burgess grew pale.

Efron then said, "I agree with Ella. I also suspect Gibbons will indeed try to contact someone here, or try to return to the station."

"Fortunately, the station is on high alert," Ella said. "With all security systems aimed toward anything approaching the station, we'll know about it, no matter the size."

"May I ask," Efron inquired, "what will happen if something does approach?"

"That's classified," Ella responded curtly.

Forster cringed. If Gibbons showed up again, there wasn't going to be a welcome committee, he thought.

"Now, on to our own business," said Ella. "We would like to access Gibbons' quarters, but it's sealed off for safety currently. We have had some trouble accessing his systems, so I assume they were damaged in the crash."

"Forster and I will look into it," said Efron.

"Thank you," Ella said with an appreciative nod.

After the meeting, Forster walked along with Efron, Ariel, and Meredith. They headed down the corridor toward Meredith and Forster's quarters. When they reached the blocked hallway, they stared at the barricade. Beyond lay Gibbons' quarters. Forster's neck hairs rose.

"Anyone else creeped out by this?" he asked.

"Yeah," Ariel responded.

"Oh yes," said Meredith.

Efron walked a few steps ahead. "Curious, don't you think? The ship crashing right into Gibbons' area." A solid, heavy door blocked further entry. The station had done its job, protecting its citizens. Outside, small bots continued to repair the exterior damage.

"When will this be reopened, do you think?" Forster asked.

"I would guess by tomorrow," Meredith replied. "The bots will surely be done by then. And it will be safe to open the barricade back up, so interior repairs can start."

"I think as soon as it's opened, we should try to get into Gibbons' quarters," suggested Forster.

"Yes," said Efron. "I would like to have a look around as well. I'm curious just how badly his systems *were* damaged." And he shot a glance behind him at Ariel and Forster, his eyes shrewd. Forster nodded.

"I wonder how long we have," murmured Ariel, "until they come back."

Meredith cast her maternal eyes on the uneasy faces surrounding her, and said, "You know what? Let's take a walk, you three. Let's go to the gardens. I could use some fresh air and some perspective."

Forster took a deep breath and exhaled in a loud *whoosh*. "I hear you."

They turned around and made their way through the various hallways of the station to wander through the conservatory. The four found a patch of moss to sit on and watch leaves sway in the artificial breeze. Ariel plucked enough lingonberries to share. Forster sat back against a tree with his hands behind his head and lowered his eyelids to slits. Efron sat with his legs folded, his back straight, his eyes closed, as if meditating. Meredith sat beside her daughter.

"That's much better," she said. "Not quite home, but it'll do."

"Well, it's not remotely like home," Ariel declared. "I am glad for the green. But I miss a real sky."

"I can appreciate that," Meredith sighed. "I hope we can see the real sky again soon."

Forster opened his eyes to look at Ariel and said, "I keep forgetting you were gone so long."

He breathed in the loamy scent of bark and soil. He had taken for granted many things: the plants, the circulating air, and the taste of real food. He chided himself. Ariel had been encapsulated for *two decades.* The least he could do was be sensitive.

The young woman shrugged, not looking at him. "It's okay, Forster," she reassured him. "I want it, though. I want *real,* fresh air. I think I want that more than anything."

"I've found it's always good to focus on what you want the most," Efron spoke up, surprising them. He remained in his lotus position, but he raised his head to admire the vines around him.

Meredith's eyes gleamed, and she smiled at him. "You'll get there, my friend."

Efron responded, "I may never get exactly what I want, but that won't stop me from being useful."

Meredith chuckled. Forster wondered what he meant. And once again, he seemed the junior member of the group, despite Ariel's youthful appearance. He felt like he would never quite fit in here. Not with them. It gave him a hollow feeling of homesickness. Not so much for a place, but for a person. And he did not know if he would ever see her again.

Efron leaned over and told him, "Stay focused."

Forster shrugged. "I don't have much choice, do I? May as well be something I love."

Ariel and Meredith smiled back at him and then at each other.

"Believe me," said Efron, "I do understand." He touched his necklace.

"Are you going to tell us whose necklace that is?" Forster asked.

Efron's eyes fell on the violet gem. He held the purple stone tenderly in his palm. He spoke very softly, almost whispering. "I said it was a gift, but...it isn't mine. It's not ever been mine, and won't ever be truly mine. I'm only glad I was able to borrow it for a time. I hope I do justice to the stone and its owner, that is all."

Forster then felt an overwhelming sympathy for Efron. He did not fully understand what the mercurial man was talking about. But he did understand what it meant to love someone, and the urge not to disappoint that person. He also grew extremely curious about this person Efron so regarded. Efron chose to be here, Forster convinced himself. He had given up a life of love to be here and help others. Forster's life had taken a similar course, after all. He realized then that he truly trusted Efron.

Efron spoke up again, startling Forster from his reverie.

"What would be home to you?" he asked them. "If you could choose where to go, that is. What kind of place would you want to live in?"

Ariel delighted in this question. "I want to travel," she said immediately. "I want a real sky again, yes, but I want more than that. I want to go places I've never been. I've been cooped up so long, I need to explore."

"Of course, because you're like your father was," Meredith said with a bittersweet grin. "He always needed to see what was beyond the next hill, mountain, atmosphere. As for me...well, at first I thought I'd like to go home again. I miss the seasons. But home is wherever my daughter is, so I want to go along with her, while she'll let me." Everyone smiled now, yet an unspoken fear and sadness lingered.

"And you, Forster?" asked Efron.

Forster thought of Auna. He remembered the two of them slipping over rocks, crossing a river. *"Used to jump these as a kid! Was quite the pro."* And then he had slid off and his feet had flown in the air, and she had laughed. He'd laughed with her.

But he said, "Well, I always did like Oregon, and we—I spent a fair amount of time there. Sometimes I wish I could see that area the way it was, hundreds of years ago, maybe longer, before anyone lived there."

"What about you, Efron?" asked Meredith, her eyes crinkled as if she was in on some secret. Efron stared upward at the ceiling and shook his head almost imperceptibly. The corners of his mouth twitched. Forster watched him cling to his amethyst.

"Ah, back to my castle in the air, I suppose," he said. "But I've got a long way ahead."

They sat and daydreamed in silence for a while. Encircled in warmth and friendship, they tried not to think about what awaited them. Forster then regretted thinking he did not fit in with them. He could become content to stay here, in this moment. But he thought about what Efron had said while he had held his secretive gem. Forster felt a rising determination. If he made it out of this alive, it was time to set other things in his life right.

# 28

# BEHIND DOORS

After dinner, Forster made his way to the medical bay. He met a busy scene. A number of people stood lined up dealing with anxiety, or real or perceived injuries from the crash. He pitied them, and yet grew a tad envious of their ignorance. *They have no idea what's really going on. If they did...*

He shook his head. He discovered a section of the medical bay that was closed off from the rest. He found a medical assistant and asked why it was closed, but of course he already knew.

"I'm sorry, that's quarantined," the assistant told him coolly.

"For Captain Spears?" asked Forster. The assistant sniffed and turned to walk off. "Can I see him?" called Forster after the man.

"I suggest you leave the med bay if you have no medical reason to be here," the assistant retorted, continuing on.

Forster sighed. He walked over to the screened area and touched the glass window.

*"Hang in there, Spears,"* he thought. *"You probably can't hear me, or maybe anything right now. I'm sorry. I'm going to try and free you from this. Just know, you're a friend."*

Forster returned to Mid Deck. He came across the barrier doors again, and snorted at himself for forgetting to go around the long way.

He had turned to do just that when the lights in the hallway flickered for a moment. He looked up. The sickly, pale lights shone steadily. He looked down, and they flickered again. Forster frowned and examined the huge, solid door. He walked forward and pressed his hand against it. He sensed and heard a low vibration, humming through the metal door. *What is that?* he thought.

He stepped back and drew his eyes all around the edges of the barricade. No light shone through anywhere, which he expected. He leaned against the door and pressed his ear to it. It hummed. The lights flickered again. Forster glanced at his arm, and immediately his silver diamond appeared.

"Efron," he whispered. "Can you come down here? I'm on the other side of the barricade near Gibbons' quarters." The diamond vanished.

Forster paced until Efron appeared several minutes later. His tall, skulking form marched through the dim, flickering lights, which winked off his spectacle lenses. Forster shivered. Efron's otherness still unsettled him. But Efron had seemed very personable at the conservatory, which confounded Forster.

"What?" Efron asked, looking down his nose at Forster. His head shone green from the overhead lights.

"There's a vibration coming from the door," Forster told him.

Efron's eyes followed the edges of the door, as Forster's had done. He drew his fingers across it and listened through it as well. His brow pinched together and his lips went taut.

"Trouble accessing the systems, so we were told," muttered Efron.

"I'm not so sure," said Forster. He glanced sidewise at Efron. Efron smirked and his eyes shone.

"I would say the bots are nearly finished repairing the outer hull," he mused.

"So the hall should be opened soon," said Forster. He scanned Efron suspiciously. "You don't think there's anything wrong with Gibbons' systems, do you?"

Efron frowned. "Oh, something's wrong all right. It's clear something is operating on the other side of that door. We need to find out what it is."

Forster could not stop himself from shuddering. "I almost don't want to," he admitted.

"Yes. I can understand that," said Efron. "The fact the ship was sent straight here, it's all quite strange."

"I don't get why it would want Gibbons' area wrecked," wondered Forster. The lights flickered again.

"I'm going to check on the status of those bots," said Efron suddenly. "Let's head back."

After several minutes, they came through their alternate hallway. Efron returned to his quarters, and Forster stared at the other side of the barricade. He stood gawking and listening, and heard the same vibration. He saw something out of the corner of his eye and jumped.

"Ariel! God!" Forster hissed.

Ariel giggled apologetically. "What are you staring at? Are you trying to will it open with your mind?" She nudged him with her elbow.

"No," replied Forster. Then he widened his eyes hopefully at her. "Can we do that?"

"Well, I've not actually tried," Ariel admitted, "but I don't think so. What's up?"

"Listen," said Forster, gesturing.

Ariel put her ear against the door. She stood very still.

"I don't like it," she said, her large, cool eyes narrowing.

"Same here. I can't figure out what the sound is, but the official excuse is that Gibbons' systems were messed up." Forster then stepped back with Ariel to study the door. "Efron's checking on some things."

Ariel folded her arms. She shared Forster's sense of unease; it seeped from her thoughts into his.

She said, "Only a matter of when, isn't it? Until she—they—come back."

"Yes," agreed Forster. "We'd better get some sleep."

"I'm not sure I will," muttered Ariel as she headed off to her mother's quarters.

Forster glanced back over his shoulder. The hallway's lights flickered. He quaked and hurried to his quarters. Efron met him at his door.

"Well?" Forster asked.

Efron sighed. "The drones stopped their repairs a few hours ago," he stated. "I looked at their status, and they're not responding."

"What? Why not?" Forster went to his own window and peeked out. "I can't see them from here," he said. "Why would they stop working?"

"Something has made them stop," said Efron.

Forster rubbed his jaw. "So we have some sort of problem with the lights, the repair drones stopped working, and there's a humming coming from the closed area. Sounds suspicious to me."

"Yes," Efron acknowledged. "If we could just get beyond that door without raising attention."

"I'm not sure we should." Forster hesitated.

"And it may be a moot point soon enough," said Efron, his fingers folded together under his chin. "Very well, let's call it a night, and try to rest as much as we can. I think we need to be prepared for anything. I'm assuming we'll get no warning when they come back."

"Not even station defense this time?" balked Forster. He did not like the sound of this at all. Surely the Top Deck folks had learned by now.

Efron smirked. "It's not that the station won't try to stop another attack. I'm just not sure they can. But they will try." And his face flickered to a more somber thoughtfulness.

"Forster, we've run out of time, I fear, and I'm going to ask you to focus with Ariel on distracting Veronica as best you can. That will buy me some time to protect everyone here."

"But what can you do? Are guns any use against this thing?" Forster asked lamely.

"Of course not," Efron replied. "It won't stop the station from trying, at this point. I will caution Top Deck that this tactic could backfire. They've already heard it from me before. The best course is simply to brace for an attack."

"If we can't fight them off..." said Forster, chewing his lip.

"Just buy me some time, that's all I ask," Efron pleaded.

"I—we—will do our best," agreed Forster. "God, I hope you have something good planned. But you're not going to tell me what that is, are you?"

Efron pressed his hand on Forster's shoulder and gave him a paternal pat.

"I'm only giving you just enough, in case something happens with Veronica. It's fair to say she's going to mess with you and Ariel. If I told you more, and your mind faltered, she and the entity would learn everything. Our best chance would be gone. Meanwhile, we have to minimize damage and loss of life."

Forster puffed out all the air in his lungs. "Are these marching orders?"

"Yes," said Efron. "Be ready. But first, try to rest."

"So easy," retorted Forster, rolling his eyes as he walked with Efron to the door. After the man had gone, Forster took in his small room. He felt sick and sad to think of what might happen to his friends, all his friends, if he failed. He curled up on his plank and willed himself to rest.

## 29

## LITTLE GOOSE

Just before waking up, Forster dreamed that Ariel was floating again, this time in his room. She was curled into a ball and suspended in the air, wearing a diaphanous green dress, her cloudlike dark hair drifting in all directions. Her eyes shut, she simply hung in the air, her arms wrapped around her legs. Forster nearly woke several times, but something pulled him back into the dream, and he tried to talk to Ariel.

*"What is it, Ariel?"* he thought to her. *"What are you doing?"*

She never answered him, and her hair and clothes drifted as if she were in a waving, shallow sea. In the dream, Forster rose and tried to approach, but he was blocked from reaching her. He held his hands up and felt an invisible barrier separating him from Ariel. He pushed in, and the shield popped like a soap bubble, and she vanished.

Forster sat up. He pulled at his T-shirt, which clung to him, soaked with sweat. It was early morning, still and quiet. He wondered if Ariel was awake. His dream bothered him, but he could not decide why. He desperately wanted to talk to her. He took a deep breath and focused on her.

*"Ariel,"* he thought, picturing her in his mind. He tried to recall her

features with her eyes open, but could only remember how she looked in the dream. This upset him. *"Are you there? Are you awake? I want to talk."*

No response. "This is stupid," he said aloud. His newly found skills were not up to hers, he figured.

Depoe squeaked. "What is stupid?"

"Oh, sorry, Depoe, thinking out loud again," Forster told his bot.

Then his door chimed.

Forster opened the door and Ariel stood before him, a bit disheveled, wiping sleep from her eyes. He sighed with relief, and guided her in. He considered her, and thought her so childlike, in her long pajamas, with her hair down her back, and her still waiflike form. He remembered reviving her from her hibernation.

"What is it, Forster?" she mumbled, blinking at the black tea he gave her. "What time is it?"

"Almost six," he replied. He sat at his small table across from her.

Ariel made a raspberry sound. "Why did you call me over here? Did something change?"

"I—not exactly," Forster said, embarrassed. "I had a strange dream about you and thought you were trying to communicate with me."

"Oh?" Ariel smiled wryly as she sipped her tea.

"Yeah. So, I was wondering if there was something you needed? Something you wanted to talk about?" Forster suggested.

Ariel tilted her head at him. "Hmm," she murmured. "Nope. Not really, no."

Forster blinked back at her expression, miffed. "You're lying to me, aren't you? I can feel it!"

Ariel grinned. "Very good, Forster. You're learning."

Forster was not about to let Ariel off so easily. Some instinct in him told him he must press her further.

"Please, Ariel, you can trust me. Tell me what's going on. Something's bothering you. And it's a stressful time, so let it out. You'll feel better. I'm happy to listen." He wanted to think of someone else's troubles rather than his own, for a change.

Ariel sighed and said, "Fine." And she stared intently into his eyes.

Forster felt as though the wind had been knocked out of him. He saw through Ariel's own vision. *"Is this a memory?"*

Ariel did not answer. Forster saw a group of young people, including Ariel, all in uniforms and talking excitedly. They walked on a long, reflective floor toward a group of what appeared to be officers of rank. Forster could not make out their insignia or their affiliation. This group of officers watched the group she walked with dispassionately, but gave them respectful nods. He could experience Ariel's feelings: a strong sense of pride and excitement.

Her memory jumped. She had turned away from her group of friends to look behind her, and she met the striking face of Veronica. Forster struggled to maintain his focus. Her resemblance to the AI of Gibbons startled him. In haste, he thought of Auna, whose face flashed in his mind before he returned to Ariel's thoughts.

Veronica's eyes bored into Ariel's with an intensity that staggered Forster. An almost predatory leer. She had high cheekbones, bobbed dark hair, and thick, dark lashes, with smoldering dark blue, almost violet eyes. Anyone would have stopped to stare at such a person. But the look she gave Ariel chilled Forster: full of hatred, even disgust. And in this memory, it hit Ariel as well.

But she made an overture. *"Are you excited?"* she asked Veronica.

Veronica bent over, inspected the sole of her left boot, and flicked something off of it toward Ariel.

*"I've never been more thrilled,"* she drawled haughtily. *"Go along, pup. They'll be needing their cheerleader."*

Ariel snapped back, *"Don't you* want *to be part of something like this? If not, why bother going?"*

*"It's—a—job,"* retorted Veronica. She glided along next to Ariel and bent down to her. *"Unlike you, I don't need it. I have my resources. This is a job for the weak. I'm simply biding my time."*

*"You sure sound grateful,"* Ariel sniffed.

Veronica gave Ariel a bright, photogenic smile, and chuckled.

"*Get along, child. Oh, what was it your mother called you? Little Goose? Heh. Go, Little Goose, go!*"

Forster felt Ariel seethe with rage.

"*Good God, enough, Veronica. Maybe let someone in someday. You'll end up alone. I pity you.*"

Veronica glared at her, then turned and walked away.

The memory changed again, and this time Ariel sat in a meeting. A number of her peers were arguing around a table. She stood and said, "*I tried to stop her. Again. She wouldn't listen to me. I'm tired of her insults. Maybe one of you can talk sense into her. I give up. She said she didn't need us, and that's the last I saw of her.*"

A young man spoke up in this memory. "*I saw her with a man, yesterday, and he seemed to know her pretty well. That's the last time I saw her.*"

"*She did say she had someone who looks after her,*" Ariel said. "*We have to go ahead with our orders. If she doesn't show up, there's not much we can do.*"

And then Ariel pulled herself from Forster's mind, so that they stared at each other in the present, holding cups of cold tea. Forster wrinkled his brow, and the young woman before him shrugged.

"There's more, of course," Ariel said. "But I don't want to drag you that far down."

Forster wished he could see more, but he relented.

"So, Veronica was part of your team, and you were about to go on a mission, and she bailed?"

"That's what we thought," Ariel replied. "She wanted to do her own thing, and she was bored with the mission. But I think she stuck with it for her own security. I guess I know now who her boyfriend was."

"Gibbons," said Forster.

"Yep." Ariel nodded. "I keep thinking...maybe she didn't really want to be with him? She was willing to do the mission, even if she didn't act like it. She would have known she might not see him again for a long time."

"Hmm," said Forster. "You may be right. And Gibbons maybe didn't take it well?"

Forster cringed. Something about this spooked him. He pushed that sensation aside, though, and moved on.

"So, now that we're going up against Veronica and this...thing. It seems like a waking nightmare for you," he guessed.

Ariel sighed.

"Yes. I guess I just feel...couldn't things have gone differently? Could I have been kinder to her? Could all of us? She just...she just made us all feel terrible. She was cruel and cold. Bitter. I was actually surprised that she might even have someone. I mean, she was beautiful, but she was just...mean. She knew she was the strongest telepath in the group. But she would never step up to lead. So I did. And on top of who knows how many other issues, that really pissed her off."

"That's not your problem, though," Forster pointed out.

Ariel shook her head. "I just feel like I messed up somewhere, somehow," she said.

Forster nodded. "I think I get what you mean. I want you to know you're not alone. I messed up too. A lot. I didn't take responsibility. I dodged a future with someone I loved. Constantly! I was afraid. Afraid of opening up like that, to anyone. I deflected. Wanted to help everyone else. Rescue people. I disappointed myself, I disappointed Auna; I sabotaged a career." And he rubbed his head.

"I think back now and I wonder what I could've done differently. But here I am, and here we are. There's no going back. We may have no time left, so I can't waste any more of it wondering how I could have changed things."

And the moment he said this, he felt freed of a yoke that had been holding him back for years. He reached across the table and squeezed one of Ariel's hands. Her eyes were full of tears.

"Thank you, Forster," she said, swallowing.

Forster smiled back. "You're welcome. Thank you, Ariel."

His messenger chimed. "Oh look," he said, "Efron."

Efron's face appeared.

"Good, you're awake. Good morning to you too, Ariel. I've called a meeting. Dome Car. Thirty minutes."

Forster lifted his eyebrows. "What's happened? What's this about?"

"Thirty minutes," said Efron briskly. The image went blank.

# 30

## STARLIGHT

Forster and Ariel joined Meredith in the hallway. Forster noted the lights flickering again. He squinted down the other end of the hall toward the barricade, expecting something or someone to walk toward him. He shivered at the thought.

He hastened along with his friends. They met up with the rest of the team as they made their way toward the Dome Car observatory. Burgess and Pop and Troy were joking back and forth, with Troy wheeze-laughing and outright guffawing. Ahead of them, the Varises strode together. Meredith and Ariel walked in front of Forster, leaving him to trail behind. He could not help thinking of Gibbons, and he felt regret.

He recalled what he had said to Ariel. He recognized his own parallels. Some of his rueful experience had come from his relationship with Auna, but the same was true of his sometime-friendship with Gibbons. He thought that perhaps he could have done more. He could have tried to understand what was happening to Gibbons, before he stowed away on Spears' ship with them to see Veronica. Would he ever have the chance to ask him now? He doubted he would, and it troubled him.

He thought about Gibbons' swift exit from the ship, somehow

dragging Veronica's capsule to a lifeboat. It was clear he was not the same man anymore, and Forster began to question their entire friendship. He realized that living on a station out at the edge of the solar system had made casual, working relationships more complex. And here they were, on the brink of probable attack, and that fact stripped everything away to the basics. His team members were his friends, and by extension, in a way, they were family. Gibbons should be here, but who knew where he was now, and what had become of him. Was he curled into a ball of pain, his mouth agape and screaming in silence? Would his eyes become crystalline? Forster shuddered.

They all arrived at the Dome Car to find it still, dark, and quiet. The field of stars that shone softly through the windows seemed so benign, so devoid of malice. On some level they all felt it: that shared memory from childhood, of having thought of starlight as beckoning and harmless. And now they knew *something* out there meant them harm. It was heartbreaking to have that peace taken from them.

In the dim light of the Dome Car, with only the starlight to guide him, Forster made out a shape off to the left. He knew it was Efron standing in darkness, waiting for them all. He recognized the shape of this curious raven of a person, who seemed to hold vast knowledge yet withheld so much. Forster understood, then, how much hope he instilled in the strange Efron. Hope was a magnet, and at this moment, Efron seemed like the only hope they had.

His quiet, yet resonant voice spoke: "Thank you for coming," and Efron stepped out of shadow to face them. His head and spectacles reflected the pale starlight, but his tidy clothes and his platform shoes absorbed it, all in black.

Efron told them, "We have very little time, I fear, before the entity returns. I realize that Top Deck has readied some form of defense, but this is an intelligent force. It will anticipate the station's actions. I think we have very few choices left to us. I've outlined them to Top Deck.

"First, station residents have the option to evacuate. I cautioned Top Deck against this. I realize many of you would like to leave the station, go to the nearest base, go to the inner worlds, to Earth. It doesn't really matter where. But the entity would surely lash out at any escapee, as it did with Captain Spears and the crew of *Alta Mira*. So I'm hoping everyone stays on board.

"I realize this opens us up for an assault, but the presence exists out here in a fledgling state. It has gained considerable power by siphoning off a powerful person, Veronica, who happens to be a telepath. As we've learned, there were a number of telepaths scattered out here decades ago. Experimental sentinels, recruited to detect any extraterrestrial presence. This backfired. It drew the entity to this part of the galaxy, where it could tap into a link of minds to increase its need for suffering. This force will metastasize, and we must expunge it before it spreads to the rest of the system. I say we fight it, and we remove it.

"Forster and Ariel are willing to distract the entity telepathically so I can try to expel it." Efron pulled forth his amethyst pendant. "This," he said, "is the only way they can avoid being tortured by the presence. I wish I had more, but I do not. This is not the only place battling this entity. In fact, it's a galactic problem."

Efron's audience stood staring, dumbfounded.

"All I can do is buy the solar system more time," he told them. "More time to grow, develop, evolve...so I hope to remove this piece from the system. It will return one day, unless we all figure out a way to eradicate it forever. For now, let's work to keep it away. That means we remove it...but it also means we must remove ourselves."

Troy held up his hand.

"Okay, whoa now. Let's dial it back for a second. What in Billy hell do you mean by 'galactic problem,' and necklaces, and whatnot? And *how* do you know all this?"

Efron nodded to Troy, and faced them all with his arms opened. The light in the room brightened just enough so they could see him better. Forster's breath caught in his chest as he watched the man tremble before them.

As he shook himself, Efron grew taller; his clothing changed, though its subtleties were hard to discern in the light. He took off his spectacles, gave a shake of his head, and a long silver mane of hair fell down his shoulders. The person before them stared down at them with silver eyes, eyes like mercury. He handed his spectacles to Troy.

Troy was so staggered, he gaped at them without understanding what they were.

"While you've known me as Efron," this tall figure announced, "my true name is Aeriod. I am here to help you battle this force known as Paosh Tohon."

Forster's eyes grew so wide they hurt. He was seeing this person, but not fully realizing it. And yet he *knew* him, had seen him before, in brief flashes. He wore the splendid cape Efron had always seemed to reach for. Forster found himself pointing at this Aeriod.

"You—you're—not—" Forster stammered. Out of the corner of his eye he noticed everyone else staring at him now.

"I am not human," said Aeriod. "Yes."

And he stood before them, an imposing, mesmerizing figure. But even Forster still recognized the man Efron within this new-yet-old form.

And Forster knew, somehow, that Aeriod was a being of extraordinary age. He even wondered if this tall humanoid form was the true Aeriod, but he stopped himself. It was too much. He took in what it meant.

Troy couldn't help himself.

"Holy shit, you're an alien!" he bellowed. "I knew it! I knew something was off about you! I mean...I mean, that's fine, dude; you don't have to vaporize me with your necklace or whatever."

"Oh my God," Forster gasped, laughing. Ariel joined him.

"This is amazing!" she said, and she turned to her mother.

Meredith stood placidly, seemingly unperturbed. Ariel opened her eyes and mouth wide.

"You *knew!*"

Meredith shrugged, and stepped up next to Aeriod. Forster thought she looked absolutely tiny next to this man. *Was he a man? Is it okay to call him a man? I'm calling him a man. For now.* He watched her. Her lined face held an extraordinary expression, of wonder, and perhaps a little anxiety? Forster wondered if he were hallucinating at this point.

"To all of you," Meredith told her astonished team, "I never knew for sure. I always suspected. And I knew it was Efr—Aeriod's place to reveal himself, not mine. I can tell you, we've been friends for many years. He has sacrificed so much to help me, and to help all of us. I trust him."

Aeriod closed his eyes as though he had received a benediction.

"Thank you, Meredith," he answered her, head bowed. "Your friendship has enriched my life and helped my cause. I hope all of you can now trust me. No more hiding. It's always been a risk, revealing myself, but we are beyond the choice now. It's time to face Paosh Tohon's power before it consumes everything."

Ella and Darren moved forward to shake hands with Aeriod, who bent his head to them. One by one, everyone came forward. The awe of the event rolled through them. Troy held the spectacles with reverence. Forster came to him last, unsure of what to say.

Finally he shook his head and said, "Wow. Well? Welcome to humanity...Aeriod." And he moved the name through his mouth with more ease than he thought he would.

He gazed up at the tall, striking person. He took in the extraordinary weaving of his clothing, its fine filigree designs indecipherable to Forster. He looked at the man's feet, and noticed the platform shoes were gone. Simple black boots took their place, also with silver scrollwork. There was no need for elevated shoes now, with Aeriod towering over everyone else.

Aeriod laughed, and that glimmer that was Efron remained. They were one and the same, after all, and Forster leaned back and let a tremendous wave of relief and great hope wash over him.

"Welcome to the galaxy, Forster," Aeriod told him, and he shook Forster's hand.

# 31

# CONFINED

As reactions unfolded across the team's faces, Forster traversed his own set of emotions. He could not help but gloat privately at his own suspicions and glimpses into the man Efron. He realized, however, that this was still the Efron he knew. Efron was Aeriod, and Forster marveled at him. He also admitted feeling intimidated by him, not merely for his striking stature and, he admitted to himself, hair envy. He quailed under the intensity of this person. Aeriod radiated the confidence of someone of immense life experience.

Forster felt Ariel's poorly veiled excitement. The young woman fidgeted, watching Aeriod. Forster thought at any moment she might bounce up and down in childlike delight. She had held back talking privately with him until everyone else had a turn in congratulating him and welcoming his truth.

Ariel moved up to Aeriod and twisted her fingers together, mirroring her mother's nervous habit, and began asking questions.

"Where are you from? How far away is it? How many...are you?" she asked breathlessly.

She had been selected for detecting alien life, but never once expected to meet, much less know, an alien on a personal level. Her giddiness bubbled off her and pirouetted into Forster's mind. He smirked. He also realized at that moment that Ariel found Aeriod attractive. And then he could not help but watch this engagement with great amusement.

Aeriod regarded her warmly, with his own sparking humor in his silver eyes. He pivoted to Meredith and cast her a wry grin. She laughed.

Ariel seemed to recognize her own over-excitement, and settled herself.

Aeriod answered Ariel and addressed all of them: "My...home, as it were, is a considerable distance away. I've not been there in decades; I spent my time working here instead. I would love to tell you more, though I think you might find it boring. I know of far more interesting denizens than I, in what you call the Milky Way.

"Thank you all for your support," he continued, and he folded his fingers together under his chin, as he always had done. "I think we need to move on to preparations for what's ahead. You have decisions to make. Stay or leave. If you stay, I'll do everything I can to try and guide you to safety. If you leave, I can't guarantee anything for you. But I'll understand your choice."

"You know we stand with you," Ella said.

Darren chimed in, "We're a team. That's all."

"We're staying!" called out Pop. Burgess nodded.

"Yep," said Troy, pulling at his white mustache. "This is home. I'd like to see anything try and kick *me* out!"

Aeriod chuckled. When he did, his eyes looked like white sparks. "Good. And I know where you three stand," he said to Forster, Meredith, and Ariel. "Thank you. Now to work."

They made quite the scene as they followed Aeriod back to Mid Deck. The confusion on people's faces thrilled Forster. *We found out first!* he thought. *They have no idea yet.* At their conference room, they met four Top Deck officials, including Dr. Singh. The expressions of the leadership team amused Forster. He watched each person waffle between awe, fear, respect, and at length, a kind of resolution.

"We welcome you, Aeriod," Dr. Singh told him. "It is a strange sensation to welcome someone who has lived here for so long, and contributed so much. You may not look like us, but I recognize our shared...humanity, if you will pardon the expression."

Aeriod said, "I understand this is an awkward situation. In many ways it might have been simpler to remain in a human form. But the circumstances demand I rally all of us. And, given the advantages I have, everyone would have found me suspicious. I have asked much of each of you already," and he nodded to Forster, Meredith, and Ariel in turn. "I fear my revealing myself opens everyone here to vulnerability from...outside forces, and I apologize for that. I saw no other way."

Dr. Singh replied, "It is clear you are willing to go to great lengths to help protect us. And we see little choice in accepting your assistance. We have completed securing the station. Ganymede command has been notified that we are under duress. But we have decided to withhold certain particulars at this time, other than to project a quarantine situation due to a new, deadly pathogen."

Murmurs of surprise wove through the team.

"Do I understand, then," Ella asked, "that no one is given permission to evacuate?"

"Correct," answered Dr. Singh. "Aeriod convinced us to consider evacuation a tremendous risk, not only to individuals, but to the rest of the system. The analogy of a pathogen works for us, so that is our official designation for this crisis. In fact, in light of events experienced by your team during its second expedition, we have decided upon radio silence until the crisis has ended. No outgoing transmissions, effective at midnight."

"If we make it through this, I wonder about the ramifications," Ella remarked.

Dr. Singh looked at her cohorts, at Aeriod, and back at Ella. "I wonder if we survive at all."

She told the team, "We are ready. I've selected a group of people and bots to secure the corridors. When the attack comes, a warning will sound, and instructions will be given in all forms for residents to remain in their quarters. We will exempt your team, given your knowledge of the situation. Good luck."

Everyone shook hands with the Top Deck officers. Forster felt relieved that everything lay open, yet was disturbed by the finality of Dr. Singh's words. He rose and began to head to his quarters, when Aeriod called to him.

"Forster," he said, "please stay behind. I would like a word."

Forster breathed deeply and exhaled. He wanted nothing more than to contact Auna, and tell her everything he had held back.

Aeriod said to him, "Do not try to contact her."

Forster gasped. "Did you…"

"I did tell you, I cannot read minds," Aeriod answered with a crooked smirk. "But I know you well enough. Please don't attempt it. The risk is too great. In fact, I wish Dr. Singh had initiated an immediate transmission cut."

Forster's eyes stung.

"I need to say goodbye to her. I need to say other things, too. I might never get another chance."

"You would put her at great risk by doing so," Aeriod told him.

Forster's shoulders sagged and he covered his face. Aeriod reached to touch his shoulder, but he backed away. He turned and left Aeriod. Walking away, he thought, *How could such a person understand what I am going through? He's not even human!*

He entered his quarters and said immediately, "Depoe. Please record this message for me. In the event of my death, I ask you to transmit it. I think you'll have to leave the station to do that." *The hell with it,* Forster thought. *I'll say my goodbye even if I can't send it now. I have to.*

Depoe obliged the command. Forster hesitated and stammered his way through his statement. This would never be enough, he knew. But it gave him some ease. When he finished, he laid his head in his hands.

## 32

# DARK

Forster found Guru at his wit's end, serving the chaotic crowd at the bar.

"Thinking Man!" he yelled, "I hear we're closing shop at midnight?"

"Not here, I hope?" Forster asked back, almost at the top of his lungs. The crowd had become restive enough that extra bouncers were brought in.

"Well, yes," Guru called back. "Probably best. I might need to do last call early tonight, by the looks of things."

Forster slipped past elbows to retrieve his drink from Guru.

"What is everyone saying?"

Guru leaned forward, his eyes harried and bloodshot, his arm and neck tattoos pulsating from the constant movement. His shock of hair sprang up like a cockatoo's crest. If Forster had to guess, Guru must have missed at least two full nights of sleep. His breath smelled of liquor.

"What they're saying I'm not understanding. I hear talk of someone on board being in disguise? Some kind of secret agent? That we're expecting another attack any minute from what hit the station earlier? It's a lot to hold together, mate."

"You seem to be managing," Forster noted.

"I'm the rum runner," Guru laughed. "Of course they don't want to piss *me* off. Here, one more for the road." Guru offered a second pour. Forster shook his head.

"Gotta stay sharp now," he said. "Thanks, Guru."

"Good luck, Thinking Man—or should I call you Fighting Man now?"

"I was always more of a thinker; you had me pegged from the start," Forster told him.

"Cheers, mate," said Guru, gripping Forster's hand.

"Cheers."

Forster's eyes searched all around the rowdy bar, and he heard *and* sensed the anxiety and questions. Obviously word had got around, but apparently not to the extent Forster had feared. Efron's true identity as Aeriod had not registered with the population. Forster guessed Aeriod kept his appearance just humanlike enough for this very scenario. The last thing the station needed was a full-scale uprising.

The drink Guru had given him calmed his nerves for a few minutes, but after that, Forster's anxiety flowed back in waves. That nervous energy coursed through him, and drifted off of other people in all directions. *If this is what it's like to be a budding telepath, I'm not sure I'm up for the gig.* And he wished he could simply toss the discomfort off. If they had more time, he would have liked some training from Ariel in blocking thoughts. So he did the only thing that worked for him, which was to think of Auna. But thinking of her at that moment made him feel anguish.

Forster walked back toward his quarters. He had almost made it to his door when the entire hallway went dark. The dim emergency lights glowed. Down the hall from his room he heard the humming sound from beyond the barrier doors, near Gibbons' quarters.

"We should have got those doors open," he muttered to himself. His skin crawled.

He checked his communicator, which still worked. The time read 8:04 p.m. He turned and glanced toward his own end of the hallway.

No one seemed to be out. He reached his room, tried to open his door, and stood staring at it. It would not open.

"What in the hell...?"

He shivered. He looked both ways down the hall, and decided to walk to Meredith's room. He tried to ring her door, and found the controls were not operating. He knocked.

"Meredith? You in there? It's Forster," he called through the closed door. He listened against the door and heard nothing. He pressed his communicator.

"Hey Meredith, I'm locked out of my room," he said to the device.

Her face came up, pale and creased with worry. "Forster, I can't find Ariel."

"Where are you?" he asked.

"I'm in the conference room, and the power's out. We can't leave the room," Meredith replied.

"I'm locked out of my room too," Forster told her. "I knocked on your door, nothing. The lights are out in the hall. Anyone else got a problem?"

"Yes, only the communicators are working, apparently. The outage must be stationwide," answered Meredith.

"Top Deck doing this?" Forster asked, his heart pounding now.

"No, we checked with Dr. Singh. She's trying to use the intercom, but it's down too."

Just then he received Dr. Singh's message: "*We are aware of the stationwide power outage. We are investigating. Please return to your quarters if you are able to do so. Otherwise report to your Deck group leaders and await instructions.*"

"Where's Ella?" asked Forster.

"She's here with me. She and Darren and Burgess. Troy and Pop chimed in; they were coming back. Maybe you'll see them in a minute. Forster, can you find Ariel? She's not communicating at all."

"Of course, I'll go look for her," he answered. "Where's Aeriod?"

"I'm not sure. He's not answering either."

"I'll contact you when I find them," Forster reassured Meredith.

"Thank you, Forster," she said. "When you find Ariel, tell—"

And her image vanished. Only the blinking clock remained.

"Meredith," called Forster. "Meredith!" He tried paging everyone else, and made no connection. "Shit," he hissed.

He hurried away from the humming barricade, and knocked on every door just to be certain no one was home. No one answered. He sped past the conference room, glad at least that some of his team members were there.

"*Ariel,*" he thought.

"*Shhhhh...*" came Ariel's response. "*I'll find you. Don't talk right now.*"

Forster pulled at his jumper, which stuck to him from sweat. He continued around Mid Deck's dim corridors, and came across a few others trying to enter their quarters. Most seemed mildly confused. He wondered if any of them knew the river of panic he traversed just then. Most moved purposefully in small groups, doubtless to their Deck safety zones.

He overheard some of their actual conversations as well as their thoughts. One woman acted unperturbed, saying dryly to her friends, "Well, there go my evening chores." Yet Forster heard her private thought, "*Dammit, how can I make a call home now? Hope it's back up soon.*"

Forster shook it off as best he could. Everyone around him seemed unconcerned, if annoyed. A few chatted about how glad they were for the break from their duties. He kept walking, searching up and down each corridor for anyone else from his team. It was unbearable to stay still. He had to keep moving. He also struggled against communicating with Ariel. He wondered why she would want him not to. He realized he was gripping his hair and stopped himself.

He headed to the conservatory. Clusters of people were walking toward him from that direction. One man said to him, "The gardens are closed. Lights are off and everything."

"Even the grow lights? The sunset lights too?" Forster asked.

"Everything except the emergency lights," the man said over his shoulder as he walked on.

That was indeed odd. The grow lights and medical bay lights held priority over all other lighting on the ship. Forster still hurried ahead to the conservatory. Maybe Ariel would be there. He reached the air shower door and found a security guard standing in front of it.

"I'm sorry, sir, but we've closed the conservatory for safety reasons," the man told him.

"Do you know what's going on?" Forster asked.

"Stationwide outage. Communications too. I suggest you head back to your room. Top Deck's orders."

"Thank you, but I can't even get *into* my room," Forster responded irritably. The guard shrugged.

Forster turned and skulked along the now-empty hallway. He decided then he should try the Dome Car, and search for any sign of either Ariel or Aeriod. At this point, he thought he would even be glad to see a mug of Troy's coffee.

He realized the lifts were out of service as well. "Of course," he muttered at the lift door.

*I am not climbing in the dark,* he thought resolutely. *Forget it.*

He checked his watch again, poked it, and still it only blinked the time. He sighed. Having given up on reaching the Dome Car, he headed up a ramp that led to the medical bay. He had turned down one corridor and meant to take another turn when he sensed something. Or rather, he sensed a presence. A hand suddenly shot out and grabbed his forearm.

Forster yelped, but Ariel blocked his scream with her small hands.

"Jesus God!" he whispered at her, scowling. He rolled his eyes and gave her a quick hug. "Glad I found you. Your mom was worried."

"Yes, she is. I can feel it," Ariel told him. "Come with me, away from here."

"Have you seen Aeriod?" Forster asked. "I couldn't reach him before the comms went out."

Ariel shook her head. She appeared wraithlike in the dim light, and Forster recalled his dream of her floating. He shuddered.

"What was that?" Ariel asked. Forster blocked her. "Fine, whatever. Listen, I think maybe I know where he's gone."

"Not the Dome Car, I hope," Forster said. "I'm not doing that climb in the dark. The lifts are down."

"I know," Ariel snapped.

Forster covered his mouth for a second. "Oh shit, we need to get to him soon, don't we?" he said quietly. They stood aside and let people pass them on the way to the medical bay.

"Forster, your arm."

Forster looked below his rolled-up sleeve and watched the silver diamond appear. He gasped with relief.

"Aeriod!" he cried. "We're looking for you...we're headed back to Mid Deck."

"Let's go," Ariel insisted, and he followed her.

Just then an alarm sounded, and the two jumped.

"What is that?" Ariel asked, as she took in Forster's taut expression.

"The station alarm. Something's happening. If we don't get to Aeriod soon..."

"We're screwed," returned Ariel. "We need that stone."

# 33

# CRIMSON

A s they ran to Mid Deck, the alarm began to warble and wail into a grating off-kilter sound. Forster saw Ariel cover her ears.

"The alarm is malfunctioning!" he yelled. "It's losing power."

"What's next?" Ariel called back.

"Never ask that!" said Forster harshly.

By the time they made it to the blocked hallway on Mid Deck, the eerie, undulating sounds of the fading alarm slowed.

*"Sounds like some kind of weird, low xylophone,"* Forster thought.

*"I can't stand it...it's fucking awful!"* Ariel thought back.

Forster swallowed and shrugged off the strange sounds as they peered into the hallway. With emergency lights casting only a dim, lurid glow, the barricade yawned like a cavernous mouth. A tall figure moved swiftly from it, and Forster stepped in front of Ariel to protect her.

"Finally!" a voice said, and next they saw the silver-bright hair of Aeriod as he moved toward them.

"Oh thank God," groaned Forster.

Ariel took her hands away from her ears. The warbled alarm now sounded like a deep, slow-rhythm gong. Each time it sounded she grimaced.

"What's happening?" Forster asked.

Aeriod glowered. "The station has lost primary power, every level is out—I've checked." His eyes searched beyond Forster and Ariel and he sighed, his bushy brows pinched together.

"What about the alarm?" Ariel asked.

"Dreadful, isn't it? My guess is it was triggered by the power outage, but as the system comms are down, we have no way of knowing."

Forster dreaded asking, but knew he must: "Do you think we're under attack?"

"That's not exactly clear, because I don't see how Veronica and Gibbons could do something like this stationwide," Aeriod replied. "I'm troubled. This could mean the agent of Tohon has grown in strength. But it doesn't quite make sense."

He turned and stared at the barricade. "Now. Let's find out what's behind that thing."

"How?" asked Forster. "Everything's locked down. There's no way to get it open."

Aeriod's eyes glowed at Forster and Ariel. "It's time for a practice run on your focusing."

"What do you mean? There's no one here to focus against," Ariel noted.

"Come," said Aeriod, and his long legs marched toward the large, closed door.

He took off the amethyst necklace and held it toward them.

"Take this and wind it around your wrists again. Just in case."

Forster and Ariel worked with the necklace to bind their arms together. Forster said, "Well, what do we do?"

Aeriod replied, "I want you both to try to open that door with your minds."

The young woman laughed. "I don't think we're quite telekinetic."

"Hmm," Aeriod answered. "Try it anyway. Focus on the door, both of you. Complete focus. Now."

Forster took a deep breath and stared at the door. *"Open,"* he thought.

*"Oh come on,"* Ariel responded. *"Let's just visualize it opening."*

*"Okay,"* Forster returned, embarrassed.

He did not grasp what he was doing, and he felt foolish. But he obliged. He stared at the door again, this time imagining himself pulling it left as hard as he could. Ariel did the same, and they both focused intently. Forster let his random thoughts float up and move away. It reminded him of repeating mantras. He remained fixated on opening the door.

Aeriod said to them in a calm voice, "How about a little help?"

He moved in between the two and held one of his hands over theirs, and the other cupped the amethyst from beneath.

"Steady," he said to them. "Focus."

Forster saw out of the corner of his eye a pale light glowing between Aeriod's hands, where the amethyst hung.

"Don't break your attention, Forster," Aeriod murmured. "Focus. Open the door."

A long, grating sound ripped forth from the door. It opened! Forster broke his concentration too soon, and found it only opened a few inches. Air whistled through.

"Perfect," Aeriod said, to Forster's surprise. "Excellent. Well done," and he grinned at them. "Look at that...the drones did their work, thankfully. The hallway is sealed off from the outside of the station."

"But it's hardly open!" Forster exclaimed. "I'm sorry. I broke focus."

Aeriod nodded. "Still, that was a good exercise. Shall we try pulling it open?"

"What did you do to help us?" Ariel asked him. She eyed the purple stone with great interest now.

"I helped activate the stone's harmonic frequency," Aeriod replied. "You and Forster did the rest. Remember what you did: you'll need to do this again."

Forster, Aeriod, and Ariel pulled at the door and dragged it far enough to let them in. They stood ready to enter the dark hallway, but Aeriod held up his hand.

"Listen," he whispered.

Forster leaned his head in. Between the bizarre, slowing alarm gongs, he heard the familiar buzzing, humming static sounds through the barricade. Now, though, they were much louder, and more familiar.

"I know that sound," Forster breathed. "That's the sound that Gibbons' AI picked up on, that interfered with Ariel's Morse code."

"Where's it coming from?" Ariel asked.

"From his room," Forster answered.

"Shall we take a look?" Aeriod asked them. Forster and Ariel met each other's gaze and shook their heads. But Aeriod had already stepped through. He turned and held out a hand.

Ariel bit her lip and seized it, and slipped through the door.

"Gah," protested Forster, but he followed.

The hallway was just as dark as the one they had left. But after blinking and squinting, Forster saw a faint, reddish light ahead. They passed Burgess' quarters, which had sustained major damage from the crash, the door warped and splayed out. Forster shivered as he peeked into the dark room. The drones had repaired the entire outer wall. It smelled metallic. Forster tripped over some shrapnel, and then realized the whole hallway was strewn with the stuff.

The three moved slowly forward, stepping over metals and composites and pieces of furniture from Burgess' room. They came at last to Gibbons' door, which stood slightly ajar, a long, slender rectangle of red light radiating from inside.

"What the hell," whispered Forster. The ruddy light mesmerized him.

"Forster," Aeriod cautioned, "don't go in alone. Let's open that door together."

They all moved in front of the door and took hold of its edge and pulled. It moved more easily than the barricade, and soon stood wide open. Forster gawked.

The room resembled a ruin of some old manor. Gibbons' collections had been knocked from their shelves by the crash of the *Alta Mira*. A strong smell of alcohol flooded Forster's nostrils. He searched the floor and found an overturned decanter of Gibbons' precious Scotch, its contents now soaked into the carpet. The entire room shone in a deep red, emanating from Gibbons' console. The buzzing static pulsed from it.

"Why is the power still on here?" Ariel whispered.

As soon as she spoke, music began playing. Forster trembled, frozen for a moment in the memory of both what he had dreamt and what he had seen in this room.

"It's harpsichord," he wheezed, his throat dry.

And as he spoke, the console's buzzing intensified. Between the deep, distant alarm gongs, the buzzing, and the tinny harpsichord, Forster wanted to run screaming from the room. Instead he stood transfixed by what he saw, a shape forming before his eyes. The second he realized it was a woman, strong arms grabbed him from behind to pull him away and out the door. He stared over his shoulder as the AI version of Veronica materialized.

Aeriod had almost picked Forster up, but Forster fought him off. The gorgeous woman in the red room beckoned with her scarlet-tipped fingernail for him to come back in. He shut his eyes tight. The door slammed, and he, Aeriod, and Ariel all stood gasping in the darkness of the hallway once more.

# 34

# PASSAGES

They scurried back to the barrier door with Aeriod urging them on. Ariel kept peeking over her shoulder.

"That—that was Veronica," she stammered, her eyes enormous in the dim light.

"No," Forster said, "that was Gibbons' AI. He made it look like the real Veronica."

"Oh, creepy," whispered Ariel. She shuddered. Forster nodded emphatically.

Aeriod sighed. "This complicates things. But now we know how the power outage came about."

"Seriously?" Forster cried. "She did that?"

Aeriod replied, "Yes; the question is why. I think we must assume that this AI is more complicated—and more *complicit*—than we thought."

"So," Forster ruminated, "is the AI in control, or Veronica, or Gibbons?"

"At this point, Veronica and Gibbons are one unit," Aeriod told him. "We just don't know exactly *when* this connection between AI and the telepath began."

"I've not known any other telepath who has done this," Ariel said, shaking her head. "Augmented with some tech, sure. But not to this level."

"So you think Veronica is controlling the AI, which is controlling the station, basically," Forster muttered. He did not like the implications of this.

"Likely," Aeriod answered.

Forster reeled from guilt for all this. He knew something had gone wrong with Gibbons' AI, and an underlying dread about it consumed him. "What happens if we try to destroy the AI?" he asked.

Aeriod took hold of the edges of his black cape and wrapped them around himself. "I think that might be unwise, currently. It might backfire and cause more mayhem."

"That could happen anyway," Ariel said.

"Of course," Aeriod agreed. "But surely this system would anticipate our meddling with it. I say we wait for them to show up, and not fall into their trap."

Forster tilted his head. "Listen," he said.

"The alarm stopped," Ariel said with a sigh of relief for the quiet. "Aeriod, should we try to go and open the door and get Mama and the others out?"

"Let's at least see if they're all right," pleaded Forster.

Aeriod shrugged off his cape. "If you insist. I'm not so sure we should let them out, assuming we can, though. I'm worried what this AI is going to do next."

"I'm gonna guess they're pretty ready to get out of that room," Forster said.

"Yes," said Ariel. "Let's do it."

The three of them began making their way around again to the Mid Deck conference room. Ariel loosed herself from the necklace, darted into the open mess hall, and grabbed several snack bars for everyone. She stuffed a few in her zippered pockets. Forster helped her back into their necklace brace. They had almost reached the conference room when they saw two bobbing, pallid green lights suspended in the air. Aeriod, Forster, and Ariel halted in surprise.

"*What in the hell is this,*" thought Forster.

"*Uh...*" Ariel responded.

A wheezing laugh echoed down to them from the lights, which began to move toward them. Forster had almost turned to run when realized that the laughter sounded familiar.

A long guffaw ricocheted off the hall walls. The light was shoved in front of Forster's face and a voice boomed, "You look like somebody pissed in your cereal!"

"Troy!" yelled Forster, simultaneously angry and joyful. Troy cackled and slapped his own leg.

"Now Troy, go easy on him—you can tell this is his first lantern," said a voice behind him. It was Pop Doogan, and he held his own lantern in front of his face and grinned, looking very like a tomten. He and Troy chuckled uncontrollably.

"Good to see you both," Aeriod told them. Troy held up his lantern to tall Aeriod, and the shadows cast in Aeriod's face hinted of a truly nonhuman expression. Forster shivered, and felt his companions' similar reactions.

Troy defused the moment by saying, "Hoo-boy, am I glad that alarm stopped. Friggin' thing got my knickers all in a twist!" Everyone giggled.

"Well, come on, let's get this damn door open," gruffed Troy back to them. "We've been trying, and Merry just about threw a hissy fit trying from her side. We heard some Southern sass, I'll tell you what!" Ariel laughed at that.

"The manual controls are hard to work," Pop told them. "Takes a stronger person than our old fogey crew, but I'll bet you guys could do it—if you were on the other side, that is."

"I completely forgot about the manual controls," Forster admitted, embarrassed.

"You're not the only one," Aeriod chimed in. Forster noticed his scowl.

"They're not everywhere, though," Pop replied.

"Hopefully most people can get out of their rooms," Troy said.

Aeriod then turned to Forster and Ariel, who glanced back at him. While he could not read Aeriod's mind, even in the lantern light his face indicated his anxiety. Forster realized Aeriod might have been correct. It might have been simpler, and safer, had everyone stayed where they were. And most would likely obey their last known command. But of course, some people would want to leave, regardless.

Aeriod announced, "We can open the door, but you'll need to give us some room." He held out a hand to Ariel. She took it, and she and Forster stepped forward.

"We're going to do the exact same thing we did earlier," Aeriod told them, "so again, you need to focus on opening the door, and I'll work the stone."

Forster let his eyelids close halfway, and he put all his thought into visualizing the door opening. He slowed and deepened his breathing. He pushed out the mumblings of Pop and Troy, the lights of the lanterns, and his own exhaustion, and envisioned the door opening. Aeriod's hands surrounded Forster's and Ariel's, and the purple stone glowed. While the stone remained cool, Forster felt his companions' warmth. He knew these things were happening, but he let them go from his thoughts, simply imagining the door opening.

And it opened! Troy and Pop gasped. Relieved cries and applause met them from the other side of the door. Aeriod and Pop and Forster gave the door a thrust, and it stood wide open. Meredith, Burgess, Darren, and Ella filed out in the hall and hugged them each in turn. Pop and Burgess hugged. Meredith linked her arm with Ariel's free one.

Darren and Burgess both wore head lanterns, while Meredith and Ella carried smaller versions of what Troy and Pop had found. Forster and Ariel downed water in the conference room and rejoined everyone in the hall.

"How did you *do* that?" Pop asked them when they came back out.

Aeriod smiled at his pupils. "They opened the door with their minds," he said proudly. "I just offered the stone's amplification."

Meredith asked, "Can you open all the doors?"

"That would take a long time," Ariel pointed out.

"And I'm not sure how much time we have," Forster said. "We have to tell you about what we found in Gibbons' quarters."

"Meanwhile," said Ella, "I propose we head to Top Deck and see if they need some help. Our comms watches aren't connecting."

They had turned to begin walking toward a ramp to leave Mid Deck when a deep *DWOOONNNG* sound rang throughout the corridors. They stopped and stared at each other, and then all around.

"The alarm again?" Ella asked.

"Yes," Aeriod replied, and a minute later, another gong sounded.

"What's it doing?" Ariel asked.

*DWOOONNNG*

"I don't know," Aeriod answered, "but we must remain alert."

*DWOOONNNG*

Forster's heart hammered in his chest. He threw a look over his shoulder as the group hurried from their hallway. He found nothing behind them, but he could *feel* something, as if eyes were on him.

*DWOOONNNG*

A piercing, crackling sound bounced all around them as they headed up the ramp. They all covered their ears. Then Forster heard something that stopped him abruptly. The buzzer static from Gibbons' quarters. It crackled continuously from every direction.

"The intercom!" Aeriod shouted over the din. "It's coming through the intercom!"

Forster squinted up and around, but found the lighting too dim to see above. He could not help but feel they were being pursued by something, and continually turned to look behind him.

"Come on!" Ariel urged, pulling at his wrist. "There's nothing back there!"

"I feel it though!" Forster shouted. "Something's following us!"

The buzzing static reverberated in his head, almost unbearable, and another *DWOOONNNG* sounded. Forster cupped one of his ears and groaned.

"Forster!" Ariel cried, and with her free hand she seized his shoulder. "Come on!"

The buzzing continued, and with one horrendous scratching sound, a voice spoke from the intercom: *"Welcome back!"*

And then, silence.

# 35

# TOP DECK

The group froze on the ramp to Top Deck. Aeriod's silver eyes shone as he looked about the corridor. Forster saw Meredith instinctively move closer to Ariel and himself. Ella stood defiantly next to Aeriod.

"What sort of crap is this?" she hissed. "Is that Gibbons' AI?"

"I think so," Aeriod answered.

Forster held up his hand. "But why would she say 'welcome back'? Unless...Gibbons is back." And he recoiled at the thought, for if Gibbons had returned, then surely...

"Veronica is with him," Ariel murmured.

"Hold on," Aeriod cautioned. "Gibbons may be back, but having Veronica would mean the entity would also be here. No one is currently feeling the signs of that, at least that we know of."

"I think we've run out of time, Aeriod," Ella said sharply. "Let's hurry to Top Deck and get a handle on this."

They moved as quickly as possible, with Aeriod jogging ahead. Forster scarcely had time to take in the dimly lit corridor, lined with art and sculpture and nonfunctioning yet elegant light fixtures. Whereas Mid Deck's public décor outside had been Spartan, the entry to Top Deck indicated the esteem and style afforded to upper management. Forster knew, also, that usually music played in this area. As this new day dawned, however, only the dreadful static and the faded alarm gong met them as they sped upward.

Aeriod stood at the first branch atrium for Top Deck, a figure devoid of light except for his long, ghostly hair and eerie eyes. It gave him an oddly disembodied look, given the darkness of his raiment.

"Go no further," he told them. "I will assess the situation. Wait here for me. In case something happens, and I do not return, I want Forster and Ariel to lead you to the Dome Car."

"Well that sounds reassuring," Forster said dryly and with a tremble in his voice.

Aeriod turned and swept down the branch. Forster wondered how well the man—or whatever he was—could see in the darkness. It made him shudder. Forster noticed its strange emptiness. Was anyone up here at all? Mid Deck at least had several people roaming the halls. He supposed they actually did listen to orders on this level. Aeriod soon returned from the first branch.

"Odd," he said. "There doesn't seem to be anyone down that way."

"I noticed it's awfully quiet up here," Meredith said, and Forster saw several people nod.

"I'll head down the second and third branches," announced Aeriod, "and the same thing applies: if I don't return, head to the Dome Car."

"Understood," Ella replied.

They watched as Aeriod made his way back from the second branch and headed down the third. Forster began to feel a sense of dread. Something seemed very off. Where was everyone?

*"Keep quiet,"* Ariel cautioned. *"I can tell that you want to say something. Don't."*

*"Okay,"* Forster thought back.

She was right. He wanted to suggest, in a loud and quite certain voice, that they needed to get the hell out of there, the sooner, the better. But he resisted.

Aeriod suddenly swirled in front of them. "Forster, Ariel, with me," and he turned and marched down the third branch.

Forster and Ariel sped to keep up, with Ella and Meredith follow-ing, and again Forster noted some of the art on the walls, and the openness of the outer walls, showing the starlight through windows, similar to the Dome Car. He had heard about its night appearance, but during the day it showed daylight landscapes of Earth, Mars, Pluto, and Titan. With the power not working, the real starlight outside the station became the default display.

Along the inner hallway, Forster saw offices. All of the housing units were along part of the first and second branches. Third branch, on Top Deck, meant all business. Why had the workers vacated their quarters? Were they holed up in offices? *Such is the life of a scientist and a manager,* he thought.

Aeriod stopped at the end of the corridor. A large, sealed door stood before them. He motioned for Forster and Ariel to come with him. Ella and Meredith stayed back.

"Forster, Ariel, we need to open this door," he told them. "Get ready."

He stood between them as they extended their thoughts to opening the large door. Aeriod surrounded the amethyst with his long fingers, and it began to give off pale, lavender light.

"Open it," Aeriod urged through gritted teeth.

Forster and Ariel both closed their eyes and slipped into their visualization. A burst of air told them the door had opened.

"Now pull," said Aeriod, and he, Forster, Ariel, Meredith, and Ella each pulled hard against the door.

A warm gust of air escaped from the open doorway. Forster real-ized then how much colder the station had grown because of the power outage. In this room, however, the temperature remained balmy. They stepped in and saw a number of lanterns in different hues, all lined up along a cabinet. Still, the light remained so dim that it took several minutes of blinking before Forster made out the shape of a person sitting at the end of a long table. A chill spread through him. The figure was alone.

"Hello?" called Ella. "Who is that?"

The figure stood and slowly walked toward them. It reached out and clasped a lantern and held the lantern in front of its face.

"Dr. Singh!" Ella exclaimed.

Forster flinched. He picked up the deep regret coming off of Dr. Singh in waves, yet her face remained stoic.

"Dr. Singh, are you all right?" Ella asked urgently, stepping forward to take her arm.

"Yes, after a fashion," the woman replied. "I am glad to see you, Ella."

"But where is everyone else? Top Deck looks empty!" Meredith exclaimed.

"I'm the only one here," Dr. Singh confirmed. "The others decided to leave, against my wishes and my orders."

Aeriod rushed forward, towering over the petite Dr. Singh. "What do you mean?" he demanded. "They left? Where did they go?"

Dr. Singh raised her head in surprise, as if seeing Aeriod's true form anew.

"Efr—Aeriod," she said. "I regret to tell you, they decided to leave the station."

# 36

# THE RECKONING

Forster watched in fascinated horror as Aeriod reached for something to hold onto. The man appeared completely staggered. Then he grew incensed.

"How did this happen?" he cried. "Did you not order everyone to stay? We all heard you!"

"Yes, I did," replied Dr. Singh, her voice quaking with sadness. "A faction decided to leave—and leave they did. I told them very clearly about what fate might await them. But I was met with 'you've been incompetent, we're done listening to you, and we're taking our chances.'"

Aeriod sat down and covered his face with his hands.

"This is bad," Forster said.

"No shit," Ariel retorted.

Meredith held up a hand. "How far do you think they got? Did they make it out before the power failure?"

Dr. Singh sat next to Aeriod. She hunched over, and appeared spent.

"They left as soon as the lights went out and the doors began closing. Some of them sprinted away. I remained here, hoping the power would be restored and I could issue further commands. I hoped I would be listened to."

Forster shook his head. It was clear now that most of Top Deck had other allegiances, and the rank-and-file had flocked to those insisting on evacuation. He grew sympathetic for Dr. Singh, as he understood how it felt not to be listened to or believed. He knew these circumstances were much worse, though.

"Could they have made it out?" Ella wondered aloud what everyone was thinking.

"Certainly they could," Dr. Singh responded. She sighed. "Command has access to its own private ship, which docks at Bottom Deck. It's essentially a larger lifeboat. Every top-tier manager knows the escape route and the human overrides. It detaches manually from the station, so the power would not have been an issue. As for what happened after they left..."

"Presuming they did leave," Aeriod responded. "And we've no way of knowing if they indeed left, nor what happened after they did so."

"I bet we'll find out soon enough," Forster muttered.

"Correct," Aeriod answered, his eyes sparking at Forster. He groaned. "I admit I did not anticipate this...this...*idiocy*! I cannot believe they actually left! With everything happening? With the fate of the *Alta Mira*? Why would they not have followed orders?"

"Aeriod," said Ariel, her voice soothing, "of course you don't believe this. Because, well, you're not...human."

Forster gulped. Aeriod turned his head and glared at Ariel. Everyone else fell silent and watched him, wide-eyed. He stood and walked over to the young woman and stared down at her, silver eyes into peridot ones.

"I failed you," he said. Ariel flinched. He went on, "You're right, of course. I've spent decades among you; I've made friends," and here he regarded Ariel's mother fondly. "I feel as though I've understood that sometimes not everyone listens to basic instructions. And yet, it is clear to me only now that of course this very thing would happen. Of course! You irrational, ridiculous, fearful, fiery people. Of course." And he said in a soft whisper to himself, "They should have sent her."

Before Forster could ask him what he meant, Dr. Singh spoke again.

"It's not your fault, Efr—Aeriod. It is mine. I am the commander of the station. I made decisions to quarantine the station and limit communications. Which, ultimately, occurred anyway. I pleaded with my fellow officers not to do this, but the impulse to run was too strong. Too human, indeed. So I take responsibility."

Ella heaved a great sigh. "Well, now what? Were they right to leave?"

"Certainly not," Aeriod replied. "As soon as the power went out, they damned themselves. And doomed themselves. We must assume they've fallen to Paosh Tohon and its siren, Veronica. Let us hope no one else followed suit."

Dr. Singh then said, "I need to address the remaining residents of the station. Given we are on auxiliary power, and the intercom seems to have been commandeered, I need you to spread the word. Let's meet in the great hall so I can inform as many people as possible of the current status. I fear if the main power is not brought online again, environmental backups will fail, and the station will become uninhabitable. I can feel the chill outside the doors."

She pulled her blazer about her shoulders and began walking out. When they all followed her out into the hallway, she turned and stopped.

"In the event something should happen to me, I cede command of the station to you, Ella," she declared. "And I ask that Aeriod lead the mission to save this station. Everything that you warned us about has happened, and I presume will continue to happen. I'm going to tell the people here that an unauthorized launch took place. And that anyone who risks this again could face potential death from the attacker. Aeriod, I presume you have your plan in place to combat this...thing and expunge it?"

"I do," Aeriod answered, nodding at Forster and Ariel, who raised their joined arms.

Forster thought, *At least someone knows what we're doing.*

Dr. Singh nodded at them, her mouth in a thin, skeptical line. "I thank you for your service in this emergency," she said. She turned back to Aeriod. "You may not have been born one of us," and she stared up at him with piercing onyx eyes, "but now you truly are one of us. We need your help, and we are grateful to have it."

Aeriod gave her a deep bow. "It is an honor," he told her.

The group descended from Top Deck, and had made it to the bottom of the ramp when they met a throng of people. A clamor arose at the sight of Dr. Singh. She stood firmly and held up her hand to quiet them.

"Good people, I apologize for not appearing sooner. I was locked inside a room in Top Deck. I understand a number of others are likely trapped in their own quarters. Let us go to the great hall, where I can discuss the current status."

A thinly veiled shout rose from the back of the crowd: "Resign!" and other voices echoed this. Yet a larger number grimly determined to follow Dr. Singh. Among them, Guru stood with his arms crossed. The crowd allowed Dr. Singh and Ella through, and Forster and the others struggled to keep up with the mass of people headed to the great hall. Lanterns bobbed among them, as though a moving cloud of giant fireflies made its way through the dim corridor of the station.

In the hall, Darren and Burgess helped set up several lanterns around a lectern, giving Dr. Singh better visibility. Aeriod hovered behind Dr. Singh, partly obscured. Forster and Ariel stood off to the side with Meredith and their Mid Deck crew. Ella's strong, clarion voice called for attention, and the undulating murmur of the crowd settled into a sea of whispers.

"Good people," Dr. Singh told them, "as you are of course aware, the station's main power has been damaged. We are currently unable to communicate within or outside of these walls. Additionally, the intercom system has been compromised. During this event, a large contingent of Top Deck decided to evacuate the station against my commands." Many in the crowd gasped at this, and a few shouts overcame the din.

"Then let's all go!" came one shout.

"Why do they get priority?" came another.

Dr. Singh held up her hand. "They were warned against this for a reason. If their ship was attacked, we cannot help them. If you chose to do the same, you would put yourself at greater risk. We do not know their status, or whether they succeeded in avoiding the entity we quarantined ourselves from.

"We learned that the force, which attacked Captain Spears and felled the crew of the *Alta Mira,* commandeered an onboard AI system of one of our crew. This crewmember stowed away on a rescue mission that failed, and took the person we wanted to rescue. I will allow Mr. Efron Aeriod to address this situation."

Aeriod straightened and stood before everyone. Forster heard a higher pitch to the murmurs in the crowd, as they wrestled with Aeriod's tall figure. He loomed in the pale lantern light, his long white hair down his shoulders, silver filigree flickering on his splendid dark clothing.

*"Do they see what we do?"* he thought to Ariel.

*"They see what he wants them to, I think,"* Ariel mused. *"I think they see someone really striking and tall."*

*"This is so weird,"* Forster thought.

*"Everything is weird now,"* Ariel thought back. *"Now try to keep your thoughts quiet."*

Forster nodded.

Aeriod spoke: "I want to begin by thanking everyone for not panicking," and a few in the crowd snorted. "What has happened here is an unfolding nightmare, but one for which I have a plan. For those of you who do not know, I spent several years researching various phenomena throughout the system. Particularly the heliosheath and out here close to the heliopause. I also recorded other exotic activity on my travels."

Forster could not help but cock an eyebrow over that remark. Ariel snickered.

"I learned of a parasitic phenomenon, for lack of better terminology, that overtakes its hosts. It entraps them in a state of profound suffering. This is what attacked Captain Spears and the *Alta Mira* crew. With each new victim, its power grows. It seems to have been drawn out here by a defunct telepathic network, with Spears and the *Alta Mira* being unfortunately caught in its crossfire.

"Its relative proximity to the station has put us all at risk. We rescued a living telepath from the network, Ariel Brant, daughter of Meredith Brant. We then attempted another rescue, Veronica Chaudron. As it happens, a member of our own team, Dunstan Gibbons, knew this person, and stowed away on our rescue ship. Ms. Chaudron had been compromised by the parasite, yet we were spared due to the connection between her and Gibbons. Gibbons took Veronica away from our ship by lifeboat, and their whereabouts are currently unknown. We discovered that Gibbons maintained an AI version of Veronica. We think that it caused the shutdown of main power to the station. This has left us all vulnerable to attack.

"The goal of this combined power is to force us to surrender," Aeriod told them. "We must not. And if we attempt to leave, it will give chase. I think it is only a matter of time until we find that the evacuees suffered the same fate as those before them who attempted to leave this area."

"What do we do then?" someone yelled. "Sit here and do nothing? They've taken over the systems!"

"We need to remove this entity," Aeriod replied clearly. "And the only way to do that is to remove ourselves. Otherwise it could easily travel inward in the system and overtake all of humanity."

"What do you mean, remove ourselves?" Guru called out. "You already said we can't leave the station." Murmurs of assent rose up.

"Correct," Aeriod responded. "I'm going to generate a force powerful enough to move the station away from here, and move the entity away from it simultaneously. But I can't do that if we don't lure it closer."

"What! How the hell?" another voice called.

"We have our own telepaths here," Aeriod told them. "They are the lure."

And he turned his silver gaze to Forster and Ariel, who stood frozen in the realization that all eyes stared at them. Between their wrists, the small purple stone swayed unseen by the crowd. Its weight pulled on Forster now, as though it wished to drag them toward the core of the station. He could not escape the duty ahead.

# 37

# FORTH

The din of confused and concerned voices ebbed and flowed. Forster sensed the worry, the fatigue, the mistrust, and sometimes the despair of people around him. He let his shoulders sag and rubbed his head with his free hand. They all needed a break, to rest and recover. He wondered if they would ever get that chance again. Even as he thought that, the dull, slowed drone of the failed alarm rang through the hall, and he groaned.

Dr. Singh addressed the audience once again. "I caution each of you as this situation continues to develop. I recommend that you return to quarters, if your quarters do not face the station exterior. Remember, the *Alta Mira* was driven into a hallway, and we may not have the capability to make repairs should another object damage the hull. If your quarters face the exterior, please seek shelter in a neighbor's quarters for now. The medical bay remains operational, but please do not overwhelm them with minor ailments at this time. We should anticipate further manipulation of our power and intercom: do your best to ignore these.

"Follow your group leader's instructions for your own safety. And lastly, given that our leadership team has evacuated, should something happen to me, I have chosen Ella Varis to lead the station. Thank you, and good luck."

Aeriod slipped away from Dr. Singh and joined Forster and Ariel. Meredith scowled, her expression clearly taciturn even in the lantern light. Aeriod gazed down at her, a frown on his face.

"Meredith, I—" he began.

"I've heard enough," Meredith said coolly. "A lure? My child is bait? You had better make sure this works."

And she turned away from him to put her arms around Ariel.

Aeriod nodded ruefully and stepped closer to Forster, looking into his eyes. "I want you to trust that I'm going to do everything I can to prevent anything happening to you and Ariel."

Forster massaged his temples. "Well, I guess we'll find out."

"Don't lose focus," Aeriod told him. "If you break focus, you're as lost as Gibbons."

The crowds dispersed, with many choosing to return to various quarters, and others lingering in small groups. Aeriod assisted Forster and Ariel with opening some of their team's doors.

"I don't think I'll ever get tired of watching you guys do that," Troy marveled.

"We're grateful," Darren told them warmly. "Think of how much work everyone else has cut out for them, opening up some of the interior doors!"

Forster managed a tired smile. He and Ariel followed Meredith back to her quarters, while the rest of their team divvied the interior rooms between them. The Varises opted to stay at Pop's, and Burgess chose to hole up at Troy's. Aeriod decided to maintain a watch. Forster noticed him cast his eyes down the dark hallway to the barricade separating them from Gibbons' quarters.

"I think I need less rest than any of you," Aeriod told them. No one objected.

Forster and Ariel fell upon every food item Meredith put in front of them. They demolished the custard pie first. Even the snack bars tasted delicious to Forster in his famished state. He and Ariel watched the annoying chain swing between them. Meredith noticed the problem, and set up two beds of quilts next to each other.

"I want more than anything to take this off," Ariel said. "No offense."

"Same here," Forster replied. "I just think if we even took the chance, we'd be risking too much."

Forster found himself lying on his quilt bed, his one arm bound to Ariel's, and the chain loosened and seemed to soften. He exhaled in relief. Ariel lay next to him, eyes closed, everything but her joined arm and her face swathed in her mother's quilts. Forster began to wonder about the chain's properties, and how it seemed to stretch or tighten as needed, when sleep overcame him.

His own snores woke Ariel, who flailed her arms and in turn jerked the necklace chain. Forster sat up in alarm, heart racing, and gawked at Ariel with huge, wild eyes.

"What happened?" he hissed.

"You snored, dumbass," Ariel snapped. "God, I just want this *off*."

They sat irritably in the dark. Meredith breathed softly from her plank. Forster envied her, for he knew he would not fall back asleep now. He plucked at his sweat-stained shirt. Ariel huffed.

"You need a bath," she sulked. "So do I—don't even tell me. I hate this."

Forster rubbed his arms, and happened to look at his forearm. The silver diamond had appeared.

"What is it?" he whispered. A tap sounded on the door.

Forster and Ariel stood. Meredith shifted and pushed herself up on her elbows.

"It's Aeriod," Forster answered. They turned the stiff, manual wheel for the door to open.

Aeriod swirled in, checking behind him as he did so. Meredith activated a lantern and its green light illuminated the man's long, white hair. His features jutted sharply, as though chipped from stone.

"What's up?" Forster asked him.

"I'm not sure," Aeriod answered. "I listened to the barrier door, and heard a voice."

"Gibbons?" Meredith asked.

"Possibly," Aeriod replied.

*I can't stand this,* Forster thought. *Can I still help him somehow?*

"Listen," he said, his free hand in his hair, "if Gibbons is there, don't you think maybe I should try to talk to him? Reason with him, give him a chance? What if he's in over his head and wants out?"

Aeriod frowned. "I told you, he's probably lost. He willingly allied with a compromised Veronica. We cannot trust him at this point."

"Maybe," said Forster. "But I want to be sure about this." He looked at Ariel. "I at least want to try."

Ariel sighed, irritated. "What about Veronica? Where is she, if she's not on the station? He came back somehow. Did he leave her out there?"

"Maybe," Forster said. "So it might be our last chance to try and get through to him before she—it—attacks us."

Ariel shook her head. "I don't really want to do this, but he's your friend, so I'll go along with this."

"Thank you," sighed Forster.

Aeriod said, "Let us hope you're right, that he is not lost, and that he is willing to listen."

Meredith gazed back and forth between them. "I'll wait here. Good luck."

Ariel gave her mother a quick squeeze, and she, Forster, and Aeriod pulled the door firmly shut behind them. Ahead of them the dark hallway curved out of sight toward the barricade. Forster stepped forward, steeling himself against the unknown. *He was my friend.*

## 38

## ADRIFT

They felt the chill of the hallway. Forster realized the temperature continued to drop, and that eventually it would be frigid. If they could not return the station's power, they would all freeze to death. He began to understand why the Top Deck people had fled. But they had not seen or experienced what he had, and he would not wish that upon anyone. He shivered from the chill and from his dark thoughts. Where was their ship now?

Aeriod, Forster, and Ariel crept up to the barrier and opened it wide enough to let themselves in. Steaming air poured forth, as did the same ruddy light they had seen in this corridor before. The sound of static met their ears, soft at first, then louder. And then Forster tilted his head to hear something more. Harpsichord music.

The three of them moved forward cautiously, stepping again over shrapnel from the collision. They found the red light glowing from the door of Gibbons' room. The music and the static both grew louder. Forster heard another sound, a mechanized sound, echoing through the hallway. He glanced at Aeriod and Ariel, and their faces, lit from the warm glow, pinched from confusion. They approached the open door of Burgess's quarters. The mechanized sound came from inside his room, and they peered in. Forster's brow furrowed as he tried to understand what he was seeing.

Two dog-sized, round, robotic forms hovered and hummed like bees in front of the area where the *Alta Mira* had ruptured a hole in the station. Forster realized they were repair drones, the kind that had fixed the exterior damage to the station. *What are they doing in here?* he wondered.

Aeriod said in a hushed voice, "They've made something," and Forster leaned in for a better look. He was right. They were weaving the final touches on a rudimentary shape in the exterior wall. It was tall and wide enough for a person to walk through, and nearly three feet wide.

"It's a door," breathed Ariel.

Forster went cold. "Those are outside drones," he whispered. "They've come inside somehow, and now they're making a door. A door for what?"

"Why hello, my good man!" a voice boomed.

The three of them jumped and wheeled around to find someone standing across the hall in front of his door. The red light of his room outlined him as a dark silhouette, yet a familiar one.

"Gibbons?" Forster asked tentatively.

The man chuckled. "Of course! Who else would I be? Do come in, you three, do come in."

Forster's pulse vibrated rapidly in his neck. Ariel's eyes protruded from her thin face. Aeriod simply brooded, his most recent default state.

"Gibbons." Aeriod stepped in front of Forster and Ariel. "You left; you put yourself at great risk. Why? What did you do with the pod?"

He slowly approached Gibbons, and Forster and Ariel followed. The static sound and the harpsichord music reverberated in Forster's mind. He began having trouble concentrating.

"Ah," Gibbons said to Aeriod. "So now we see your true nature. Yes, Veronica told me you might do this. She did." And now they faced the man.

Forster felt a gut punch of remorse. His old friend's face looked aged, pruned by decades, his hair gone white. His grin was more of a slash in his face, as his eyes did not wrinkle in smile. His eyes! His eyes flicked up, and down, and around. Those wheeling eyes briefly settled on each of them, then continued their restless journey.

*Was Aeriod right? Was he lost?*

Forster stepped beside Aeriod. "Gibbons, we're here to talk. I wanted to talk to you; I want to help you."

Gibbons turned his head to one side, still grinning horribly, his eyes swiveling. "Forster! My good man. Come in, now. Come in."

Forster glanced, questioningly, up at Aeriod. Aeriod lowered his head slightly. Forster stepped in, and drew Ariel in with him. Ariel, meanwhile, had calmed herself, and scowled.

With all of them inside Gibbons' quarters, the man bowed and held his arms wide. "Isn't it grand?" he asked, and he spun around to his harpsichord music. Forster took a close look at the AI controls. They flashed and flickered and thrummed with the static buzz.

"I have all the power at my command," Gibbons told them, raising and lowering his arms to the music. "I am a conductor! What a gift, eh? A little gift from Veronica."

Forster flinched at this remark.

"Gibbons," he said, "the station is without power, and it's getting colder by the minute. We need the power restored. Can your AI turn it back on?"

"Oh, Veronica can do anything, anything, my lad," Gibbons laughed.

"Which...Veronica?" asked Ariel.

Gibbons halted in his steps and sulked reproachfully at Ariel. For a moment, his eyes stilled.

"Naughty Little Goose," he said, spittle flying. "Were it not for your mother...but then again Veronica has no need for you. And who am I to say no to her? After everything. You'll get what's coming to you, my dear."

Ariel held her head high in defiance. Forster could see the steely resolve of Meredith welling in her daughter.

"He's mad," Aeriod declared.

*Dammit, man,* thought Forster. *He's messed up, but can't he be saved?*

"Well, sure, but he's still my friend," said Forster. "Gibbons, come on, man. We were—we're friends, remember? Do you remember us having Scotch and just...just hanging out?"

Gibbons had returned to pirouetting to the music.

"Gibbons," Forster said again. "What's going on? Why is the AI controlling the power? What are you doing out there with those drone bots?"

Forster clutched the man's arms and tried to make eye contact. Gibbons' gaze drifted everywhere but to Forster's eyes. Something fiery arose within Forster, revulsion combined with anger.

"What did she do to you?" Forster cried, trying to hold the man by his shoulders. "She's hurt you, Gibbons. She's made you older. You're not in control of yourself, don't you see?" His eyes stung.

Ariel tugged on the chain. At first Forster did not look at her, but eventually he glanced down impatiently. She shook her head. Forster wanted to ignore her, but her eyes haunted him. He did not want to accept what she was trying to tell him, even without sending him a single thought. He knew what she meant.

"Gibbons," Forster said, letting the man go, and bending his own head down. "I want you to try and fight her, fight this thing that's not even *her* anymore. This force has destroyed Veronica. Used her. She can't ever recover from this, and now it could drag you down with her. And then...and then the rest of us, all of us, like Spears, like the *Alta Mira*. Please, Gibbons, please try to fight her."

Gibbons shook his head and covered his ears, and his feet danced back and forth. But then he abruptly stopped. He stood very still and gazed straight into Forster's eyes, in one moment of lucidity.

"There's no going back, my good man," said Gibbons in a clear voice. "You cannot fight this force, you cannot imagine its power. Better to let that go. I had one chance to save Ronnie, which is why I came out here. I waited, and I waited, and then you came along. And you unlocked everything. For that I thank you. I had the chance to be with my love again. Farewell, good man, and I am truly sorry for any trouble I've caused. I'll not be without my Veronica ever again."

And Gibbons jumped in place and began dancing again, his eyes lolling, his tongue wagging. Forster stood numb. The buzzing and the static increased, and he watched something working up from the floor near Gibbons' feet. A form rising next to the man. Aeriod seized him and Ariel.

"Go. Now," commanded Aeriod.

Forster hesitated, staring at the form. Up it grew, a tall and curvy shape, and the shepherdess appeared: Veronica. She smiled at Forster with her perfect teeth, and she curtsied. She reached out a slender hand to him. Her eyes, while deep indigo, sparkled strangely, as if poorly veiling the diamond eyes of their original owner.

"Forster, so good to see you again," she said. "It is time, darling, so why don't you stay?"

Aeriod and Ariel both pulled on Forster, but he resisted, for he wanted to behold this phenomenal creature once more.

He only heard buzzing now. His friends' voices never made it to his ears. "Let him go," he managed to say.

"Oh I won't be letting anyone go," the gorgeous figure told him. "Now I have everything I want and need; now we can be whole."

A distant creaking and grinding sound echoed down the hall. Aeriod took hold of Forster and shook him. "Go!" he screamed, and he and Ariel pulled and pulled until Forster fell back.

Forster shuddered and looked up. He saw Gibbons take the woman's hand. A screech of metal echoed in the distance. Forster blinked. What was happening?

"Run!" shouted Ariel.

Forster stumbled and stood and began to run. He took one last look behind him and saw Gibbons leave his room with his AI. *How did it get out?* he wondered briefly as he ran down the hall. The three glanced at the open door to Burgess's room. Forster blinked, confused, and Ariel pulled on him again.

"Come on, Forster! Hurry! It's coming in!"

*What was coming in?* The drone bots had stopped their work, and their door was opening. They hovered on either side of the entrance and attached themselves to an oblong shape just outside the door.

Forster wanted to go back and see, but Aeriod and Ariel took hold of him and nearly dragged him away toward the opening of the barricade.

"Shut it! Help me!" Aeriod yelled. Forster shook his head and tried to concentrate. He and Ariel helped Aeriod pull the barricade door shut with a *thoom.*

Aeriod panted. "It's here!" he cried.

"What is it?" Forster asked, gaping at Ariel's look of horror.

"Her pod," Ariel gasped. "He's brought in Veronica's pod!"

Aeriod hissed, "It's worse than I feared. His AI is part of all of this. Now the AI will join with Veronica, and as a result, with Paosh Tohon. We've got to get everyone out of this corridor *now.*"

Forster grew nauseous. He glanced down at the tiny purple stone binding him with Ariel. That small jewel was all the protection they had.

# 39

## GLOAMING

Forster, Aeriod, and Ariel hurried to open the doors along the Mid Deck corridors to let everyone out. The barricade remained closed for the time being, but they kept looking nervously back in its direction as they hastened away from the area.

"Where to?" Ella asked them all, as they met with another small cluster of people near the ramp to Top Deck. Dr. Singh stood among them, holding a lantern to illuminate Ella.

"It might be best if everyone stayed in their quarters elsewhere," Dr. Singh responded. "Naturally I wouldn't have expected any of you to do this, with that thing on board in Mid Deck."

"Soon it won't matter where that thing is," Aeriod pointed out. "We're stuck on here with it if we don't get rid of it soon."

*More like immediately,* Forster thought.

"Do you still think we shouldn't evacuate?" Ella asked.

"It's all of us or none of us," Aeriod replied flatly. "That thing will follow us everywhere. Now it has control of the station. We have to get it out of here."

A disturbance caught Forster's attention. He thought he heard a distinct shriek and raised voices coming from the Dome Car area. *Oh no.*

"What has happened?" Dr. Singh called as a younger man came running up to them.

"I'm sorry, Dr. Singh," he said, his hands trembling so hard he clasped them together. "A body just drifted in front of the Dome Car."

"Whose?" Dr. Singh said hoarsely, but she was already walking rapidly that direction.

"We should probably stay away from any windows," called Aeriod. He groaned. "Useless telling any of you this. Fine, let's see what's happened."

They hurried up to the Dome Car to meet a crowd of people. Some of them were leaving in a rush, others halting, in tears and hysterics.

"Dear God!" Darren said, and Forster followed his gaze to the star field outside the huge window. It was not one, but three bodies floating, each one contorted. Forster felt sick. Their faces bore the same twisted, anguished looks as Captain Spears'. Only they were dead and frozen.

Aeriod exhaled loudly. He turned to Dr. Singh. She stood, horrified. "My team," she murmured.

"Come away, Dr. Singh. I am so sorry," said Ella, and she and Meredith helped her turn away from the awful scene.

"They were the evacuees, weren't they?" Ariel asked softly.

"It looks that way," Forster replied.

Aeriod said, "So there is no escape. Whatever happened to their ship, they never made it far."

A desolate pall fell upon all of them. They could not leave, but they could not stay.

Ariel clasped Forster's hand. They looked to Aeriod.

"Tell us what to do," Forster said urgently.

"Everyone away from the windows! All windows!" Ella called out to the crowd. "Return to your quarters and stay alert!"

Fear crackled off of everyone like arcing currents, and Forster had a difficult time clearing the sensation from his mind. He could feel a migraine threatening to form.

"*Ariel,*" he thought to her.

"*No! Don't, she'll—*"

A crackling sound burst over their heads. The intercom blared in Veronica's voice: "*Won't you stay with us, good people? You can't leave now. Just relax! Get out and about! No need to be prisoners.*"

With a crash, every closed door flung open down every hallway. Some people peeked out of them; others remained huddled inside. Forster swung his head back and forth, watching what everyone was doing.

"Why would they do this?" he asked. Aeriod eyed him balefully.

"It's just speeding up the process," he shot back. "Come. We need to put a stop to this, before things get worse."

The intercom crackled ominously again: "*Come on out! Don't be shy! Just relax! It will all be over soon!*"

Some people sobbed and gasped. Others looked wild. Forster caught sight of Guru holding up a rod.

"Let's get this thing!" he shouted. A roar sounded as people raised various makeshift weapons.

Aeriod yelled, "Stop! What do you think you're doing? Sticks? Against this force? Ridiculous! Think for a second before you make things worse!"

"How can they be worse, eh?" Guru snapped. "We're trapped in our own homes. Nobody's taking *me* without a fight!"

Aeriod stepped swiftly over to the man and whispered something to him. Guru backed up a step, still clinging to his rod, but he let it fall a bit. He nodded.

"Follow me!" Guru then shouted, and a large group followed him, clamoring, away from Aeriod.

"Where are they going?" Forster asked. Aeriod cocked an eyebrow.

"Focus, Forster," he responded lightly. "Are you ready?"

The intercom crackled yet again. This time the team groaned in annoyance.

"*Now there's no sense getting testy!*" came the musical voice of Veronica. "*You don't want this to be any worse for yourselves, do you?*"

Troy came up to Forster and Ariel and said seriously, "You've gotta get rid of this skank-ass dark force, invading harpy *freak*. Do it for Gibbons!" He clapped a hand into Forster's.

Ariel touched Troy's arm. "Troy, Gibbons isn't the only person possessed. Veronica is too. It's not her fault."

Forster stared down at her. "Where are you going with this, Ariel?"

"I'm telling the truth, and you know it," she fumed. "Stop blaming her for this. For all her faults, she's—she *was* human."

Forster nodded guiltily. "I know. I just...he was my friend."

"And she could've been mine," Ariel said sadly. "Let's go. The only way to help them is to set them free."

Troy nodded vigorously. "What you said," he agreed, and he shook her hand too. "Come back to us, come back to Merry and all of us, okay?"

"We'll do our best, Troy," Ariel said. Troy peered at Meredith, and Forster followed his gaze.

Meredith twisted her hands together, but her eyes streamed. She blinked back the tears. Forster leaned in to let Ariel give her a long hug. Forster's own eyes welled. Why did this feel like goodbye? Was this really the end for them, for everyone? And he still could not give a final farewell to Auna. That hurt him more than anything else.

Aeriod bent and also put an arm around Meredith. They formed a circle around her. Unspoken love and support entwined them all.

"You can do this, Little Goose," Meredith said firmly. She wiped away her tears, and wiped away her daughter's. Ariel nodded. She could not speak. Forster understood how she felt.

He and Ariel and Aeriod left them and made their way back to Mid Deck.

# 40

## RELINQUISHED

The three approached their old hallway leading to the barricade. Every door stood open; every room lay dark. Forster took what he thought might be his final glance into his old room. Would Depoe and Bandon ever be able to send his final message? He hoped they somehow would. He caught sight of his porthole window. Where once he saw possibility, now he envisioned only memories.

Forster turned back to Ariel and Aeriod, who watched him.

"This was never your real home," he said to them. "But it was mine. For a little while."

"Well, it was mine too, then," Aeriod replied, looking above and all around him. "Now remember, whatever I ask you to do, you must concentrate fully on it. Remember opening the doors? *You* did that, as a team. Put your trust in each other, and follow my lead."

Forster took a deep breath, and Ariel squeezed his hand. Hers was slick with sweat. The air temperature had risen as they approached the barricade. Yet Forster knew Ariel did not sweat from heat, but from fear.

The hallway glowed red. Forster knew then that the barricade must be wide open, as all the other doors were. He heard no music this time, only the constant static buzz from the AI. They moved forward gradually, as if the hallway stretched into eternity. Forster wished, anyway, that it did, that they never needed to arrive.

The intercom fizzled and crackled again.

Veronica's sultry voice announced, *"Entertainment has arrived! Now if you would just relax! No need for tears or panic! All we need are these two telepaths. We'll let the rest of you go! No need to worry anymore!"*

"That won't be necessary!" cried a voice from behind them. Forster jerked his head around and found two figures standing with weapons in their hands. Was it Guru and his band?

They stepped forward into the dim red light. It was Officer Derry and Lieutenant Marshall, his interrogators. *Why are they here?* he thought.

The two officers quickly moved in front of Forster and Ariel. Aeriod watched with consternation. "What are you doing?" he demanded. "You put your lives at risk being here!"

Derry and Marshall marched down the hall and faced the doorway to Gibbons' quarters, where the tall figure of Veronica waited, Gibbons by her side. Forster noticed Gibbons carrying something on his back.

"We are here to retrieve the telepaths," declared Lieutenant Marshall. "As officers of MindSynd, we order you to stand down from this attack, and we will take the telepaths into custody!"

Veronica met this proclamation with a long, merry laugh, bright and cheerful yet somehow menacing at the same time. A sparkle of electric charge surged through her form.

She called out over the intercom: *"We welcome new contestants in our little game! Listen closely, everyone!"*

And she spun Gibbons around. Attached to his back, a hunched, warped, darkened shape faced the group. Brilliant diamond eyes shone out of it: the sunken form of the true Veronica. Forster watched as if in almost slow motion, Lieutenant Marshall and Officer Derry shrieked and doubled over in pain on the floor.

The tall, AI Veronica kept her hand on Gibbon's shoulder and she laughed and laughed. Overhead the intercom reverberated every shriek and every laugh. Her voice echoed horrifically through the hallway and into Forster's brain.

*"Hear that, my dears? Please don't do that. Please don't put up a fight!"*

A flash of light appeared and Gibbons grunted. Officer Derry had fired off one shot before seizing up into a locked, fetal position. The gun burst struck Gibbons in the leg. Veronica's face changed. Her megawatt smile vanished, to be replaced by an expressionless, waxen look.

The diamond eyes of the true Veronica bored into Forster's, and her thoughts struck like a blow against his face.

*"You made a mistake coming here,"* she thought to him and Ariel. *"You've brought your little government friends with you. All they want to do is tether you, don't you see? That's all they ever wanted to do. Keep tabs on you, then drag you in when you're stepping out of line. They would have come for you one day, Forster. They wanted their own control. That's why I never agreed to it, Ariel. We could have escaped their grasp."*

*"And done what?"* answered Ariel. *"Where would we have gone? The experiment was our last chance to start something new. To go beyond them. And then this happened."*

*"You could have opened up your mind to so much more, Ariel,"* Veronica urged. *"You still can. Do this, so you can set the station free. Set your mother free!"*

*"Don't trust her, Ariel!"* Forster pleaded. *"She's not in control of herself anymore. It's Paosh Tohon talking."*

As soon as he thought the name, the AI version of Veronica cackled. She pointed at Aeriod.

"You thought they could handle this, didn't you? You really thought that?" she said to him with a wild smile. "How low you are, Aeriod. No wonder you're here in this backwater. You seem *impressive* to them here! How embarrassing for you."

"They are better than you," Aeriod responded. "They deserve a better fate, as does everyone. I will never stop trying, and helping, to be rid of you and your malice."

"You will never succeed," Veronica said smoothly. "You will continually put these fledglings at risk trying to recruit them in your cause. How can you blame me for wanting them to be better and stronger?"

"The only thing you want is their suffering, for your own strength and power," Aeriod spat. "Anything I can do to stop you, I will do."

Veronica simply smiled back. The overhead intercom rustled and crackled again.

*"It's about to get interesting, my dears! Hold on!"* and with that, a strange sensation, a tremor, ran under their feet. Forster felt his stomach lurch.

"Gravity is off!" Aeriod yelled.

The station still spun gently, but would soon come to a full stop. Forster floated up and bobbed over, flailing. The chain between him and Ariel loosened.

"The amethyst!" Ariel cried, and she and Forster grabbed for the stone just as it almost slid off their hands. Aeriod bumped into them and touched the chain, and it tightened again. Now they all drifted, except for the AI Veronica, who remained anchored where she stood. She held Gibbons and his ruined passenger down with her hands. Forster watched in horror as the torture-frozen forms of Lieutenant Marshall and Officer Derry drifted about and struck the sides of the hallway. They were alive, trapped in their pain, and yet unable to respond.

Forster experienced Ariel's tremendous remorse and sadness. *"Can't you stop this, Veronica?"* Ariel begged, daring to plead with the sparkling eyes of what remained of her former coworker. *"Can't you fight this? Fight for all of us. Fight for yourself. You didn't ask for this."*

*"Oh but I did,"* Veronica thought back. *"I asked for independence, and for power, and I got it."*

*"But look at Gibbons,"* Ariel thought desperately. *"He's your lover, he's Forster's friend, and he's not himself anymore. This thing has warped him. Is that what you want?"*

*"Dunstan is alive, and we are together again. It was the only way I could save him. Why don't you come with us, Ariel? We could do so much. Together we would be so strong."*

*"I will never leave my mother again,"* Ariel responded emphatically.

"*You've doomed yourself, Ariel,*" Veronica told her. Forster almost caught something. A tiny spark of regret buried deep in this former person, someone who was once full of life and passion. It was a bit like picking up Ariel's mayday.

He sent a thought to that little spark: "*You can still try to stop this. Help us. Make the AI respond to you, and get the station power going again. You still have a chance.*"

"*Mr. Forster, I do not,*" Veronica replied. "*Goodbye, Ariel.*"

And the darkened shape slumped down upon Gibbons' back, the diamond eyes nearly closed. Forster could not hear her anymore.

The crow of the AI Veronica's laugh jerked Forster back out of the telepathic link.

"*I have all that I need up here! Time for a show!*"

And before Forster could ready himself, the balled-up form of Lieutenant Marshall was sent hurtling at him, bashing him into the wall behind him. His head lolled and he watched the dim red hue of the light and the ghostly pale form of Ariel screaming, and then he saw blackness.

# 41

# THE DUMBBELL

An amorphous, floating, red world greeted Forster as he blinked. *What's it like in the womb?* he wondered. *Is it like this? Am I beginning, or am I ending?*

He felt so very tired. *Can't I just go to sleep, can't I rest? I just want to rest now.*

*"Forrrrrrsterrrrrrr,"* a high voice called through the swimming red. Something yanked him. Was that his umbilical cord? Was he about to be born?

Then a small, cold object pressed into his forehead. *The world is cold out there. Do I have to go?* But he jerked at the sensation. He blinked, and blinked again, and then he coughed.

At once the sound and the sensation hit him, and he felt his body go straight as an arrow, as if trying to stand in the weightless hallway. He gasped, for in front of his face, Aeriod's silver eyes met his, almost nose to nose.

"He's all right," Aeriod announced. Ariel wept.

*"I thought you were dead—I couldn't hear your thoughts anymore."* And she pushed herself to move toward him and hug him for a moment.

*"What happened?"*

"Forster!" cried Aeriod. "Deflect any more thoughts coming from Veronica. She's delayed us."

Forster watched as the AI Veronica marched along the hallway, little balls of electricity bouncing off of her stiletto-heeled feet with each step on the soft floor. She pulled a slack-faced Gibbons along behind her, like some large balloon. Forster flinched from a haze of malevolence all throughout the hallway. He knew that the moment that got out to the rest of the station, no one could escape.

"Focus!" cried Aeriod. "Put your thoughts on closing that barricade door!"

Forster and Ariel closed their eyes and visualized the door. Aeriod placed his hands over the small floating amethyst, and it began to glow. "Close it!" he cried. Forster could picture the door in his mind. He thought of shutting it immediately, and Ariel followed suit. They door closed with a clang.

"Focus on keeping that door closed," Aeriod told them, "or she'll just open it again!"

Veronica had hesitated at the closed door. Then she walked casually back into their view, and laughed.

"Every door you close, I will open! Nothing you and your piece of jewelry can do will stop that!"

The intercom hissed in her voice: *"I did warn you not to fight! I did tell you to relax! But if you won't, it's time I came for you all. It's time you —"* and a stream of static and buzzing and popping sputtered from the intercom.

Forster watched in amazement as the form of Veronica sizzled and flickered before him, and then burst apart and into thousands of sparks. Gibbons jerked about in his weightless form.

*"What did you do?"* Veronica thought to Ariel and Forster.

Aeriod gave a sharp laugh. "You're probably wondering what's happened, Veronica!" and he floated in the air toward Gibbons and turned the man around. He drifted in front of Veronica's diamond eyes and glared fearlessly into them.

"See, the thing about humans," he said airily, "they always want a good fight. Any form, really. Why not? It's part of who they are.

So for once, I decided to give them one. It doesn't have to be a fist-fight, or a firefight; sometimes it just takes a human with a stick, after all."

Gibbons gasped and choked. "You...you've cut the power to the AI! Veronica!" and then he remembered suddenly what he was carrying. He screamed. "No! What did you do! It was all I had left of her!" Even as he said this, the shriveled being on his back jolted.

"No!" said Ariel, her eyes glittering. "Veronica was always out here. You didn't need to make some fantasy version of her! You have her with you *now*, so deal with it!"

"*Paosh Tohon is still here,*" Veronica thought to Ariel and Forster. "*That is what you must deal with! There is no escape. I can control anyone and anything on this station now. I am strong enough.*"

And Gibbons let out a shrill sound and clutched himself all over. "Ronnie! Ronnie, help me!" Forster watched as every limb on the man tensed and every finger curled, and he became clenched further.

"No!" Forster yelled, and he reached for Gibbons. As he did so, his hand wiggled free from the amethyst necklace. Ariel gasped and Aeriod charged forward to try to reach Forster. Pain entered him like an electric shock. It sprang down his arm like tiny razors pricking him. He began to scream, and then he fell silent.

Aeriod swiftly entwined the necklace around Forster's hand once more. Forster simply stared up at him, blankly. "I can't feel my arm," he said, and he grew sluggish.

Aeriod looked at Ariel. His face seemed inscrutable to Forster.

"That was too close," Aeriod said. "Forster, I'm not sure about your arm."

Forster said, "But what about Gibbons?"

"Forget him for now. We have to stop this thing from going any further!" And then Aeriod ducked. The shapes of Officer Derry and Lieutenant Marshall came flinging at them. The three of them swerved awkwardly to avoid the projectiles.

At that moment they heard a strange grating *thock* down the hall-way, and a vibrating sound traveled along the walls.

"God, what was that?" Forster wailed.

Ariel turned her head to look back. "Something down the hall, maybe in Burgess' room."

"Ah!" exclaimed Aeriod. "Quick, grab Gibbons! Let's go to that room. I have an idea. Maybe we don't have to excise part of our station to get rid of this thing."

With his free, healthy hand, Forster seized hold of Gibbons, whose aged face remained warped into a silent scream. *"Where are you taking us?"* Veronica's thoughts asked petulantly. *"You cannot escape."*

*"We'll see about that,"* Forster shot back. He pushed himself and his load and they catapulted down the hall. He and Ariel and Aeriod worked themselves into a sweat goading along the awkward bundle of Gibbons and Veronica. Veronica meanwhile continued mentally hurling the two officers at them to try and stop them. They struck the walls with nauseating thuds. Forster and Ariel grew enraged together, and the combined energy of their rage hastened them.

Finally they made it to the door, just as Veronica decided to lift pieces of shrapnel as missiles. One struck Ariel in the thigh, opening her skin; another struck Aeriod in the head, with no apparent effect. Forster ducked in time to miss a shard in the eye. They craned to look inside the room.

"What the hell?" Forster cried. "The door is open, the one the drones made." Strewn aside, the old capsule that had held Veronica drifted in the room. The drone bots, now defunct, hung motionless. Aeriod pushed himself forward to investigate.

Forster saw Aeriod's eyes gleam even in the dim emergency lights. "Ah!" the man said as he worked his way toward the door in the wall. Forster watched, agape, as Aeriod pulled himself through the hole.

"What are you doing, Aeriod?" Ariel screamed. "Come back! Oh God, will he be sucked out into space?"

Forster had thought the same thing, but then he said, "No...wait. We would all be blown out that door by now if it was wide open."

Sure enough, Aeriod soon reappeared. He dodged a glancing blow from a piece of hurled metal.

"There's a ship," he announced breathlessly.

"What?" Forster and Ariel said in unison.

"It's empty," Aeriod continued, and his eyes flashed around the room. "Quick, get them in it!"

"Wha—" Forster began, but Ariel pulled ahead and gave Gibbons and Veronica a push.

Veronica laughed inside their minds. *"What do you think you can do? Send us back out there? We'll just return. We'll ram your station until it bursts. Nothing can hurt us now."*

*"Wrong,"* said Ariel to her mentally. *"You've already hurt Gibbons. You've hurt yourself beyond recognition. We gave you a chance and you blew it. It's time for you to go."* And Ariel raised her feet and gave the bundle of Gibbons and Veronica a shove into the hole in the door.

*"No! You'll be sorry for this, Ariel,"* Veronica said venomously. *"You can't escape us. You can run away, but we will find you again!"*

*"Good luck with that,"* Ariel retorted.

*"Gibbons, I'm sorry,"* Forster said lamely. *"Goodbye, old friend."*

"Now!" shouted Aeriod. "Close that door with your minds!"

And he held out his hands to cover theirs, with the small, cool purple gem suspended inside their entwined fingers. A glow emanated, and Forster and Ariel focused on the door.

*"You will regret this,"* Veronica's thoughts came to them once more.

The door shut with a loud clang.

"Focus again!" Aeriod urged them. "Do not break the link with each other, the stone, or with me. Think of another door opening. Think of the biggest door you can possibly imagine, and then think of a bigger one, and then another, and another."

Forster imagined a huge gaping door, larger than the docking bay, larger than the largest hangar he'd ever seen. Ariel did the same. Together they envisioned a gaping maw.

"Now stretch it farther," Aeriod commanded. "Farther beyond all the edges of your mind, beyond all your imagining. Larger than this station. You can do this! Focus!"

Forster trembled. A great darkness yawned before him, a door into a vastness he could not understand. But he continued to focus and grow the image.

"Now, pinch the door in the middle. Pinch it into the tiniest point you can fathom, smaller than the smallest thing you can think of, so small you could never see it."

Forster tried hard to imagine it. He was struggling. He kept slipping. He wondered what would happen to them all—would this kill them? He thought briefly of his bots. Would they survive? Could they send his goodbye message for him?

*Laughter.* "*You can't do it!*" Veronica hissed, but she sounded very far away, beyond his immediate thoughts, and her words seemed warped like a Doppler effect.

"*Forster!*" *Tug-tug.* "*Focus, Forster!*" And Ariel's voice drifted off in another direction.

"Pinch it! Pinch it just between the station and that ship. Do you have it? Focus!" cried Aeriod, grasping their hands powerfully with his, squeezing them almost too hard.

"*Watch me, Forster—I think this is what he means.*" Ariel appeared in his mind, but not the grown Ariel he knew. A tiny, younger Ariel, somewhere sunlit and green, smiling and laughing. She held up a small, elongated, inflated balloon, and took it in her wee dimpled hands and twisted it. She formed the shape of a dumbbell. Then the little girl vanished, and Forster found his giant door again.

There it was. There was the tiniest point. Forster pinched and twisted and did everything he could, thinking of that tiny point.

Sounds became muffled, and he thought he heard Aeriod calling from far away, nearly out of hearing range, "Hold it! Hold it there!"

Forster's mind held that tiny point, and he thought for one moment, "Goodbye, Auna, goodbye." And all around him he heard a roaring, and beheld a blinding light, and then many colors flashed by all together, and then he looked below him. Beneath him were stars, only stars. He hung, suspended, with nothing above or below. He tried to scream, but no sound came out. He tried to flail, but could not move. And then he closed his eyes and slid away from everything.

# 42

# LUX

He stared up and blinked. All Forster knew were dark eyes, a broad, smooth brow with a wry little furrow in it, and warmth. "Goodbye, Auna," he said to those eyes. "Goodbye." And his tears pooled in his eyes. Surely they would float away soon. But they did not. They ran down his cheeks. That was funny. Shouldn't they be floating, like him? But he felt very heavy. *Why am I not floating?*

"Goodbye, Auna," he said again.

A clucking sound met his ears. "Why does he keep saying that?" a voice asked.

He blinked again. He wanted to wipe his eyes, but his hand wasn't working very well. It was numb and sagging. *At least it's not the arm with the chain on it,* he thought dully. Forster twitched his arm. Then he sat up sharply.

"Oh Jesus!" he cried. "Where is it? Where is it?" and he flung off his covers. He shook his head. "The stone, the stone. Oh God."

Someone giggled. Another, deeper voice chuckled too, and then it coughed. Who were they? He knew both of those voices, somehow. And they were different from the first voice he had heard. That one had also sounded familiar.

"Where am I?" he asked, and he blinked and blinked. He was starting to see more clearly through his blurred vision.

Forster squinted. "Ariel?" he asked tentatively.

*"Of course, silly,"* came her merry reply. She sat up from her bed and gave him a wave. Frail and pallid, with dark circles under her eyes, she favored her injured leg. But it was Ariel. Forster thought back, *"Are we in the Med Bay?"* She nodded.

"Hey buddy," came a deep voice. Another cough. Forster twisted around to see where it came from. He stared, and then rubbed his eyes, and stared again.

"Spears!" Forster shouted. And Spears answered him with a long, baritone guffaw. "I can't believe it!" And tears sprang again into Forster's eyes before he could help it.

The huge man beamed at him and laughed again. He spread his arms wide where he sat in his bed. Captain Spears' muscles had atrophied, so to Forster he appeared emaciated. His dry, reddened eyes haunted Forster with a hollow staring. But he was definitely Spears.

"Good to see you, Forster," Spears said cheerfully. He gave Forster a smirk. "Now, are you gonna keep ignoring her or what? She's been hovering over you all this time."

"Huh?" Forster asked, and then he turned back around and raised his head. Her inky eyes shone at him under her wry, long brows, her hair now fringed in bangs. Forster opened his eyes as wide as he could and stared at her, noting only briefly that she wore a flight suit. Its patch read "Kein."

"Auna!" he shouted, and he reached for her and pulled her onto the bed. Her familiar, tangy-wild smell of fir, woodsmoke, and honey awakened his entire body. He wrapped every limb around her, buried his face in her neck, and burst into tears.

"How, how?" he asked, as the lithe woman pushed herself back up, disheveled and blushing. "It's you, isn't it? Am I hallucinating? Did we all die?"

"No!" cried Ariel, and she laughed out loud. "We moved ourselves. Remember?"

Forster still clung to Auna's hands, which were trembling. Her own dark eyes flowed with tears, and Forster watched her fight them. Auna the fighter.

"But, how are *you* here?" Forster asked her softly.

Auna bit her lip. "I arrived just before...before you...moved us all," she said. "I couldn't find an open bay anywhere, and nobody answered my hailing." She shivered. "I couldn't figure out what was going on, so I took my ship around the station, and I saw—I saw—" and she shivered again.

"You saw the bodies," Ariel interjected.

Auna turned to her and nodded. "Yes. And I...well, I kind of panicked after I saw them and a ship just drifting and damaged. So I circled around, and then I found a small makeshift bay, so I docked."

Forster held Auna's hands and thought about everything.

"You must've found the little bay door Gibbons and the drone bots made," he mused. "And no one was in there at the time?"

"No, and everything was dark, and the gravity was off," Auna answered. She was biting her lip again. "I was glad I still had my suit; at first I didn't think there was any air, either. I didn't know what the hell was going on, and it was pretty spooky. I feel like I'm going to have nightmares about it for a while." She shuddered.

"Where did you go?" Forster asked excitedly. He had a feeling he would be asking for this story again and again over time so he could picture it all in his mind. He imagined telling her about his own story, and those of Ariel and Aeriod.

Auna ruffled her hair. She said, "I made it out into a hallway and pulled myself along until I reached a landing. And a group of people came out of the ceiling—that was bizarre."

Forster sat and watched with amusement as her face flickered between confusion and concern.

"Out of the ceiling?" he repeated.

"Yes, a group of people, led by a big guy, who I soon learned is called Guru," Auna told him. "Apparently they had gone in between decks and cut off a certain room's power supply. Pretty rough work, by the sound of it."

She noticed Ariel was leaning into the conversation too, owl-eyed, so she turned enough for her small audience to hear her better.

Auna continued, "Let me tell you, that was not the most polite meeting I've ever had. He had a pole or something, and he yelled, 'Who the fuck are you?' And I thought for sure he was going to hit me, but another bloke said, 'No, mate, look, she's with the Commerce League!' And so, luckily, I didn't get my head smashed in!"

Forster gasped and laughed. "I'm going to have a word with Guru," he said. "I'm sorry that happened."

Auna straightened herself and tossed her head. "Yeah, well, I told him, 'You touch me, and I'm gonna beat your ass six ways to Saturn and back again,' and then everything was okay."

Spears roared with laughter, which set off his coughing.

"See?" he called to Forster. "You'd better not muck it up this time. She'll whoop your ass, boy!"

A sky-blue, bulbous-headed Medic bot rolled in with hen-like clucks of concern and asked, "Does anyone require assistance?" This set them all off laughing again.

Forster felt warmth flowing over and through him. At first he sensed it as love and humor. And then he began to grasp his sensation: the temperature was warm again. The climate controls had returned to service. The gravity was returned; the power was back on.

"So, where are we?" he asked.

Auna smiled at Forster, and there was a strange look in her vivid, dark brown eyes. She turned to face Ariel.

"Are you up for a walk, do you think?" she asked the patients. Forster nodded eagerly. "Not you, Spears, doctor's orders. Maybe soon though," and Auna smiled at him apologetically.

Spears gave a resigned shrug.

"Fine by me. I can wait a little longer. Not going anywhere anytime soon. Now if you could talk to somebody about getting me a decent meal?"

"Sure thing," said Auna, and she walked over and patted Spears on the arm.

Auna then pressed her comms watch. "Hi," she said to someone on it. "They're ready. Do you want to come?...Okay, I'll wait for you."

Soon the Medic bot returned and gracefully announced, "Miss Brant and Mr. Forster, you have visitors. May I allow them in?"

"Yes, thank you, Medic," Forster replied. Ariel agreed as well.

In swept Aeriod, his long cape flapping, with Meredith alongside him. Forster could not resist watching Spears' reaction to Aeriod. Spears caught his eye and nodded as if to say, "I told you so!"

Forster grinned and took Aeriod and Auna's arms, and he stood. His legs felt leaden. He glanced at Ariel, who despite her leg wound seemed nimbler, holding her mother's hand.

"Forster!" Meredith said, her face warm and open and peaceful in a way he had never seen before. "I'm so glad you're up and about. You were out like a light, earlier. She kept a good watch." And Meredith nodded to Auna, who smiled back.

"How is your arm?" Aeriod asked Forster.

Forster looked up at the man's impassive face. *How can he just casually walk in here like nothing's happened?* He noted, fleetingly, that the silver chain with its small purple gem hung once again around Aeriod's neck.

Forster rubbed his arm. "The feeling is coming back. It hurts."

"That's good," Aeriod reassured him. "That means you're healing." And Forster watched as the man sighed and smiled a bit.

"Where are we going?" Forster asked.

"To the Dome Car," Aeriod replied.

"So...it worked?" Forster persisted. "We did it? Is everything really working again? The controls seem back online."

"They are, for the most part," Aeriod agreed. "Just a bit more of an adjustment, but you'll see."

Forster squinted at him. "Where are we?"

"Come and have a look," Aeriod said.

"You're always cagey," Forster sighed, exasperated. Aeriod dipped his head.

The group walked along, and Forster marveled at the lit hallways. Everywhere, people walked and chatted, and he noted their excitement. He sensed no fear among them, only vigor, although in some cases, it was accompanied by a bit of sadness. He dragged his feet as he feebly walked, but he kept on, and he checked from time to time to see if Auna was still there, holding his arm. She was, and that thrilled him constantly. He noticed she carried a small bag on her shoulder.

Forster then remembered his vision of her, cramped inside a small ship, and it dawned on him that he had seen her en route to Mandira Station without realizing it.

*What if she hadn't made it?* he thought.

He squeezed her warm hand. She entwined her fingers with his.

As they entered the Dome Car, the Mid Deck crew all met Forster and Ariel with cheers. Ella and Darren clasped their hands and kissed their cheeks. Burgess and Pop gave bear hugs and backslaps. And Troy took in the sight of Forster, and Ariel, and Auna, and he sniffed loudly.

"Forster!" he said hoarsely. "You look like..." And Forster felt his own grin spreading. "...you look like...you look great, man."

"Oof!" said Forster, as Troy barreled into him with a fierce hug. He turned and marveled at Auna, and his face lit up.

"Auna," said Forster, "this is Troy, and that's Pop and Burgess, and Ella and Darren."

"Very pleased to meet you!" Troy said enthusiastically, lingering maybe a few seconds too long on Auna's striking features. "I'll have to invite you and your old lug over soon," he said. "You can try some of my special brew." And he winked.

Forster snorted. "Oh Jesus Christ, no."

"Oh!" cried Auna brightly. "That reminds me," and she lifted her bag off her shoulder and opened it. She pulled out a small silver capsule. It had a little window in it, through which Forster noticed something leafy and green inside. Auna held the capsule up. "Who ordered coffee?"

Forster leaned back and guffawed, and every other member of the Mid Deck team chuckled too. Aeriod beamed. Forster noticed, and he squinted again at Aeriod. But the man took hold of his cape and wrapped it around himself. Forster blinked, confused by all the light shining behind Aeriod. After all, it was the Dome Car, where everyone went to gaze at the stars.

"And now, Forster and Ariel," Aeriod said to them, "come and see what you have done."

The pair stepped forward tentatively, bolstered by Auna and Meredith, and faced what lay beyond the window. They beheld a nearby star, which for a moment reminded them of the sun. The star's light shone around the edge of a world that filled their entire field of vision outside the window. As the day dawned on that side of the planet, it shone vividly with rich turquoise water, broken up by green land in a way Earth had not been, and its atmosphere spun with white clouds.

"We did it," Ariel breathed. She leaned her head onto Meredith's shoulder, and her mother held her that way for a long time.

Forster moved closer to the window, with Auna at his side. He took her hand in his. Everyone stared out at the warm and welcoming planet. "A new world," he said.

# 43

## IKA NUI

Forster could not stop asking questions. To his relief, Ariel volleyed her own inquiries and interjections, and generally kept Aeriod on his toes. This amused Forster greatly. He watched her push and pull with Aeriod. She clearly fancied him, on one hand, but on the other, she felt guarded. *Well, she could hardly be blamed,* thought Forster. He was an alien, after all.

That thought stopped him.

"We're all aliens out here, aren't we?" he asked Auna.

They were lounging in his room, which he realized he had missed greatly. He had made Auna a bed of Meredith's quilts on the floor next to him, so he took the hard plank instead. She sat up and smoothed her short hair and considered.

"I suppose that's true," she said slowly. She studied him. Five days had passed since the Great Move, as they jokingly called it. More questions than answers seemed to be the rule. People were readjusting to their homes on board the station, but restlessness stirred among some. Auna recognized that feeling. Of course, she had not lived on the station, so it was not going to feel like a familiar home to her, anyway.

"Do you want to go?" Auna asked him.

Forster crossed his legs and looked longingly at her. Whether they stayed or not didn't matter to him. He would happily go where Auna went—she was the adventurer. She lowered her eyes.

"Auna," he said. "I'm sorry. You couldn't have known what you were getting yourself into. I mean, I'm guessing you had a full life back there. And—and now you can't return."

"Mm," said Auna. "How far did Aeriod say it was?"

Forster ran his fingers through his hair. "I don't remember. On the other side of the galaxy—that's all I care about."

"So, I guess we're stuck here, then," she murmured. She put her chin on her knees. Forster could not help himself; he reached down and smoothed the bangs from her broad forehead. She avoided his gaze. "Still, the view is nice. I wonder what it's like on the surface?"

"I've heard it's tropical," Forster said. "Warm, humid, rampant plant life."

"But are there mountains to climb? Crashing waves? Tall forests?"

Forster smiled. "Like our old hiking days in Oregon."

"I need those things," Auna declared. "Nothing against the tropics, of course. I need the wind, and the sea, and the trees, and sometimes the rain."

"Well, it's a big galaxy," Forster mused. "Maybe we could ask Aeriod...."

Auna snickered and reached up to take his hands. "Later," she said, and he slid off his plank down to her.

After some time, Forster ultimately chose not to ignore the messages coming in. Ella had called for a meeting, and Forster received another invitation from Guru to drop by the bar. And yet another message announced a stationwide conference the next morning. Mandira Station civilians would attend a memorial for those lost during the attack. First, though, his door chimed.

Auna worked with Depoe and Bandon's diagnostics, and in doing so she unsealed Forster's message. She now sat covering her mouth and trying not to laugh.

"Hey!" Forster cried as he headed to the door. "It's not funny, you know. I thought I'd never see you again."

Auna stifled, but could not prevent, a fit of giggles. Then she subsided, her smile faded, and she gazed at Forster with tears in her eyes.

"You kept telling me goodbye when you came out of it," she reminded him. He groaned.

He opened the door and found Troy, looking suspiciously eager.

"Hullo, Troy," he drawled. "Come in?"

"Hey, hey," Troy answered, and he bounced back and forth on his heels. Forster noticed he held the silver capsule Auna had brought with her. Troy peeked in at her.

"I just wanted to say...thank you, again, for the coffee bush. I'm hoping I don't kill it just yet! Not until I get my first harvest!" And Troy wheeze-laughed. "But I was curious: how'd you get hold of this thing? I mean, now that we're out here in the ass-end of nowhere, I figure you can tell me, right?"

Auna chuckled and shrugged. "That was a special order. Pretty insistent customer. Excellent profit for me. Not that I can spend it now, of course, but at least I don't have any debts on the other side of the galaxy."

"So," Troy muttered, "who ordered it?"

"Not sure; it was anonymous. I decided to deliver it myself because...well, I'd heard something was going on at the station. Thought I might visit," and she smirked sheepishly at Forster.

"Hmm," said Forster. "Well, you'd better *not* kill it, my man, because Auna risked her life getting it here."

"I'll take the best care of it," Troy reassured them seriously. He stroked the capsule lovingly. "Only thing is, I think the conservatory might not be the best place for it to grow. You know what I mean?"

"You're not thinking of taking it down there, are you?" Forster asked incredulously. "What would that do to the environment?"

"Well," confided Troy, "I was talking to Aeriod about that very thing, as a matter of fact. And he said maybe we could build a greenhouse or something like that. He seems to think it would work."

Auna glanced sidewise at Forster.

"Does he now," said Forster thoughtfully. "Well, I'll tell you what: once you get that up and running, invite us over for coffee, will you?"

"My pleasure!" Troy beamed. "You headed to the meeting?"

"Yes, in a bit," Forster answered. "See you there." And Troy waved to Auna and Forster.

The two walked down the corridor, stealing glances at each other, finding their fingers interlaced out of long habit. Forster wanted to keep walking with her, and never stop.

Aeriod helmed the meeting, and Forster knew the man was bracing himself for a barrage of additional questions. But before they came, he quieted everyone by raising his hand.

"I want to give an update on repairs. Everything seems to be back online and in working order, though of course the clocks are out of sync. I don't think you'll be needing my ship for any further repairs."

Forster wrinkled his brow. "What ship?" he asked.

Aeriod smiled. "Well, when you and Ariel moved us here, a beacon in orbit of the world below us alerted my fleet and sent a ship out here."

"Your...fleet?" Forster began, but Aeriod frowned at him.

Aeriod went on, "So I used the ship to aid in repairing the station. It's docked at Bottom Deck. You can see it later if you wish," and he glared with a tiny scowl at Ariel, whose eager green eyes glowed with excitement.

"I'm getting many questions about traveling to the surface, so for the time being I am willing to ferry passengers down in my ship. I realize the remaining craft on the station are not suitable for planetary descents and landings until they are retrofitted. That will take some time. But my craft is capable, of course."

"Thank you, Aeriod," Ella said. "If I were you, I would be prepared for a deluge of passengers. We might need to use a lottery system."

"Oh, nobody's going to go for that, Ella," Darren objected.

"You just want shore leave," Ella quipped.

"I confess I do!" admitted Darren.

Meredith cleared her throat. "About tomorrow," she began.

"Yes," Ella said, and she nodded. "We need to decide how to honor Gibbons at the memorial."

"But we're not sure if he's...dead, are we?" Forster asked cautiously. Ariel squirmed.

Aeriod's eyes transfixed Forster, and for a moment, he was reminded of Efron's spectacles. "While we don't know his exact whereabouts," Aeriod answered, "we can declare him missing and presumed dead. We all knew Gibbons, and his loss is keenly felt. Who would like to speak on his behalf?"

Forster raised his hand. "I'll do it."

"Thank you, Forster," Meredith said, and everyone else murmured in appreciation. She shifted in her seat to face her daughter, who for a moment did not return her gaze.

"Ariel, would you like to speak on behalf of Veronica?" Meredith asked. "Officer Derry and Lieutenant Marshall have offered on behalf of the other telepaths who passed away, though the network never served in MindSynd. And for all intents and purposes, MindSynd does not exist out here. You have some time to think about it."

Ariel nodded but said nothing. Forster prodded her thoughts: *"You don't have to do anything. But it might help you."*

*"Sure,"* was all she thought back, and Forster was surprised at her immediate building of a wall between their thoughts. Was he losing a friend?

Forster enjoyed hearing the interest in the world below. Every team member wanted to visit, and it soon became clear that Troy wanted more than a vacation.

"Oh, I'm moving down there," he said assuredly. "I want to get this coffee bush up and going! Guru already has a distillery planned. Maybe I'll have my own roaster, if I can clone this thing. I'll make coffee by a beach one day!" and his eyes glazed over with the prospect.

Ella continued on with business.

"So we're all doing shore leave, and Troy wants to relocate, but what about you?" she asked Pop and Burgess.

"I'm staying here," Burgess said firmly. "Pop and I have it all worked out."

"Can I rely on you to keep some day-to-day activities running up here until I can recruit new people?" Ella asked.

"Sure thing," said Pop. "We'll take a vacation, but we're not leaving our home."

Ella straightened in her chair. "There will likely be a mix of feelings about this is the sense I'm getting from the other group leaders. Now that we are beyond Earth authority, we kind of have to start from scratch out here."

"With the caveat that we aren't alone," Darren remarked. Ella nodded.

"And also with the realization we have more capabilities here, and more resources, than we ever had before," Ella noted.

"One day," Meredith said, "you'll decommission the station, I'm sure. I don't really want to be around for that."

"You're coming with me, Mama," Ariel insisted.

"That's right," Meredith said, with a wide, relaxed smile. "But I do have questions. Aeriod, how safe are we out here? From...Paosh Tohon."

Aeriod's half-lidded silver eyes opened up at the name. "Excellent question," he stated. "Paosh Tohon is known throughout much of the galaxy. We are not immune from the risks on our travels, but we have our own unique defenses. This system is under my jurisdiction, as are a few others. It will take some time to explain everything, but trust that here, you are safe."

"Sounds like a good reason to stick around," Troy said.

"And you may, of course," Aeriod said graciously. "You've been through more than enough. Just...try to be a good neighbor, for you will have company."

"And what are you going to do now?" Forster asked.

"It's time to check in with my own coworkers, as it were," Aeriod said archly.

"You'll be back, yes?" Ella asked.

"Of course, from time to time," Aeriod replied. "I trust you'll keep things running smoothly out here, and I have my own surveillance network around the system, which can detect any intrusion."

"It seems like you're kind of important," Pop noted. Burgess nodded.

Aeriod grinned and his eyelids lowered again, but he said nothing.

Forster mulled over everything he had told them. "What if," he said slowly, "we don't want to stay on the station, and we're not wanting to settle on the planet? And anyway, what is the planet called?"

"The planet's name is not translatable to any human language," Aeriod replied, "but I was given a suggestion, and so you're welcome to go with that. I believe it was Ika Nui? Guru chose it. Anyway, it is of no great importance to me what *you* name it."

*How many planets does this guy manage?* Forster wondered.

"Now in answer to your first question, I think what you're wondering is, can I take you somewhere else?"

A thrill of excitement jolted through Ariel, who did not contain herself, so Forster felt its full brunt. She sat up, radiant, and her eyes became huge.

Forster smirked. "Well, yes, that's what I'm asking."

Aeriod steepled his fingers and rested his chin on them. The egg-shaped amethyst glistened on his chest. He stared upward for a moment. "I think that can be arranged. In fact, it could be quite useful. Let me see...I know just the place—a safe world, also in my jurisdiction."

Forster's heart raced. Auna was out for a walk around the station, but he would have seized her hand if she were there. "I think we might be interested," said Forster, thinly concealing his delight.

Ariel asked, "What if we just want to visit...all of your worlds?" And Meredith chuckled.

Aeriod laughed. Then he gave her a look that Forster read as endearing, and indulging. "If that is what you want," he said carefully. "It may not be safe everywhere, though."

"But you have that necklace," Ariel pointed out. "And if we traveled with you, we could use it if we needed to."

Aeriod smiled, but his eyes shone wistfully as he touched the amethyst. "Sooner or later I will give this back. But I could use a telepath during my travels from time to time. You could hone your skills, and maybe I could introduce you to other people with similar abilities."

"Other aliens?" gasped Ariel. "I mean...I mean...other species?"

"Of course," Aeriod said with a shrug. "You're all the sojourners here, for humanity. So you might not meet any of your kind again for some time. Something else to consider."

"But," Meredith asked, "if we wanted to, could we come back here, to Ika Nui?"

"Certainly," Aeriod replied.

"Please take us with you," Ariel pleaded.

"One thing at a time, and one group at a time," Aeriod said. "First, let's think about shore leave to Ika Nui. And second, Forster, maybe you could help choose the group of people with similar interests to yours, before I take you on your journey. I should warn you, it's rather far from here. You might not be able return quite so frequently. Pick resourceful people."

Forster closed his eyes. His thoughts wheeled and overwhelmed him. "I'll think it all over and let you know later."

## 44

## WINDWARD

The weeks blew by for Forster. The memorial had gone well, but he still lingered over the tragedy of Gibbons and Veronica. Hearing "Dunstan Gibbons" on the list of names called out had been a disturbing jolt. It had made everything so concrete for him, that he would never see his friend again.

Dr. Singh hosted a ceremony to celebrate Ariel, Forster, Aeriod, and Guru's group. Again, Forster grew disoriented upon hearing Dr. Singh read his full name.

"Linden Deming Forster, for your outstanding bravery and heroism during the recent events..."

He did not hear the rest, as he was all in a fog, and Auna had to nudge him to get him to rise and walk up to the stage in the great hall.

Ariel had seemed more removed lately, even as she became more social with the rest of the station. Forster was happy she had mingled with people more her age. He supposed she must have the feeling of being out of her time, with twenty years lost in hibernation. He sighed. Of course she must start a new life over, as all of them must, and he could only wish her well.

When the day came that Aeriod dropped by his quarters to say,

"Ready?" and Forster's eyes took in his small room, and the parcels stacked up to move to Aeriod's ship, he held back.

"I just want to take one more walk," he said, and Auna nodded. That was the grandest thing about Auna, among many grand things: she always understood. She and Aeriod stayed behind to sort the parcels for loading, with the help of Depoe and Bandon, who would be joining them.

Forster walked down the corridor to the area that once housed Burgess and Gibbons' quarters. The "dumbbell" had pinched Auna's ship clean off its bay, leaving a tunnel jutting out from the closed little bay door. No one seemed to be interested in fixing it, and he wondered if it would always stay that way. Burgess' old room had therefore become something of a memorial, adjacent to Gibbons' old quarters.

Forster walked in the open door of Gibbons' room, for now it held a makeshift library. He could not help thinking that Gibbons, in another life, would have enjoyed that. The defunct AI had been dismantled and destroyed, but all of Gibbons' furniture and books and art remained. The hallway outside echoed empty and hollow, and Forster sensed not many people made their way here. Perhaps one day they would, he pondered. They might want to recall how they had all arrived out here so far away from their home sun and its orbit.

He looped back around to his friends' quarters to say goodbye. They were waiting for him in the hallway—Troy swearing while telling some joke to Pop, who guffawed; Burgess, standing with his arms crossed and his smile broad, his eyes as sleepy as ever. Spears had come along to say goodbye as well, as he continued recuperating. Aeriod had promised him passage to anywhere among the local systems he wished, but Spears had chosen to stay, and maybe visit Ika Nui from time to time.

"I'm staying here on The Conch for now," Spears said. He still bore a tired, vacant look. "Thanks for fixing everything, my man."

Forster nodded.

"Feel better, Spears," he told his friend.

Ella and Darren hovered near Meredith and Ariel, and Auna stood aside with Aeriod and watched Forster's expression.

Forster said, hoarsely, "Thank you all. You gave me a home here, and you were my family. I'm going to miss you. So much." And he swallowed. He held his hands out to Ariel and Meredith, and they took them, and the tears flowed.

"I hope to see you again someday," he told them. "But if I don't, I just...thank you."

*"Goodbye, Ariel."*

*"Goodbye, Forster."*

Auna and Aeriod stepped forward, and Auna took Forster's hand. Her warm fingers heartened him. They walked away and down and out to Bottom Deck, where Aeriod's ship awaited. Forster did not look back at Ariel or his former coworkers.

The sleek vessel fit neatly into the bay. While the bots helped load the belongings of Forster and twelve others who were joining them, Forster took one more look around the home he had known. Auna nudged him. She leaned her head into his neck.

"Will you miss it?" she asked softly.

"I won't miss the place," he said solemnly. "I'll miss the people."

He sighed and climbed aboard, with Auna by his side.

Aeriod had been right about the distance. He and Auna slept comfortably as the ship raced through space and met what Aeriod called a "junction."

"Close your eyes for these, Forster," Aeriod had advised him. "Don't need any more migraines."

Forster shut his eyes while the light pulsation of the junction seemed to flow through the cabin of the ship. He was not certain he wanted to make that kind of journey a regular habit.

"I hope I won't be needing that necklace of yours," Forster remarked at one point. "When will you give it back?"

Aeriod smirked. "When the time is right, I suppose."

"So, whose is it?" Forster pressed. He had endured enough dodging from Aeriod, and now seemed like a good time to corner him.

"Why don't I show you," Aeriod replied to Forster's surprise. "Come," and he led Forster and Auna into an alcove near the cockpit.

Aeriod waved his hand over a part of the wall, and Forster watched a hologram form. He could not hold back, and exclaimed, "Oh my God!"

Auna laughed and nudged him with her elbow. "Hey, knock it off!" she teased him.

"Wow," Forster said. "Now I know why you would wait for her." Auna smirked, and Aeriod rolled his eyes. "But she looks—"

"She isn't," Aeriod said evasively. "That is a tale for another time. Well, we need to strap in again. We're approaching the system."

The ship entered the space of another world, with large ice caps at its poles, and large oceans. Forster and Auna clamored to see more of the planet as they coasted toward its atmosphere. After a turbulent descent, Aeriod perched his ship on a landing pad in a small village along a crescent-shaped bay. The vessel steamed as sheets of rain lashed it.

Aeriod gave them ponchos, and said, "These will have to do for now, but you had better get used to the weather. I'll help you settle in, but after that, you're on your own for a while. Remember: you can call for me if you need to," and he glanced at Forster's arm.

Aeriod informed the passengers to step carefully in the village. He cautioned them that its denizens were used to off-world types, but still liked to keep to themselves. Forster hoped the group he'd helped choose could handle the strangeness.

Forster and Auna ran into the rain, hand in hand, and headed straight for a cliff nearby to view the ocean. Tall trees, strange plants, and sea rocks filled their vision. They pelted forward, flushed with excitement, down a trail to the shore. Auna sat promptly on a rock among smaller pebbles, and let rain soak her hair as she looked out at the broken clouds on the horizon.

"It looks like Oregon, just like Cape Perpetua," she said, motioning to Forster to sit next to her on the rock. He hesitated. He drank her in, sitting there, and watched her dark eyes grow enchanted by what she saw.

"Auna," Forster said, and she turned to him. He met her unflinching gaze and held it. "Do you want to try again?"

A tiny smile formed in the corners of her mouth. "I thought you could read minds."

Forster blushed. "I mean, yeah, I guess," he said.

"So read mine right now," Auna said. She met his eyes directly. He blushed again. She took his hands. "Just to be sure," she whispered, "yes."

## 45

## LEEWARD

Guru had begged Ariel to come to the bar, for a surprise. She had rolled her eyes, but decided to go for it.

"You sure you want to leave?" he asked, whisking something in a glass for her. She pressed her lips together and avoided his gaze. She felt waves of attraction from him for her, and she did not want to inflame it.

Not that he wasn't handsome or charming enough; he was that in spades, and intelligent as well. But Ariel felt more than ready to move on.

"Yes," she answered.

"Too bad," he replied, and she watched his tattooed forearms pulse as he adjusted a garnish on a glass. He had pushed three little red fruits onto a stick and placed the stick horizontally on the glass.

"Are those cherries?"

"No," said Guru, winking at her, and she blushed this time. "Aeriod brought them up from Ika Nui for me to try out. I'm going to go crazy with the fruits down there! Might finally get to use my degree."

He slid the drink over to her and she sniffed its rich, tropical headiness.

"Thank you. What is it?"

Guru rested his chin on his hands and looked at her with intense longing.

"Thought this would be perfect for you. Forster told me all about the Morse code thing."

Ariel arched an eyebrow at him.

"It's called Three Dots and a Dash," he said, and winked at her again.

Ariel tossed her long hair back and laughed out loud.

"Maybe I'll drop back by for a visit. Some day."

Now she sat in her room and smoothed her quilt and felt herself let go of any regrets. She knew she might never "return" to Ika Nui, and that was fine with her.

So many people had come and gone over the past couple of months. She sat in her mother's quarters, traced her own name on the quilt, and sighed.

Ariel was accustomed to hearing the words so many times that on this occasion it did not register with her.

"Well?" said a voice, with some impatience.

Ariel looked up and started. "Oh! Aeriod! What?"

Aeriod pressed his lips into a thin line. "Are you ready?" he said again.

"Oh. Yes!" she replied, and then more emphatically, "Definitely."

Meredith ventured back into the room. They had already said their farewells to everyone else, and Ariel had been in a dreamy state. Meredith watched her daughter keenly.

"You're missing him, aren't you?" she asked. She pulled Ariel's long, black hair away from her neck.

"Yes," Ariel admitted. "I miss chatting with him, in our minds, you know."

"Well," Aeriod spoke up, "the ship isn't going anywhere until you do. Shall we?" And he held out his arm for Ariel to take.

She accepted his offer and gawked at him, still with a bit of awe at the sight of him, and for a moment she had forgotten all about Forster. Sometimes she had dreams about Forster and Veronica fighting. Sometimes she felt suffocated, waking in a sweat, thinking of what had happened to Veronica. She was now putting her trust in someone else for a change, someone other than her mother, and someone other than Forster.

"He was a friend," Aeriod said simply, watching her. "You will make more friends."

Ariel's eyes stung. "I wonder," she said.

"You will," Aeriod assured her. "Would you like to meet some of my friends?"

Ariel's eyes lit up. Aeriod smiled at her.

"I would like for you to meet someone," he said casually. "You have just the same look right now that she—" and he stopped, and straightened his back.

"Will we get to meet her then?" Ariel cried. She glanced at Meredith, and they shared their mischievous spark. They had whispered many times over who this person was, the owner of the gem.

"Maybe you can help me take this back to its proper owner," said Aeriod coolly, holding the small amethyst in his palm.

"So we are going to meet her," Ariel said firmly.

"I do hope so," said Aeriod, his voice wistful.

They boarded his ship and began their journey, and then Aeriod gasped and said, "Oh, I forgot! I have something for you." And he gave Ariel a small blue box.

"What is this?" she asked, admiring its silver filigree.

"Open it," Aeriod urged.

Ariel opened the box, and immediately holographic images began to play for her. "It's Forster!" she cried. "Look, Mama!"

Meredith leaned over to see.

"Ah, he's in his new home," she said fondly. "There he is with Auna...Wait! Is that a baby?"

They marveled as the images turned past. One image showed Forster and Auna holding a tiny baby. In another, they walked with him on a pebbled beach. In another image, a smaller baby had joined the brother, and so on. In one image, a greying, bearded Forster hiked with his wife and children on a tall bluff.

"What, how..." began Ariel, her eyes flooding.

"They live a long way away," Aeriod told her gently. The images continued, but Ariel set the box aside and collected herself.

Meredith mused, "This must be what it is like for you, Aeriod, watching our lives fly by you so quickly."

Aeriod raised his eyebrows. "Yes," he agreed.

"Are they still alive?" Ariel whispered.

Aeriod said nothing at first, but she furrowed her eyebrows, daring him.

So he said, "They very well may be, and if so, maybe they are grandparents now. You could keep looking."

"No," said Ariel firmly. "Not right now. And besides, I want my own life now, out there."

Meredith held Ariel's hand, and Aeriod nodded at both of them. They sped onward among the stars.

THE END

# ABOUT THE AUTHOR

Dianne dreamed up other worlds and their characters as a child in the 1980s. She formed her own neighborhood astronomy club before age 10, to educate her friends about the universe. In addition to writing stories, she drew and painted her characters, gave them outrageous space fashions, and created travel guides and glossaries for the worlds she invented. As an adult, Dianne earned a Bachelor of Science and spent several years working in both academic laboratory and nonprofit clinical research. On the side, she painted watercolors, made quilts, and took many road trips (a hobby she still enjoys). Today Dianne lives with her family in Southern California, and they all make up a house of serious nerds who enjoy talking, creating, and eating Dianne's baked goods.

jdiannedotson.com

facebook.com/jdiannedotsonwriter
twitter.com/jdiannedotson
instagram.com/jdiannedotson

CPSIA information can be obtained
at www.ICGtesting.com
Printed in the USA
LVHW020501050422
715325LV00009B/625